When Josie awakened, the room was empty, and the sun cast late afternoon shadows from the window across her naked body.

"Rourke?"

There was no answer. She slipped from the tangled covers and looked beyond the drape into the other room.

It too was empty.

Returning to the bed, her eyes suddenly fell on the new silk chemise lying across it. It was a delicate, pale pink, with lace at the bodice and a satin sash of lovely deep rose.

And lying in the garment's center were two gold sovereigns.

Josie picked them up. She lay them in her palm and, as the sun glinted off their shiny surface, she began to weep silently.

The convict girl, Cora Lee, had been right, she thought. All women in this God-forsaken place who aren't wives are whores.

All except one.

Suddenly, for no reason she could fathom, Josie began to hate Annie Hollister.

Rum Colony

Terry Nelsen Bonner

A DELL / JOAN HITZIG MCDONNELL BOOK

Published by
Dell Publishing Co., Inc.
1 Dag Hammarskjold Plaza
New York, New York 10017

Dell ® TM 681510, Dell Publishing Co., Inc.

ISBN: 0-440-07469-X

Printed in the United States of America

First printing—September 1982

PROLOGUE
England
1787

THE cart hurtled down the rutted lane behind the frenzied horse. Each time an unpadded wheel hit a pothole the cart would lurch precariously, almost unseating its occupant.

The frightened young girl, her auburn hair flowing behind her, sawed upon the reins and tried to soothe the horse.

The mare had been spooked by a fox running across her path a half mile back. And now it seemed there was no calming her as cart, rider and horse careened between the hedgerows beneath a canopy of tall trees.

You were a fool, the girl told herself, *a fool to remain in the village so late!*

Though her face was now contorted with fright, there was no masking the beauty of her high cheekbones, her firm chin that bespoke character, and the startling green of her emerald eyes.

Now those eyes anxiously noted a wide bend in the lane fifty yards ahead. The fragile wheels of the cart would never hold the ground if the bend were rounded at such speed.

"Whoa, girl . . . whoa! Ease down!" she cried, her hands grasping the reins tightly.

She leaned the upper half of her body far back, bringing the reins with her until the hands holding them were pressing hard against her throbbing breast.

The mare's head came up, higher, higher . . . but still she fought the bit and thundered ahead.

7

In seconds, cart and horse lurched into the bend. The girl could feel the wheels begin to slide. Closer and closer they came to the hedgerow. Once there, the stout foliage would catch the hubs and spin the cart crazily to God-knew what end.

Her face drained of color, her knuckles chalk-white on the reins, the girl prayed.

A quarter of the way through the bend.

Half the way.

And then she screamed.

There, directly in front of her, appeared a black-cloaked rider. His horse was stretched out in a full gallop. There was no time to swerve, and, indeed, nowhere to swerve. The lane was too narrow for passing.

She opened her mouth to scream again, but the sound erupted in a long gasp of wonder. Powerful arms encased in a white cambric shirt emerged from beneath the folds of the cloak. The rider bent low over his horse's mane, and, as if he had used the strength in his arms, the steed rose from the ground. Up, up they went, horse and rider together as one, until they appeared like a black spectre against the moonlit sky.

And then they were over the hedgerow and out of sight, the thundering hoofs fading into the distance.

The girl marvelled at such horsemanship. But she had little time to dwell on it. Her own mare, in shying from the oncoming rider, had veered too far to the right.

It all happened in seconds. There was a grinding, shearing sound as wheel and hub met the hedgerow, and then the cart lifted. It spun dizzily, and the girl felt the reins yanked from her grasp.

As if she had been thrown from a catapult, her body lifted and arched through the air. Her cloak caught the top of a thorny hedge and was ripped away. Over and over she turned, and then came crashing to earth with a sickening thud.

She lay, not trying to rise, as the patchy moonlight played games with her eyes through the trees. Her head spun crazily, and her chest and back ached. It was hard to breathe, and an elbow throbbed with needle-like pain. There was a warmth running down her cheek she suspected was her own blood.

But I'm alive, she thought gratefully. *At least I'm alive!*

She started to roll to her side, but a jolt of sharp pain beneath her right breast halted her in mid-motion, and brought a groan of agony to her lips.

She settled back, coolly assessing her predicament. She was still five miles from home. It was obvious she could not walk the distance. She was late. Perhaps her brother and her father were already looking for her. If they weren't, they soon would be. But would they find her? She had taken the shorter way from the village, the dangerous way . . . the route her father had told her never to go.

She closed her eyes, trying to force her mind to think clearly.

And then, suddenly, she heard the heavy tread of booted feet moving toward her.

Her eyes flew open, her body tensing in alarm.

"Damme, a girl!"

It was the cloaked figure who had nearly run her down. The cloak's cowl had fallen back from his head. She could see a mane of shaggy black curls, and beneath them an unbearded face of chiseled features. His skin was smooth and tanned and, as he knelt beside her, she could see eyes that were as black as his cloak.

"Where do ye hurt, lass?"

She shook her head. "My back, my side . . . my arm."

Gentle fingers probed up and down both of her arms. Their touch brought an odd, soothing effect to the rest of the body.

"Nothing broken there," the stranger said, his voice a deep rumble in the still night. "Only a bruise or two."

"No thanks to you," she hissed.

"I believe, lass, 'twas your horse that was not under control."

His tone was coldly accusing, and when his black eyes fell again on her face, a shiver went through her body. She had never before met such a penetrating gaze. It somehow made her shrink within herself.

" 'Twas not my fault . . . a fox spooked my mare," she stammered. And then she bridled. Why was she making excuses to him when she was not at fault! "I would have calmed her once around the bend. Any rider knows to slow in such a blind spot at night. You did not!"

His dark head nodded in a mock bow and his lips parted, revealing even, white teeth in a rakish smile. "Aye, I'm afraid I couldn't."

"One would think, sir, that you fled the King's men, riding so recklessly . . ."

The night was filled with his low, mirthless chuckle. It rang in her ears almost ominously. "And what would put that thought in your pretty head?"

"Because these woods are filled with robbers, men of the road, those who . . ." Suddenly her body tensed, her mind whirled. His dress, his horse, the way he rode . . . and at night? "Dear God, you are a highwayman!" she cried.

"Among other things," the stranger said, emitting another low chuckle from between those gleaming teeth. He reached out and cradled her head in his hand. He lifted her slightly and turned her face into a patch of moonlight. "Damme, but I've found me a real beauty now, haven't I?"

Her green eyes grew wide with fear. She had heard tales of what these men did to women on the high road at night.

Instinctively she started to struggle from him, only to be brought up short again by the pain.

Gently he eased her head back to the grass and removed his hand. "Where?"

"My leg . . . my side."

"Which leg?"

"My right one. What. . . ?" His hands were beneath her skirts, lifting her petticoats, sliding beneath the cinch of her pantaloons. "No! How dare . . . ohhh . . ." She couldn't move. Each time she did, the pain wrenched agonizingly at her side.

The stranger's hands moved up over the flesh of her thigh. Closer and closer they came, alarmingly close. No man had ever touched her so intimately. She groaned, tensed her body. Her mind willed his hands to stop. And then she relaxed as they did move away. Her skirts were replaced, and she sighed with relief.

"Nothing broken there. Again, only a nasty bruise. What is wrong?"

"Methinks . . ." she said, her face flushed with embarrassment but her chin thrust forward in defiance, ". . . methinks you go further than necessary in locating a broken bone!"

He shrugged and his lips again curled into a broad smile. "Forgive me, but such softness I haven't touched in a very long while. Now, I've little time to worry about your modesty. Which side?"

"My right side, here . . . ohh!"

His hands deftly loosened the laces on her bodice.

"Must you . . . ?"

"I must."

Her hands flew up to stop his, but they were too late. Her dress fell open and his hands were already beneath her bodice, the fingers gently probing. Through the thin material of her chemise she could feel the heat of his hands warm her flesh. To her surprise she found herself almost enjoying his touch.

Suddenly the heel of his hand brushed against the fullness of her breast and a ripple swept through her.

"What is it?" he asked, seemingly unaware of the stir he had caused in her body.

"N-nothing," she replied, curling her lower lip between her teeth and biting down hard.

The fingers drifted lazily beneath the swell of her bosom and then brushed the soft, tender spot beneath her arm where her breast blossomed from her side.

Again she felt a flutter within her she couldn't fathom, but it was quickly replaced by a twinge of pain.

"Aye, lass, you've broken or cracked a rib or two."

The next few moments were lost in the deft swiftness of his movements. He removed her petticoat and rended it into strips with his powerful hands. Gently he sat her up and pushed her dress to her waist.

Modesty was gone now, replaced by the aching throb of pain, as he wound the strips tightly around her.

At least, she thought with relief, he didn't insist on removing her chemise. Had that been necessary, no amount of pain could have removed the embarrassment of baring her breasts to a man . . . and a perfect stranger at that!

"Ohhh . . . must it be so tight?"

"Aye, 'tis the only way. Can ye manage to dress yourself?"

"Of course."

"Good," he said. "I shall be right back."

"Where . . . ?"

But he was gone, a dark figure moving panther-like through the trees until he disappeared around the hedgerow.

Painfully she struggled to her feet. But there her movement ended. One step told her she would be walking nowhere.

And then he was back at her side, a strong, heavily muscled arm winding around her thin waist.

"The cart is kindling, I fear. The traces must have broken. And your mare is nowhere in sight."

"She knows her way home."

"An' where would that be?" he asked. She pointed the direction. "Damme, just where they'll be comin' from," he murmured.

"Who?"

"Never mind. How far?"

"Five miles."

"Damme," he hissed again, his heavy brows drawing into a scowl above his flashing eyes. "Can ye walk?"

"No, I . . . I tried."

His dark face grew even darker, and lines of worry suddenly creased his broad forehead. "Well, there's nothing for it. Let's hope you're not the death of me, lass!"

Suddenly she was in his arms, cradled effortlessly, as if her weight were no more than a child's. With her hands on his shoulders and her head lolling against his neck, she suddenly felt and realized the size and the power of his body.

As if she were a feather, he lifted her to his saddle and then vaulted up behind her.

"Hang on to my neck, lass. You can ease the jolt yourself that way. And sit across my thighs!"

She did as she was told, and sighed with relief when the horse's gait caused very little pain.

They had gone about two miles when the sound of thudding hooves reached their ears. The riders were directly in front of them, and riding fast.

"Damn, the distance is about what I expected."

Before she could question his words, he broke the horse into a canter and then to a full gallop. Shortly he spotted a break in the hedgerow and reined through.

"Do ye know this country?"

"Aye."

"Then where can we not be seen or heard until they've passed? They'll have an outrider or two in the fields off the lane."

"You *are* a highwayman!"

"Aye, lass, I told ye I was . . . an' more. 'Twas odd, your guess, for the riders ye hear are indeed the King's men . . . and if they catch me this time 'tis the gibbet for sure."

She searched his dark eyes and handsome face for only an instant before making her decision.

"There, to the left, beneath that rise. There is a heavy stand of oaks with a small clearing in the center!"

He spurred the stallion, and shortly they were hidden in the darkness of the trees. And not a moment too soon. They had barely reined up when the horsemen thundered down the lane, passing the very spot they had just left.

"They're gone," she sighed.

"Wait . . . shh!"

In silence they waited, another five minutes . . . ten. And then two riders, their voices hushed, their horses barely making a sound in the soft meadow grass, passed near the oaks.

When they were out of sight, she turned to him. "How did ye know?"

A broad grin flashed across his face. "When ye've run as long as I have, lass, ye learn how to survive."

"But you're not that old!"

"Nay, not in years . . . twenty-five 'tis all. But years mean nothing when ye live as fast as I've been forced to live, lass."

For the first time something in his voice struck her. "Your accent . . . you're Irish!"

"Aye, lass," he chortled, "you've hit it. A wild Irish rogue and rebel I am, who'll come to no good end. But, mark me, when 'tis over they'll know I was here!"

He kept the horse's pace at a gentle walk for the last

three miles, and then stopped just a few yards from the cottage she called home.

"A pretty place," he said. "Cozy."

"Aye."

"I grew up on a farm, meself . . . in Ireland."

A lump grew in her throat when she saw the misty, far-away look that suddenly filled his eyes.

"Can you never go back?"

"To Ireland? . . . aye, I'm headed there now. But to the farm, never."

He had been watching her face, bathed in moonlight, and as he studied her fine features, his own face seemed to relax. The smile, when it touched his lips now, was more sad than reckless, and the look in his dark eyes struck her as a look of longing.

"You're truly a picture, you are, lass . . . beautiful. You should always wear green. It does lovely things to your hair . . . your eyes . . . your eyes . . ."

It was like a dream, as if she were in a web of gauzy silk, being drawn closer and closer to its center.

And the center was his sensuous, full lips.

They were warm and seeking as they found and pressed against her temple. Then, slowly, they brushed her eyes and moved across her cheek. His mouth trailed slowly to hers, leaving a searing sensation in its wake that made her whole body tremble in his arms.

Then she tasted his lips on hers, pressing them open until the tips of their tongues met. She was moving against him, responding as she had never, in her young years, dreamed she could respond.

The sweetness of his kiss seemed to last forever. And still she responded, willing it to go on and on, until she was sure she could stand it no longer. Her breasts crushed against his broad chest until she was breathless, stunned by the incredible sensations she was experiencing with this man she didn't even know.

She gasped as his mouth left hers. Her breasts rose

and fell as she took in short, quick breaths. Her whole body felt light, as if she were floating.

His eyes, as they melted into hers, told her that he too sensed the wild currents that flowed between them.

"Ah, ye are a beauty, lass, and a woman with true passion in her soul. 'Tis a pity we couldn't have met in another time . . . another place."

Abruptly but gently, he lowered her to the ground, then with a finger tilted her chin upward, his black eyes locking on hers.

"Give me a name, lass, that I can remember on dark, cold nights."

"Annie . . . Annie Hollister," she gasped.

"Annie Hollister," he repeated.

"Aye."

"I'll ne'er forget it. Good-bye, Annie Hollister."

He leaned forward and lightly brushed his lips over hers before reining around and spurring the horse into a walk.

His lips had worked some strange magic in her body and brain. Now she swayed, almost on the verge of swooning. Never had a man touched her body, nor kissed her, in this way.

Now, in one short evening, she had experienced a man's lips on hers, his hands on her body. And she was sure she had seen some depth of emotion in the dark stranger's eyes as they seemed to devour her at the conclusion of their kiss.

"Wait!"

He reined around. "Aye?"

"Give . . . give *me* a name to remember!"

"Phillip, lass. Phillip Conroy."

And then he was gone, topping a far hill, again appearing like a black spectre against the night sky.

PART ONE

SYDNEY COVE 1789

Port Jackson, New South Wales

1

"SAIL, ho!" the lookout's voice boomed, his arms waving excitedly toward the narrow mouth of Sydney harbor.

Several long strides of Captain Steven Rourke's powerful legs propelled him through the misty rain to the top of Lookout Point. He halted beside the convict-lookout, dwarfing the smaller man by several inches.

"Where?"

"There, sar, jest breakin' the fog bank!"

Rourke's pale blue eyes squinted through the mist and heavy fog that had blanketed Port Jackson and the cove since early that morning. Slowly his gaze pierced the mist until he could make out the ship's fore topsail. It seemed to barely inch through the fog's snake-like fingers.

"Damme," Rourke hissed, more to himself than to the lookout. "But is she the *Venture*?"

"Can't see her bow markings yet, sar."

"Give me the glass!"

The lookout thrust a seaman's glass into Rourke's hands and, with a sharp intake of air, he brought it to his eye. Slowly, ever so slowly, the crosstrees of her mainmast materialized, and then the mast itself cleared the fog like a giant arm pointing skyward.

"Blimey, Captain, I think they're goin' to make it!"

"Aye, it would seem so. He looks dead center in the channel between north point and south point."

And then the long, black-sided prow broke the fog bank and ran toward the quay like a sleek racehorse.

"Thank God, 'tis indeed the *Venture*," Rourke said, dropping the glass from his eye. His broad shoulders sagged in relief and a slight smile of triumph creased his broad, tanned features.

"Thanks be to God for the men aboard," the lookout said.

"Aye." Rourke nodded, but he cared little for the seamen who now scurried over the *Venture*'s teak deck.

He was far more concerned for what lay beneath those decks, in the sleek ship's cargo hold.

The lookout had spotted the bark at dawn, two miles out, in a clear, calm sea. Then, suddenly, the fog had descended and all trace of the ship—and her precious cargo—was lost.

Until now.

Rourke offered up a silent prayer of thanks to Captain James Cook, who had insisted on this particular ship design for the exploration of the South Pacific. The wisdom of his choice was still evident almost two decades later. Had the *Venture* been anything other than a Whitby bark, she could have been wrecked on the treacherous shoals that so jealously guarded the entrance to Sydney harbor. But this ruggedly built, coast-wise vessel was sufficiently shoal of draft to venture into uncharted waters.

And the *Venture*'s cargo was far too precious to be lost in the angry foam of the sea, or to be made kindling against a jagged coral reef.

They had not seen a ship since May, when the *Sirius* had arrived from Capetown, their first visitation in seventeen months from the outside world. But her cargo of wheat had been only a temporary relief. Now, in September, the famine was increasing again, clothes and uniforms were wearing out, and many of the men were going barefoot.

The whole colony, King's marines and convicts alike, was only weeks from starvation rations. Thieving, which for a while had been held to a minimum, was now on the upswing.

Neither the private gardens tilled by the more industrious of the convicts, nor the farms owned by the free settlers were immune. No man or woman could take to their beds at night without posting one or more guards to watch their crops until dawn.

Hopefully the *Venture* would be laden with livestock, fruit trees, unspoiled seed, farm implements, and other much needed provisions for the colony.

But that was not the part of her cargo that interested Captain Steven Rourke. In addition to the wheat, cattle and farm implements, the *Venture* would be carrying a far more precious load.

Rum.

For in this God-forsaken colony thousands of miles from the English mother-land, rum was like gold, and often more powerful in barter. A man could purchase extra food, extra seed, weapons, bricks from the newly built kiln with rum. With the precious liquid a man could buy a woman, or even the death of another man.

Aye, Rourke thought, *let 'em all . . . convict, soldier and free settler alike . . . haggle over the rest of the* Venture's *cargo.*

It was only the rum that interested Captain Steven Rourke.

Rum for food. Rum for boots. Rum for timber. Rum for the convicts assigned to him: it was the most effective spur to make the bloody bastards work.

And this lot was his; all his. As a senior officer in the elite New South Wales Corps, he was entitled to trade his credits to buy the entire cargo of the American ships which were beginning to appear in Port Jackson. And with the scheme he was about to propose to the captain of the *Venture*, Rourke would soon be able to charter his own ships to run to the Cape and the East for purposes of his own trade.

The tall man with the mane of blond hair and the ice blue eyes allowed himself a slight chuckle as he stood watching the three-masted bark inch its way slowly to dockside.

"Sar?"

"What?"

"You spoke, sar?"

"No," Rourke replied, turning to the smaller man, "I was only thinking what a great relief it will be to rise from a table with a full belly again."

"Aye, sar, that it will," said the shifty-eyed little convict. And then as Rourke moved away he added in a low mumble, "As if any of the *Venture*'s cargo will dribble down to the likes of me."

The big man paused, spinning around on the toe of one boot, and leveled his gaze.

"What was that?"

"Er, nothing, sar," the man said, shivering beneath his rags and wrenching his own eyes away from Rourke's cold stare.

There was a moment's pause, as if the Captain would return, but then the lookout heard his boots retreat down the path. Slowly he turned his head, stealing one more glance at Rourke's broad back in the deep scarlet tunic.

Even seeing Steven Rourke from the rear make the little man shiver and remember the look from those depthless, penetrating eyes.

Some said that looking at Rourke was like looking into the face of an eagle with blue eyes . . . and just as dangerous. One woman convict even claimed that she had seen his soul through those eyes, and it was black.

"Like the devil," the lookout muttered to himself. "For if the devil walks the earth, he does it as Captain Steven Rourke."

The object of the lookout's fears moved down the

hill from Lookout Point with long, military strides.
Two marines at the wattle and daub makeshift fort
halfway down the hill snapped to and executed a
crossarm salute with their muskets.

Rourke carelessly returned it without breaking
stride.

He did smile.

He always smiled when he saw Port Jackson's "defense fortifications". The fort, constantly manned and
armed with two cannon from one of the ships of the
First Fleet, was a joke.

It wouldn't last minutes after a well-fired ball, and
none of the men who manned it were trained in artillery.

But it met the home government's specifications:
". . . a fort shall be erected for the defense of the
colony."

Defense, Rourke thought with a laugh. Defense
against whom?

Who would make war against a penal colony, except
those who lived in it?

As far as he was concerned, who would want this
God-forsaken hell-hole in the middle of the South
Seas? There was even a rumor that the Crown was
thinking about giving up Port Jackson. It was said the
colony was costing too much to maintain, and it would
be years before it would be self-sufficient.

A likely place to move the fledgling colony would be
Northern Canada. There it would be closer to England
and much cheaper to supply.

Rourke cared little either way. He had found a way,
here in Port Jackson, to grow rich. By the time they
moved the colony, if they moved it at all, he would be
wealthy enough to quit the King's service, quit all colonies, and, perhaps, quit England forever.

As a youth, before entering the military college at
Dartmouth, he had taken the grand tour. Paris was to

his liking, with perhaps a small summer chateau in the south of France.

In many ways it was the only road open to Steven Rourke. He had few other expectations because of his checkered military career.

Thoughts of his career brought a wide smile to his full lips as he walked toward the main camp.

The same month he had been born in Surrey, just outside London, his father had died bravely an ocean away, fighting the French and heathen Indians at Fort Ticonderoga.

The senior Rourke's widow had been a good and kindly mother, but not a parent of strict discipline. Rourke's youth was filled with a delinquency and precocity far beyond his years.

In college itself his affairs with women—from milkmaids to ladies of title—became legendary. Wisely, he attached himself to the richest and most influential of his schoolfellows, the young Earl of Welbourne.

It was Welbourne who frequently saved him from being cashiered.

But Welbourne couldn't save him from being posted to the American colonies upon graduation. There he had fought bravely and earned high honors. But he never forgot his ambition to live as well or better than those officers he shared command with, but whom he couldn't compete with in lands, titles, and money.

It was never proven, but often rumored, that wherever Lieutenant Steven Rourke did duty, the blackmarket in underground goods flourished.

Near the end of war, he returned to England with a captaincy and a very full purse.

But Rourke was never one to stand still. Upon his arrival back in his native land, he immediately began to look around for ways to increase his wealth.

As a lad women had adored him, as they always did a handsome and daring young rascal. As a grown man, handsome and even more dashing, with a carefree yet charmingly sardonic smile, women couldn't resist him.

Rourke used it to full advantage.

As an aid in his schemes, he chose the Lady Budmore, wife to Lord Alfred Budmore, His Majesty's Minister of Trade. Lord Budmore was not above lining his own purse with speculations on cargo imports and exports, along with surreptitious ventures in the African slave trade.

When Rourke discovered this, he concentrated all his efforts on Lord Budmore's young and beautiful wife. The Lady proved not only amiable, but very receptive to the attentions of the handsome blond giant who was twenty-five years her husband's junior.

In a fortnight Rourke was privy to the Lady's bed, and in just over a month equally as close to the secrets of her husband's speculations.

For nearly a year Rourke rode high. Then disaster struck. And it was the Lady Budmore herself who brought him to ground when she discovered the mistress he had been keeping.

More confident of her husband's adoration than Rourke had expected, the Lady contrived and succeeded in having her husband discover them in a very compromising tryst.

She immediately begged her husband's forgiveness. Lord Budmore demanded satisfaction. Rourke had no choice.

Forty-eight hours later Lord Budmore was dead with a ball in his heart and Rourke was standing trial for his life in the old Bailey, while the Lady Budmore became a very rich widow.

His plea was self-defense, but only because of his brilliant military career was he found not guilty.

This, however, was not an end to his troubles.

He soon discovered the true power of status and wealth. Powerful friends of the deceased quickly maneuvered him into a position from which he could not escape.

A new penal colony was being formed in a place called New South Wales. They needed trained officers as wardens over the thousands of convicts who would be sent to the colony.

He was given a choice to go or face financial ruin and an end to his career in England.

Rourke chuckled mirthlessly to himself as he made his way through the mud of Port Jackson toward the quay. In many ways they had done him a favor. His time in Port Jackson had hardened him, given him a cold resolve. He had learned how much men respect fear. He had also acquired a bitterness that made him a man of cold steel, totally without emotion.

Captain Steven Rourke had become the perfect survivor, in a land that let few survive.

Without seeming to pay any attention, his eyes surveyed everything around him in the misty rain.

To his far right, on high ground, was the newly erected Government House. Though not quite completed, it had the only brick foundation of any structure in the colony. The brick kiln itself had only been finished two months before. The only two other structures of any permanence were the hospital and the new barracks. The rest of the colony was made up of wattle and daub huts, with leaky thatch for roofs.

"A hell-hole indeed," he muttered to himself. "But good in that it gives a man the desire to be out of it!"

Port Jackson was indeed a hell-hole, a fit place for the dumping of England's human trash: convicts. For that was its only reason for being, since the Crown had lost its former dumping ground, the American colonies.

Rourke reached quayside, and turned to walk along the water toward the landing wharf where the *Venture* was tying up.

Beyond the ship's rigging, the fog had lifted enough to make visible the harbor mouth.

It was an ideal harbor, almost totally land-locked, with a deep-water estuary running inland for many miles. Once inside the narrow heads, one had the sensation of being on an inland lake with the long arms reaching away on every side into secret coves and hidden bays. It was much more promising than the flat, featureless and barren area of Botany Bay a few miles to the south, where the present governor, Arthur Phillip, had landed with the First Fleet.

The thought of Phillip brought a foul taste to Rourke's mouth and a frown of anger across his high, wide forehead. He spit to rid his mouth of the taste, but the frown remained.

The man was a spineless weakling preaching fairness and compassion to all, including the convicts.

"One day this will be a great land," he told them often. "A land that you will be proud to have been a part of at the beginning!"

To Rourke, New South Wales would always be a pest hole inhabited by scum. And one day, if Phillip kept insisting on conciliation with the filthy natives and the slovenly convicts, they, and not Phillip and the army, would be ruling New South Wales.

If Rourke had his way, each and every one of the bloody bastards, men and women alike, would be flogged daily.

Scum.

He spat again.

Convicted of everything from stealing a loaf of bread or pickpocketing to armed robbery and murder, they were being transported by the thousands to both Van Dieman's Land and New South Wales. The hideous conditions of English prisons—inhuman crowding, food shortages, filth—were being rapidly duplicated in the new colony. Women convicts prostituted themselves for food; the streets swarmed with their illegitimate brats. Petty criminals could work as domestic servants or farm laborers; the worst of the criminal offenders worked on chain gangs in irons, like the scum of the earth, for the New South Wales Corps.

Over all, oppressive and persistent, stultifying every enterprise, was that dead, sullen atmosphere of a jail. A man in fetters, dressed in a coarse blue and yellow prisoner's jacket and working in a chain gang, was hardly likely to throw himself into the creation of the new colony with a sense of burning enthusiasm. For him it was simply another jail.

But useful scum they were, Rourke reminded himself. He had twenty-seven of the bastards assigned to him, and with any luck he would own half of the next lot, which had just set sail for Southampton and was due to arrive in Sydney Cove in three to four month's time, depending on the weather rounding the Cape.

He was close to the wharf now, elbowing his way through the milling people who had crowded around to watch the *Venture* unload. Most were convicts, men in tattered sackcloth shirts and filthy breeches and women in makeshift skirts, with any remnant of castoff clothing hiding the upper parts of their bodies.

Several of the women had brats clutched to their breasts or wound around their legs. The older children, also in rags, were the castoff children of the colony's prostitutes. They maneuvered through the legs of their elders, with a cunning in their eyes borne of a constant desire for food. If any chance box of cargo were set on the wharf for seconds without a watchful eye, these young thieves would have it before its marine guard could blink.

On the fringes of the convict crowd stood the free settlers. As a group they were good, honest men, who had left England with hopes of finding something better in a new land.

In many ways Rourke admired them, for they had the grit of true pioneers, and they truly did want the colony to grow and to prosper. But he also looked down on them as idealistic fools. For they were too few, and they would grow fewer as more and more lazy convicts arrived to steal the fruits of their hard labor.

A couple of these farmers called out to him as he passed through their line. Rourke chose to ignore them, and pitched himself forward through the steamy bodies of the convict crowd.

He was nearly through them to the line of marines holding them back with crossed muskets and fixed bayonets, when a tug at his sleeve and a husky female voice arrested his progress.

"B'gar, Cap'n, you'd think you was to oversee the unloadin' yerself, yer in sech a hurry!"

He paused, looking down, and smiled.

"Why, Cora Lee, I thought you'd gotten a man and gone upriver to stake a shack and garden."

"That I did, Cap'n. Married him even, I did! Jeff Capp by name. A lifer he was."

"Was?"

"Bloody natives got 'im . . . split 'is skull, they did. They'd a got me but I hid under the hut, I did."

Rourke's smile broadened. "Good for you, Cora Lee."

"And good fer you, Cap'n," she replied, moving against his arm.

Like the other convicts, she was dressed in a ragged skirt and there were no shoes on her feet. A laced leather shirtwaist was the only other piece of clothing she wore. And she wore nothing beneath it. Rourke dropped his eyes to her sharply pointed breasts. They could be seen clearly between the laces, and bulged invitingly in the vest's opening as she pressed their fullness against his arm.

"Why is that, Cora Lee?" he asked, willing himself not to bend to the animal pull of the young prostitute.

"Be there a bit of rum in that cargo, Cap'n?" she whispered.

"Aye, there may be," he replied in the same hushed tones.

"Well, if there be and some of it be yours, mayn't we take up where we left off?" She smiled coyly.

Rourke remembered the many nights, months before, with this winsome young wench. She had been the pick of the camp then, and, from the looks of her, still was.

He was tempted. But now he had other, more important things on his mind. However, Cora Lee might be of another use.

"I've a new hand since you've been gone . . . name of Jack Moran."

"So?"

"So, when this day's work is done, I'll owe him."

There was a pause as the meaning of his words sunk in, then her lips curled down in a pout. "And what's fer me, if I takes care of 'im?" she asked, still pressing her breasts to Rourke's arm.

"Rum."

Her eyes widened and her full, sensual lips split in a smile. "I'll be in me shack."

Chuckling, he reached around her slender body and squeezed an ample buttock until she squealed.

"For rum, lass, you'd bed the devil."

"Aye, I would," she said, laughing and shrugging away from him, making her breasts dance inside the vest. "And have! . . . fer haven't I bedded you, Steven Rourke?"

2

"DINGO!"

With a groan; Annie Hollister bent to pick up the little calico dog from the floor, wrinkling her nose and sticking her tongue out as she returned it to her baby brother where he sat squirming and tied into the roughhewn high chair.

Billy shrieked and gurgled with glee, and promptly propelled the stuffed dog back to the floor.

"Dingo! Dingo!" he cackled, loving this game of throw-doggie-to-the-floor, watch-Annie-pick-it-up-again.

"I'm going to Dingo you, you little imp!" Annie laughed, once more retrieving the animal and burrowing it into Billy's chubby little fist. "Ma will have my hide if this floor isn't scrubbed to a fair-thee-well when she gets back!"

Billy gurgled his complete understanding, and planted a gooey kiss on the dog's lone button eye.

Shaking her head, Annie pulled herself to her feet and looked around with satisfaction at the gleaming room. Clean it was, and backbreaking to make it that way. The wattle and daub home was more like a hut than a house, but it was all they had. And at least it was theirs.

Overhead, the thatching was parting in places, and she made a mental note to remind her brother Tom to repair it. Luckily they had secured a few lengths of discarded canvas months before to place over the worst of the thatching. But now it was rotting and they had only newly woven thatch to take its place.

She made to move into the hut's only other room, her mother and father's bedroom, and then thought better of it. It could be cleaned later. Her back ached like the very devil, and her knees were raw from the scraping they'd taken on the rough plank floor.

"But at least we have planking," she murmured with some satisfaction, "while most still do with packed dirt and rushes." .

With a sigh she moved to the hearth, and stirred a stew simmering in their one iron kettle above the fire. Closing her eyes she leaned forward to inhale the enticing aroma of fresh cabbage and onions mixed with a few bits of precious meat.

"Meat," she said, running her tongue across her lips and again bobbing her head toward the stew.

She couldn't remember the last time she cooked a stew that had meat. And there wouldn't be meat in this one if her brother Tom hadn't run across a pair of natives who had just killed a roo. Skillfully he had gotten their trust and then bartered a few vegetables for a generous slice off the kangaroo's rump.

And thank heavens, too, for a meat-flavored stew would celebrate the day.

It was a special occasion. Her parents and Tom had hitched their tired old mare to their wagon early that morning and driven the five miles into Port Jackson. A ship was due in port from America, and with any luck it would have much needed farm implements, maybe even some livestock that Ben and Mary Hollister could afford.

Although the land was fertile along the Hawkesbury River, good for growing corn and grain, there was a crucial shortage of spades and axes needed for clearing the land. Annie sighed as she thought of how difficult the past year had been. This New South Wales was so different from what they had known in England. There was no botanist or geologist on the island, and practically no one who could advise them about that most difficult of all things which they had set out to do: to make European plants grow in land that was utterly alien to them, a country where winter fell in summer, where there was no manure for the soil, where no one knew from one day to another what the temperature was going to be, where the wind was going to come from and at what velocity, or whether or not rain was going to fall.

No one had foreseen the extreme toughness of the timber to be cleared, nor the aridity of a soil that was baked iron-hard by the fierce summer heat. No one had anticipated that no limestone would be found for the making of mortar, or that long droughts would be followed by floods that would wash away the surface soil from their fields.

They had no horses to plough with, and once their provisions were exhausted, no reserves of any kind. Of necessity, they had taken over some of the aborigines' hunting grounds, and the natives were bound to try and defend their rights and to take reprisals.

And worst of all were the convicts themselves, the main reason for Port Jackson in the first place.

Living far from London, the Hollister family had no idea of the extent of overcrowding in British jails. When they heard of this new place called New South Wales they believed it to be some kind of paradise where there was land for the taking. No other nation had claimed it.

Now Annie knew why. No other nation had wanted it.

They had been told of the penal colony, but not how large it would be and how fast it would grow, with more and more convicts and fewer free settlers.

And not enough food for any of them.

The sheep-stealer, the pickpocket, the forger, the house-breaker, aye, even the highwayman and murderer, had plied their trade in or near cities in England. They knew little of farming and country life.

So when they were dumped in this uncivilized land, where survival meant working with one's hands to make the ground yield grain, most were either too ignorant or too lazy to do it themselves.

Consequently they stole from those who did, like the Hollisters; the Hunnicutts, a neighboring family of free settlers; or from the few convicts who were willing to work the land.

Annie mused with helpless frustration. It was a situation that bordered on lunacy. How could they hope to survive in this arid and hostile place?

Benjamin Hollister was a huge, powerful man, but even with his son Tom's help, he was beginning to show the strain of the backbreaking work of clearing the land of rocks and battling the infernal mallee.

They had never heard of mallee before coming to New South Wales a year ago from their native England. Although almost everything about the new frontier was different from anything they had known, mallee was proving to be the most intractable. It was a dwarf eucalypt with slender stems that grew in bunches, making it look like a bush rather than a tree. Before the land could be cultivated, the farmer had to get rid of the mallee, which was easier said than done. He could chop it down, if he had an axe; pull it down, if he had a horse and plow; or burn it down. Either way, within a few weeks it would once more be dense enough to get lost in.

And it wasn't only the men who wore the brunt of such a hard way of life. Her mother, Mary, was also showing the strain. Already her face had aged greatly in the single year since their arrival.

Idly, Annie turned her large, almond-shaped eyes to her own reflection in the cracked mirror above a makeshift wash basin, and made a face at what she saw there.

Yes, she too had aged, but not as severely as her mother, and not in the same way. Gone were the peach-tinted cheeks and alabaster complexion that was her natural color. In its place was a golden brown that set off the lightness of her auburn hair, hair that had lightened in the sun until it was nearly the color of burnished copper.

She still had the high, prominent cheekbones and the smooth lips that were just short of being too full and provocative when she smiled. Her nose was almost aristocratic and perfectly straight, with a slight upward tilt at its tip.

Her eyes, under delicately arched brows, were a deep green, and when they flashed with anger, as they often did, they seemed flecked with orange.

Now they looked sad, almost lusterless, mirroring the distress and despair she felt in her heart.

She was tall and full-figured yet trim. Her soft, full curves, even in cheap lindsey-woolsey skirts and blouses, never failed to draw catcalls and leering glances on her infrequent trips to Port Jackson.

Her body suddenly quivered at the thought.

Convicts.

Other than her own brother, the only young men she had seen since their arrival were prisoners. True, many of them were boyishly handsome, and often their only crime had been to purloin a loaf of bread to fill their starving bellies. But they were still convicts, and no matter how much awe and open admiration she detected in their eyes when they stared at her, Annie knew that there would never be a beau from that quarter.

Indeed, she thought ruefully, there might never be a beau for her unless she one day returned to England. Already she was seventeen, and the thought had lately entered her mind that her lot in life would be that of an old maid.

"Enough of such moody thoughts, Annie Hollister!" she scolded herself, planting her fisted hands on her hips and again gazing about the room. " 'Tis a life you've got here, with a family you love and who loves you. 'Tis enough now, so back to work!"

"Gaa-ffftt!" little Billy cried out in reply.

"Aye, you're so right, little one," she said with a laugh.

Shrugging her recent thoughts from her mind, she ran the back of her hand over her forehead to brush a few stubborn strands of auburn hair from her face, then knelt once again beside the wooden bucket on the floor.

Splashing the rag into the hot water, she wrung it out and began scrubbing the pine planks beside Billy's highchair. She scrubbed with a vengeance, determined to finish this distasteful chore as quickly as possible. Then she would treat herself to a long, hot bath, and be fresh when her Pa and Ma got back from Port Jackson.

"Goo-daa-gaa-ppft," came the small voice from above her. Then, "Dingo!" with a shriek, and Annie got a faceful of water as the little calico dog fell with a splat into the bucket.

Soap dripping from the end of her nose, she looked up at Billy where he peered cautiously over the arm of the highchair, his eyes wide with fear of the spanking he was sure was coming.

"Dingo?" he whispered.

Annie tried to be cross, but that chubby, innocent little face and brown eyes as big as saucers tugged at her heartstrings. In spite of her exasperation, she burst out laughing.

"Oh, Billy, I should take the switch to your little bottom," she said, shaking her head. "But Dingo *was* ready for a bath!"

"Ba-ba!" Billy chirped as he watched her retrieve the dripping toy from its watery grave.

Annie shook the excess water off the dog, plumped up its straw stuffing, and set it near the fire to dry.

"There you are, Dingo," she chuckled. "Just don't shrink!"

"Is it toys yer still playin' with, Annie Hollister?"

Annie whirled at the sound of the voice, and the sarcastic giggle that accompanied it.

Josie Hunnicut stood on the stoop just beyond the open door, a shawl thrown over her shoulders and her baby brother, Joseph, in her arms.

"Hello, Josie . . . I was just . . ."

"Jest doin' the same as me, I'll wager," the girl interrupted, the corners of her rosebud lips curling into a pout. "Tendin' to the brats while everyone else goes off to Port Jackson."

"Aye, they—"

Again the girl interrupted. "Mind if I come in fer a spell? I got bored at the home place, and onc't the sun peeked out I thought I'd walk a bit."

"Of course, come on in. I'll make some sweet tea."

"I'd rather have a tiny dram o' rum, if ya have it . . . or a spot o' wine?" Josie said, giggling again and flowing past Annie to a corner cot. Once there, she unceremoniously dumped her sleeping brother.

"I . . . I might find a glass," Annie replied after a moment's hesitation. Rum was gold, and wine was silver. Her father usually saved it for very special occasions. But, Josie was a guest.

Annie moved into the other room and rummaged in a trunk until the precious bottle was found. Returning, she came up short when she saw that Josie had removed her shawl and was now smoothing her hands over what was obviously a new dress.

"Ya like it, Annie? Ain't it lovely?"

"Yes . . . yes, Josie," Annie stammered, quickly quelling the burst of jealousy that had filled her breast at the sight of the dress. "It's very pretty."

And it was; the material was of a deep blue that accented the lighter blue of Josie's eyes. The sleeves were full, elbow-length, and the neck was deeply scooped.

Josie's small, pert breasts rested alarmingly high above the bodice and seemed about to pop free with every move she made.

Another pang of jealousy struck Annie when she saw the lacy top of a chemise peeking just above the neckline.

Annie didn't own a single chemise, and suddenly the rough weave of her own skirt and blouse grated against her bare skin.

"Very pretty," she said again as an afterthought, and turned to search for a wooden cup.

"It ain't like it was grand silk or satin or anythin' like that," Josie chattered on, "but at least it's better'n the sackcloth and lindsey-woolsey I usually got to wear."

The back of Annie's neck burned thinking what her own much-mended clothing must look like beside Josie's new finery.

The other girl must have caught Annie's mood and the sudden tenseness in her body. She moved up to Annie's side and grasped her gently by the elbow.

"Oh, Annie, I didn't mean . . ."

"It's all right, Josie," she quickly replied, turning to look down at the shorter girl, "I know you didn't mean anything."

She handed Josie the cup half-filled with wine, and turned back toward the fire to prepare herself a cup of sweet tea.

"If your Daddy wants to risk growing a little tobacco so he can buy you a new dress now and then . . ."

Josie whooped and whirled around the room. "Oh, I didn't get this dress with no 'baccy," she said, nearly convulsed with laughter. "There's other ways!" Suddenly she stopped, leveling her coquettish blue eyes on Annie. "If ya know what I mean . . ."

Annie didn't, not really. But she didn't understand much of what Josie Hunnicut said any more. Josie and her folks had come over on the same ship with the

Hollisters, and on the crossing the two girls had become friends. Then, Josie had been a petite, pert girl filled with a zest and enthusiasm for a new life in a new land.

That had quickly disappeared when Josie saw the new land and discovered all the hardships that went with it. She soon became sullen and withdrawn. Her previously impish features had become pinched, until there was a tautness around her pouting mouth that often suggested cruelty.

Even though they were both the same age, and John and Abigail Hunnicut were farmers like her own parents, Annie found herself drawing further and further away from the girl during those first months after their landing.

But now, in the last two months, Josie had reverted to her old self. At least a part of her old self, Annie thought, staring at the girl across the room.

She was still pretty, with her golden blonde hair, her blue eyes, and her petite, compact figure. But now there seemed to be a tart, almost cheap, quality in the way Josie looked. And the former innocence of her impish face had been replaced with a hardness that was caused by something beyond the hardships of their life. That hardness was now in Josie's eyes as she stared back at Annie.

"What you thinkin', Annie Hollister?"

"Nothing," Annie replied quickly. Then suddenly she laughed. "Yes, I was. I was thinking that I might grow some tobacco myself this year. Even if Governor Phillip has made it against the law to use grain land for it, the men still want tobacco almost as much as rum!"

"I tol' you, Annie, 'baccy didn't get me this here dress."

"Oh? Then how did you get it, Josie? I mean, it seems like every time I see you, you're wearing a new frock."

"Never you mind how!" the girl shouted, a sudden flush reddening her entire face.

"I . . . I'm sorry, Josie . . ."

The sudden outburst of anger confused Annie. What could be the reason for it? There was no doubt about it, Josie had changed. She was talking and acting very strangely. And now that Annie thought about it, this unreasonable anger over apparently nothing had happened before.

Annie knew Josie's folks were as poor as her own. Neither family had money to spend on luxuries.

If it wasn't a harmless illegal sale of tobacco that had gotten the girl her new finery, what had?

But before Annie could press the point, Josie spoke again, calmly moving the discussion to something else.

This was another thing about Josie lately; her moods changed quicker than the weather.

"Your folks in Port Jackson meetin' the ship?"

"Aye." Annie nodded, wishing now that the girl would leave.

"Mine, too. They need a new plow or somethin'. I wanted ta go with 'em, but they said I had to mind the baby."

"Me too," Annie said, wondering why Josie had come by, if it was only to drink her father's liquor and argue.

"Did . . . uh, did Tom go with 'em?" Josie suddenly blurted.

So that was it. Annie had noticed that whenever her older brother was around, Josie would suddenly appear on the scene, all decked out in a fresh clean dress, her honey blonde hair shining and done up with fancy ribbons. Not that Annie could blame her. Even she had to admit that Tom was good-looking. He was stocky and strong, his thick black hair always tumbling out of control across his handsome, open face.

At one time, not too long ago, Annie would have

been thrilled at the idea of having Josie as a sister-in-law. But not now. Not with the new Josie.

"He went along to pick up supplies at the public store house," Annie replied, a slight smile touching her lips. "They won't be back much before dark."

Josie's pretty face screwed into a petulant pout, then brightened, her blue eyes twinkling with mischief. "Makes no never mind. I've got another . . . friend . . . anyway."

"Oh?" Annie's brow arched in interest at this new bit of gossip. "Who?"

"Oh, not anyone you'd know," Josie said with a shrug. "He lives in Port Jackson. He's real important. He thinks I'm beautiful, and he . . ." The girl stopped, her eyes leveling with Annie's, the mischievous twinkle being replaced with a look Annie couldn't define. "Really, Annie, you should spend more time in Port Jackson."

"Oh, Josie, you know I can't."

"I'm serious, Annie. There are men there . . . powerful men . . . with money . . . and . . ." She checked herself midsentence. "Well, you just should, that's all!"

Suddenly Josie was by her and tugging her little brother up in her arms.

"I'd better go, I had. Pa will more'n likely tan me good if supper ain't on when they get back. Damme, that's all we are in this hateful place . . . babysitters, weed-howers, cooks, scrubbers . . ."

At the door she paused mid-sentence and again whirled to face Annie. Her face was crafty now rather than impish, and there was an icy quality in her clear blue eyes.

"Maybe one day, Annie Hollister, you'll grow to hate this place like I do. Maybe some day you'll come down off yer holier-than-thou highhorse and want a new dress yerself, so you can look and feel like a lady again."

"Josie!"

But she was gone, flouncing across the yard and through the gate.

Annie watched the girl as she set off down the dirt lane leading to the Hunnicutt farm. Then she shook her head and moved back into the cottage, closing the door behind her and leaning against it.

Josie really could be infuriating at times.

But where did she get all those new clothes?

And why did she accuse me of being holier-than-thou?

3————————————————————————

CAPTAIN Steven Rourke cursed under his breath as he elbowed his way through the last of the milling crowd around the wharf. At last he broke the line of marine guards and reached the foot of the *Venture*'s gangway. Once there he paused, casting an eye back over the crowd.

He could practically read the minds behind the anxious faces. The convicts were wondering what they could steal, and the bloody free settler farmers were fearful that the chits they held wouldn't be enough to purchase the provisions they needed.

The farmers came to Port Jackson only rarely, and when they did they usually returned to their grubby little plots empty handed. The uncouth oafs hauled in their sacks of corn and grain, queued up before harrassed government clerks who registered all commodities brought in for sale or barter, and in turn handed out chits that could be used as currency. The farmers hoped to barter their meager wares for a bolt of cloth, a pair of new boots, or maybe some timber for a new silo.

Bloody fools, Rourke thought.

He almost had more respect for the convicts. At least they had been forced to come to New South Wales. Rourke couldn't imagine any man volunteering his soul to such a place.

Again scanning their anxious faces, his mouth set in

a sardonic smile. He had the only thing worth bartering.

Blessed rum.

"Cap'n!"

Rourke turned, his eyes searching for the source of the voice, his convict aide, Jack Moran. He spotted the giant at the end of the gangplank, making fast one of the ropes.

The man's huge hands worked deftly, and with each movement the corded muscles in his enormous arms rippled and tensed. Moran was an ominous figure, even in broad daylight. He had a bull-like neck and a thick forehead that lay like a shelf over narrow, darting eyes.

Rourke's eyes held on Moran's hands, and a slight shiver passed up his spine. They were more like the paws of a bear than the hands of a human being. Rourke knew those hands could crush the life from a man in seconds.

He had seen them do it.

Moran was dressed in an open-necked broadcloth shirt, more tattered than whole, and equally ragged breeches that barely contained his log-like legs. Unlike the other prisoners who hadn't owned a pair of shoes for months, Moran, because of his status as Rourke's chief bully, wore knee-high rolled boots.

The most imposing part of his costume was a wide leather belt held with a huge iron buckle. Many a prisoner had felt the lash of that belt and the bite of that buckle on their skulls when they hadn't jumped quickly enough to Moran's commands.

Rourke had spotted the man's talents at once. Like himself, Moran believed in rule by fear.

But that didn't mean that Rourke liked the bull-necked giant. Actually he despised him. Moran had a quarrelsome, volcanic temperament, and Rourke suspected that the man would slit his back from gizzard to earlobe for the right price. But he was useful for Rourke's purposes for the time being.

"Odds blood, Cap'n, where ye been!" the big man

roared when Rourke reached him. "Cap'n Brownlee is waitin' on ye fer the bills of lading, an' his men are a might eager fer a touch o' dry land . . . not to mention the feel of somethin' soft and curvy under 'em!"

Rourke laughed and patted his inside uniform pocket where the proof lay of his ownership of this cargo. "Then let's not keep the good Captain waiting," he replied.

Then he moved closer to Moran and spoke in a low voice from the side of his mouth.

"Offload the supplies and tools first, Jack. That will draw this crowd to the supply house. There's no need for the swine to know the bulk of the cargo."

"Aye, Cap'n, ol' Jack gets yer drift."

"See the job done well, and there'll be a little extra warmth in your bed tonight."

Moran chuckled. "You mean there's a whore in Port Jackson I ain't had, Cap'n?"

"Aye, and one you've wanted," Rourke replied with a slow grin. "Cora Lee." He could practically see the drool slide from Moran's slack mouth. "She'll be in her shack when you've finished here."

"Damme, Cap'n, yer a saint!"

Rourke threw back his head and roared with laughter, then clapped Moran on the back and vaulted up the gangplank.

The narrow eyes became slits as Moran watched the red uniform tunic cross the deck and disappear. "And yer a bloody bastard," the giant added under his breath, "but I'll take yer leavings, fer now."

But Jack Moran did look forward to a night with the convict wench, Cora Lee Fenner. He'd lusted for her months before, when she was Rourke's regular woman. A time or two he'd almost raped her. But she ran her tongue off to the Captain, and Moran had paid with twenty strokes of the cat across his back.

Thinking of her now, he could still feel the burning welts.

Aye, lassie, he thought, *tonight ye'll pay for every one of 'em.*

"File! Carnes! Get yer bloody arses down into that hold! An' mark me, if there's a seal broke on a single keg ye'll both be pig-meat by sundown!"

Toby File and Hazer Carnes were both small, wiry men with narrow shoulders and sunken chests. At times of extreme exertion, when they breathed deeply, it seemed as though their belly-buttons touched their spines.

Beside Jack Moran they looked like ferrets as they scrambled down the ladder into the *Venture*'s hold. Moran watched them jump to his command, and a wide, gap-toothed grin broke across his leathery face.

Weasels they were. But they were as useful to Moran as he was to Rourke. For a bit of rum they would do anything. Anything, that is, short of murder.

But then File and Carnes were never called upon to kill anyone. Jack Moran did his own killing.

The two men hit the soggy bottom of the hold and began moving among the crates and boxes . . . and what they realized were a good number of kegs.

"Blimey, would ya look at this!"

"Damme, lad, 'tis rum! Kegs an' kegs o' rum!"

Their eyes met in open awe. Even the lowliest convict in Port Jackson knew about the orders concerning ships' manifests. Seed, farm implements, clothing and food stuffs took precedence over rum in all cargoes. It was a rule for survival.

Even though File and Carnes could neither read nor write, they could count. Far above half of the *Venture*'s cargo was rum.

"Cap'n Rourke?"

"Aye, who else?" Toby File replied. "The man's a devil, but a smart one. With this much rum he could buy Port Jackson."

"An' well he might before he's done!"

Just then Jack Moran's bullet head appeared in the

hatch opening. "Step lively, lads, platforms and line comin' down. An', lads, the boxes and crates go first. I'll be fer tellin' ya when to unload the kegs."

Captain Richard Brownlee sat at his ease in a tall, carved chair, his doublet untrussed, his strong legs stretched before him, a pensive smile playing about the full lips that were nearly obscured by a thick, graying moustache. The man's face looked like leather tanned from many years of curing in the elements, his thick mop of black hair salted with gray matching his moustache. Despite his appearance, Rourke knew Brownlee's age to be near his own, thirty-two, maybe a year or two more. Young, to have command of such a prestigious ship as the *Venture*. But, from what Rourke had heard about Brownlee, the American captain was ambitious, a skilled seaman—as evidenced by his maneuvering the *Venture* through the tricky fog that very morning—and not above entering into a shady deal or two if it would profit either his pocket or his position.

Rourke was counting on that reputation.

As Rourke entered the cabin, Brownlee rose and bowed from his great height. "Captain."

"I bid you welcome to New South Wales," Rourke said, extending his hand.

"And a bloody rotten welcome it was, too," Brownlee grinned. "That confounded fog nearly shoaled us!"

" 'Tis fortunate that you are so skilled a seaman," Rourke replied. " 'Twould have been a grave loss of good men . . . and good rum."

"And methinks you would have grieved more for the rum," Brownlee chuckled, a twinkle lighting up his dark eyes. "Will you sit?" He spread a hand toward a chair by a small table on which perched a half empty flagon. "And speaking of rum, would you care for a drop of the cargo that I have risked life and limb to deliver to you safely?"

"Which brings me to a point. Your manifest?"

"Aye."

Brownlee extracted a sheaf of papers from the desk's center drawer and thrust them toward his visitor.

Rourke rifled through them until he found the page he wanted.

And then he smiled.

"As procurement officer for Port Jackson, I approve the ratio of your cargo. Where do I sign?"

Brownlee handed him a quill and indicated where to put his signature on both copies. Rourke signed with a flourish, and pushed one copy back to the captain before he spoke.

"You did get my letter in Capetown?"

"Aye." Brownlee nodded. "There's a hundred more kegs of rum in the hold than is recorded on the manifest."

Rourke couldn't suppress a smile. "I believe a toast is in order for your gallant bravery."

The captain of the *Venture* poured from the flagon into two cups, and handed one to Rourke. "To future health and wealth, my friend," he said, touching Rourke's cup with his own.

"In point of fact, 'tis on that very matter I have come to speak with you," Rourke replied, the smile disappearing from his lips, the expression on his face now deadly serious.

Brownlee didn't miss it. He looked across the table at Rourke, suddenly uneasy, his body stiffening in wariness. "Oh?"

Rourke's gaze never wavered as his eyes met the captain's. " 'Tis been brought to my attention that in the past you have engaged in, shall we say, questionable private enterprise that, were it brought to the attention of the American government, would result in the loss of your ship, if not your neck."

Brownlee came abruptly to his feet, his chair crashing over behind him. "Sir," he blazed, "you insult my reputation!"

Rourke laughed. "I make free with it, perhaps. But please spare me the righteous indignation, Captain. One of my trusted colleagues had the misfortune to be first mate on the *New Boston*."

At the sound of the name, Brownlee blanched. Slowly he sank back into the chair.

"Ah, I see you remember the *New Boston*," Rourke growled. "Yes, the pride of the new American Navy, lost on its last voyage, presumably to the elements. But you and I know that was not exactly the case, do we not, Captain? It was not a sudden gale or squall that scuttled her, but another ship . . . another *American* ship, at that. A ship who pretended distress until the *New Boston* drew alongside . . . and whose crew then boarded her, massacred every poor soul on board, looted her entire cargo, then set her afire and scuttled her. A ship whose captain was Richard Brownlee!"

Brownlee's black eyes blazed. "To call me a pirate is to say a foolish thing, sir," he hissed in a soft, deadly voice.

"A bit strong, perhaps. But I perceive you are growing rich with the fruit of thieving upon the seas," Rourke replied coldly.

"And *I* perceive that *you* are growing rich with the treasures of the ships that arrive here, and the labor of convicts who are no better than slaves under your command!" Brownlee raged, jumping to his feet and towering over Rourke. "*You* are growing rich with the blood of dead men!"

A sneer flickered over Steven Rourke's face. "Then it would appear that we have common ground, sir. We both desire to grow rich. Would it not make more sense for us to combine our resources and become *doubly* rich?"

Brownlee's weathered face grew thoughtful, his

black brows contracting until no more than a single deep furrow separated them. Then slowly a smile appeared. but not a gentle, open smile. It was a smile of resolve and determination that invested his brooding eyes with a gleam that was mocking, crafty, and almost wicked.

"Did you have a particular plan in mind, my friend?" he said softly, easing back into the chair.

Rourke smiled and raised the cup of rum to his lips. "As a matter of fact, I have," he said, taking a long draft of the sweet liquid. When he looked at Brownlee again, his eyes glinted like cold, hard steel.

The skipper of the *Venture* shifted uneasily in his chair and averted his own eyes from the other man's steady glare. As a slave trader making the Gold Coast to Barbados run, and later as a smuggler who supplied the illegal auction houses around New Orleans, Captain Richard Brownlee had met and bested some hard men.

He was a man who could size up another man at first glance. It was a talent that had saved his life many times. He had already sized up Captain Steven Rourke, and decided that here sat a man he could not bluff, and dared not cross.

"As you may know, Captain," Rourke continued, "the New South Wales Corps was formed for the express purpose of taking over from His Majesty's marines here in Port Jackson."

"Aye, I've heard."

"Governor Phillip will be leaving soon. When he does, Lieutenant Governor Grose will take command. I have chosen to shift my commission from the marines to the Corps, and stay in Port Jackson rather than return to England."

Brownlee's eyes opened wide and he leaned forward with a smile. "I pride myself, sir, in reading a man. If a man such as you opts to stay out here at the end of the world, I'd say he had a good reason."

"Then you would be correct, Captain Brownlee. Grose is a man who believes that the convicts are what they are—scum. He won't coddle them as Governor Phillip has done. And neither will all the rewards go to the free settlers. Major Grose is a commander who believes that his men come first."

Brownlee nodded with mock severity. "And well they should, for the hellish duty you have here."

"Too true, too true." Now it was Rourke's turn to lean forward and lower his voice to a conspiratorial tone. "As you may know, we of the New South Wales Corps will have, when Major Grose assumes full command, a rather . . . unique . . . position."

"It would seem so."

"It is up to us to maintain authority and discipline over the rabble that the Crown courts dump on these shores from England. 'Tis a distasteful business, to be sure, but one that needn't be without its rewards. Major Grose has seen fit to give us permission to pool our credits in England and to buy the cargoes of the occasional ship that finds its way to this Godforsaken place."

Brownlee nodded. "Of that I am aware, obviously, Captain Rourke, since it is you who now owns the bulk of the *Venture*'s cargo. What is your point?"

"My point is this, Captain. There are too few ships coming into Port Jackson, and too many members of the Corps to share them with."

The meaning of his words slowly dawned on Brownlee, bringing a smile to his lips. "And you would prefer, shall we say, a more . . . private fleet?"

"Exactly," Rourke replied, matching the captain's smile. "I will buy all the rum you can provide, from any source, no questions asked. You could make two runs a month with ease to South Africa, and deliver the cargo to me at a point south of here, near Botany Bay. Send a runner to notify me of your arrival, and you can be off-loaded and on your way within two days' time."

Brownlee leaned back in the chair and raised the cup of rum to his lips, his brows furrowing as he considered Rourke's proposition. Running short, relatively easy voyages between New South Wales and South Africa was far more appealing than battling the North Atlantic between America and the Continent. What would he use as an excuse to his superiors? Having the *Venture* down for repairs would salve their curiosity for several months. His scurvy crew would keep their mouths shut if he made it worth their while. And, besides, Rourke had a sword of sorts hanging over his head. How in thunder had he found out about the *New Boston*?

With a sigh he leaned forward across the table, his massive palm extended. "To rum," he declared.

Rourke's eyes pierced into Brownlee's. "It is important that you understand clearly, Captain. No one else is to know of our little arrangement."

Captain Brownlee shook his head as he met Rourke's icy stare. "I'm no fool, Captain Rourke. I like my head attached to my body."

"Good," Rourke growled, "then it is settled." He reached out and gave a perfunctory shake to Brownlee's outstretched hand. "I shall expect the first delivery within three weeks' time. Now, shall we celebrate our newly minted partnership with a decent meal and something to drink besides this gawd-awful rum?"

The crowd beneath the thatched overhang of the commissary hut was a noisy morass of bodies. On the fringe of the shouting men and women stood Ben Hollister and his son. Two meager sacks of seed, an axe and hatchet, some powder and shot, and a single slab of hardtack lay in the bed of the wagon beside them.

" 'Tis a bleak day, lad," the older man said with a

groan. "All these months to wait for a ship, and this is
the best we can do!"

"Aye, Father." Tom Hollister nodded with a solemn
frown.

Ben Hollister had the look of a hard-working man, a
man who spent nearly all his time in the outdoors. His
face was tanned a deep brown and crosshatched with
fine lines. His eyes held a perpetual squint from constant combat with the broiling sun. He was tall but
stoop-shouldered, as if there were a weight on his
broad back that couldn't be lightened. His gray eyes
seemed to mirror this mood as they shifted from their
meager purchases to what was left of the *Venture*'s
cargo inside the commissary hut.

"Ma and Annie are gonna be bad depressed. They
was countin' on maybe a dress apiece to lift their spirits some."

"Somethin' jest don't seem right," Ben said, his voice
low, as if he were speaking more to himself than to his
son.

From his shorter height, young Tom looked up to
study his father's expression. "You thinkin' the Corps
is holdin' out fer themselves, Pa?"

"Wouldn't be the first time, would it?" Ben's jaw
took on a solid set as he laid a hand on his son's shoulder. "Stay here a mite, lad, and watch the wagon. I'm
after havin' a look at the rest of the unloadin'!"

Without another word, Ben moved off through the
mud and the milling crowd. Deft hands patted his
pockets, searching for a purse, but Ben was used to it.
He slapped them away with a grunt and mumbled
curse.

He moved briskly past the area that held the officers'
barracks and the cooking ovens. The pungent smell
emanating from the kitchens told him that the convicts
would be dining tonight on their regular fare: watery
potato soup.

Idly, he wondered what the members of the Corps

and the higher ranking marine officers would be eating tonight. He didn't doubt that it could be kangaroo steak and kidney pie, washed down with aged lager from the Netherlands.

Since Major Grose had arrived, things had changed. And Ben was sure they would change even more. In the beginning, he had been hopeful. Even with the thieving natives and the thieving prisoners, they had produced two good crops, with enough extra to feed the tiny herd of new lambs.

But what good did it do to have credits, when the ships coming into Port Jackson brought nothing to trade them for?

Poor Annie and Mary. It was a hard place and a hard life for anyone, let alone two decent women.

Not even a dress to lift their spirits and bring a smile to their pretty faces.

Ben couldn't remember the last time he had seen his wife smile. For that matter, he couldn't remember the last time he had smiled himself.

Ben's pace quickened as he rounded the Tank Stream and made for the wharf. A few hoots and jibes reached him from the blockhouse where the male convicts were held, but he ignored them and hurried on past the belching smoke of the blacksmith to dockside where the *Venture* was moored.

One glance halted his steps, and his breath hissed through his teeth. His face became a mask of agonized anger.

It was no wonder the *Venture*'s cargo was so short on much needed supplies.

"Rum. The bastards overloaded her with rum!" he growled, his hands balling into fists at his sides. "What in God's holy name can we grow with rum!"

4————————————————————————————

DOCKSIDE was nearly deserted. The *Venture*'s crew struggled hastily to offload the last of the cargo. It was evident on every seaman's face that they wanted to finish the task and get on with the pleasures of being in port after a long voyage.

The two captains walked to the gangplank. Brownlee shouted last minute orders at his First Mate to oversee the rest of the unloading, and reminded the man set up a watch.

Rourke, in turn, quietly instructed Jack Moran to oversee the First Mate.

They quickly walked away from the wharf, toward the main camp's makeshift buildings. In minutes they approached the shouting crowd around the commissary store.

A few noticed the men's uniforms, and detached themselves from the others. In seconds Brownlee and Rourke were surrounded by potential purchasers angling for an inside line on merchandise that might not be in view in the store. Bony old men in convict yellow tugged at their sleeves. Prostitutes offered themselves in exhange for a meal, and their bastard children begged for a crumb of anything.

"Good lord, man, this is worse than Cheapside in London," Brownlee hissed in distaste as he shrugged aside one scrawny whore's whining pleas and caught up with Rourke as he strode toward a shabby wooden building next to the blacksmith shop.

" 'Tis exactly the same," Rourke hissed. "Our good King has filled his prisons to overflowing at home, and you Americans deprived him of another dumping ground when you won your war for independence, so now he ships the scum to us. It matters not whether the wretch has committed murder, or merely disagreed with the Crown's politics, the end is the same. We cannot build prison facilities fast enough to handle the influx, let alone grow enough food in this God-forsaken place to feed them."

"Do they all run loose like this?"

"Most," Rourke replied, as at last they cleared the crowd. "And why not? They've no place to go. Overland they would fall prey to the black savages, and the ocean is full of sharks. A few, the worst, are kept permanently in chains. They are the real incorrigibles, the ones who murder for the sheer joy of killing."

Brownlee's face went white. "Why aren't they hung?"

Rourke shrugged. "They most probably will be. . . one day. They were granted reprieves in England and sent here because they could afford to buy this instead of swinging from the noose."

"God, a week in this place and I'd be ready for Bedlam myself!"

Again Rourke shrugged. "At first it bothered me somewhat. But now I realize that they are all worthless and I would do better to direct my concerns elsewhere."

"Aye, if I had your duty, I'd line my pockets with gold as well," Brownlee declared.

The look Rourke shot back at him made him instantly regret that he had made the statement.

Then Rourke relaxed somewhat. "You are naive as to the realities of this new frontier, my friend. The only thing that matters here is survival."

"Aye, and none of us will survive, as long as those at

home let the likes of you steal the food from our table!"

Rourke paused, letting his icy stare fall on the speaker, a big, raw-boned man with thinning brown hair turning to gray.

"You spoke to me, sir?"

"Aye, for they tell me you're the officer that signed ashore this pittance we've got to pick over."

"You're a free settler, aren't you?" Rourke said, eyeing the man's clothing.

"Aye. Ben Hollister. This is my son, Tom. We've a hundred and fifty acres on the Hawkesbury. Fair land it is, but little good it does us."

"I don't know what you're talking about, Hollister. As a free settler you have first pick of the cargoes. If you don't have the credits—"

"To hell with your credits, sir!" Ben Hollister cried, pulling chits from his pocket and waving them in Rourke's face. "What good are they unless I want to buy rum!"

Rourke and Brownlee exchanged looks.

Two marines, bayonets fixed on their muskets, appeared at Rourke's elbow.

"Trouble, sir?"

"Aye, there's trouble when an honest man can get no reward for his honest labor!"

Hollister was shouting now, and Rourke noticed that several men around the commissary hut had taken notice. It was just this sort of thing that could start a mob riot.

"No trouble," he told the marines, waving them away and then stepping forward for a closer confrontation with the farmer. "Mister Hollister, I think you know the bartering value of rum."

"Aye, for these poor souls . . ." He paused, waving his arm in the direction of the massed convicts. " 'Tis oblivion they seek in rum. 'Tis no wonder they won't work without it."

"The convicts are not your affair or your problem, Mister Hollister," Rourke said coldly.

"Damme if they aren't, man!" Hollister bellowed, his hand flashing out to grip Rourke's shoulder. "When they steal my crops to buy your filthy rum!"

Rourke's own hand came up to grip the other's wrist. Though Ben Hollister was the same size and build of the Corps officer, and his sinewy muscles had been hardened with labor, his grip was no match for Steven Rourke's. His face flinched in pain as Rourke grasped and twisted his arm.

"Pa!" Tom took a step forward.

"Stand off, lad," Rourke hissed in a low voice, then turned back to the older man. "Now I suggest you take your chits and obtain what rum you can, Hollister."

"At your prices, I suppose?" Ben growled through gritted teeth.

"Aye, at my prices. And take what you can trade it for and go back to your place on the Hawkesbury."

"The devil I will!" Hollister replied, jerking his arm free at last. "Your Major ain't the law here yet. Governor Phillip is a just man. We'll see what *he* says about your rum trade!"

"I wouldn't do that, Hollister . . . and besides, it isn't *my* rum trade. It's the Corps'."

Ben Hollister stopped in his tracks. The anger on his face turned to disgust, and then gloom.

"Aye. The bloody Corps. You'll have us all dead and buried with your profiteering before we've had a chance to begin."

Steven Rourke shrugged, turned on his heel, and moved on with Brownlee close behind him.

"Damme, Rourke, what if the farmer counted the kegs?"

"What if he did?"

"But if he tells the Governor—"

"If he tells the Governor, I'll get a reprimand. I'm no longer a marine, Brownlee, I'm in the Corps. And the Corps is Major Grose. Things are changing in Port Jackson . . . and here is one of them."

Brownlee, trying to still his fears about the false manifest he had been a party to, followed his companion through the rough-hewn door of what appeared to be no more than a one-story hut.

Once inside. Brownlee came up short.

The room before him was not opulent, but it was a far cry from the squalid conditions existing just outside the door. It was set up as a dining room, small but comfortable, with a half dozen tables and cane-backed chairs. A carpet of woven foliage covered the plank floor, and the air was filled with the aroma of freshly cooked victuals.

Rourke chuckled as he watched the expression on the sea captain's face. "Another one of the little rewards of being a member of the Corps," he said lightly, and gestured to a table. "Such refinements would be wasted on the riffraff outside, don't you agree? In any event, we in the Corps need a respite from the impossible conditions of the settlement, and a place where we may entertain our guests. Robbie!"

As Brownleee eased himself into a chair, a canvas curtain in the far wall was pulled aside and a slender young man with huge brown eyes and delicate, almost feminine features hurried into the room.

"Good afternoon, Captain Rourke," he said, his voice almost a whisper.

"Robbie, we have the honor of entertaining Captain Brownlee of the *Venture*."

"Captain, sir," the young man said, bowing slightly from the waist to Brownlee. "An honor, sir. How may I serve you, gentlemen?"

"You may start by bringing us a bottle of chilled white port," Rourke replied. "And then instruct Ming to prepare a wild pheasant, with rice and fresh fruit. We must convince Captain Brownlee that we are not all savages here!"

"Very good, sir. I shall bring the port straight away," the young man replied, and disappeared behind the curtain.

"A trifle young, and . . . frail . . . to be in the Corps, isn't he?" Brownlee asked when Robbie was out of earshot.

Rourke leaned back in the chair and roared with laughter. "Good lord, man, Robbie's not in the Corps. He's a convict! I understand he comes from a damn good family. That's probably why he can set a table."

"What did he do?"

"Murdered his lover, fit of passion, I understand. The fellow wanted to leave Robbie for a woman."

Brownlee raised an eyebrow but said nothing as the young man returned with the port and two wooden goblets.

"We had some pewter when we first arrived," Rourke chuckled, "but it was stolen to melt down and fob off to the natives as weapons."

The meal came, and both men fell to it with healthy appetites. At last they were sated, leaning back over a dram of rum.

"Filthy stuff, actually," Rourke said, "but really all we can get out here." He raised his cup. "I prefer brandy or a good claret myself. Here's to the day when I can enjoy them both with a long-legged, big-bosomed French filly, far from this pesthole!"

"Hear, hear!" Brownlee chorused, and tipped his cup. When it was drained, he leaned forward across the table with one eye cocked to the door. "In the absence of a French filly, Captain Rourke . . ."

"Say no more," Rourke interrupted with a nod. "Nearly every female on this continent is a whore, in one way or another. Most of them are what you saw in the streets . . . underfed, filthy, and diseased. We try to keep one or two of the more healthy ones for ourselves."

He made the statement so matter-of-factly, it oc-

curred to Brownlee that he could have been talking
about cows or sheep, rather than human beings.

Brownlee wondered if Rourke really cared about
anything, or anyone. He didn't think so.

But at this point, he didn't care. It had been a long
voyage.

"Listen, my friend, I don't care if they are bow-
legged, knock-kneed and cross-eyed . . . I haven't
been between a woman's thighs for nigh onto two
months now, and more than my belly is hungry for sus-
tenance!"

Rourke chuckled. "Then I suggest we move, before
some of my comrades finish their meal and the same
urge comes to them. The girls tend to tire quickly, I'm
told."

He rose and gestured Brownlee through the heavy
canvas drapery in the far wall. On the other side was a
hallway, with the door to the kitchen leading off to the
right, and another door on the left.

Without knocking, Rourke opened the second door
and entered, with Brownlee close behind him.

It was more cell than room, airless and windowless,
and illuminated by candles placed in wall sconces.
Once his eyes became accustomed to the dimness,
Brownlee made out three alcoves off the main room.
They were also lit by candles, with sheets of worn can-
vas hung for privacy.

"Damme, it's a sty!"

"Aye, not much more," Rourke agreed, "but it
serves the purpose. The cats in the cubicles are de-
loused daily, so at least you have no fear there."

Then he stepped aside and Brownlee's eyes lit on a
rush mat against the far wall.

Sitting on the mat were two women. One was a mere
girl, really, Brownlee mused, guessing her to be no
more than thirteen or fourteen. Much too young for his
tastes. He preferred his women a bit more mature,
more experienced, with lots of meat on their bones, ca-

pable of giving him a good, healthy romp. The child looked as though she would break in two if you breathed on her.

The older one, however, was a real beauty. She was a woman of perhaps some twenty years, of a beauty entirely Castilian. Her face was a warm olive hue, and was gracefully framed by the mass of ebony hair surrounding it. Her eyebrows were finely arched, and her eyes, when she lifted them, were a deep, soft brown under even darker lashes.

Her only clothing was a threadbare lavender robe, but it was silk and hugged her body like a second skin. The robe was belted beneath her sharply pointed breasts.

Dropping his eyes to the fullness of the woman's breasts, Brownlee could feel the erotic pull of her body.

As the two men studied them with a calculating eye, the younger girl began to shake visibly and inched backward on the mat, drawing a pillow up around her like a shield. The woman stood and faced them squarely, with a contemptuous fierceness flashing from her dark eyes.

Without a word, she loosened the tie at her waist and shrugged her shoulders slightly, letting the silk robe fall in a puddle to the floor.

Brownlee gasped as her voluptuous body was laid bare to his gaze. Her breasts were spectacular, ripe and full, the tiny veins leading in a delicate spiderweb to large chocolate brown nipples, the aureoles of which were beginning to pucker from exposure to the air.

Brownlee felt desire tighten in his groin as his eyes traveled down her naked body, to the slenderness of her waist, the womanly smooth and rounded belly. His gaze fastened onto the tufts of jet black hair that formed a perfect vee between her legs.

"You want her?" Rourke growled from beside him.

"She's almost worth a free load of rum," Brownlee croaked, tearing at the buttons of his trousers.

"She's a whore," Rourke hissed, and advanced toward the young girl where she cowered at the head of the bed.

Instantly, the woman came alive, her eyes blazing. "Leave her alone!" she spat, her words heavily accented. "I'll take care of both of you!"

Rourke whirled on her. "You do not give me orders, whore," he said, his voice like ice. "I will take what I want whenever I want it."

"No, *por favor*! She . . . she cannot give you the pleasure I can give you! See? . . . she is mere child, I am woman!" Her hands came up to cup her breasts, forming them into two huge thrusting cones in front of his face.

Rourke glared at her, then a slow smile creased his face. "She is a virgin."

"No! She . . . she is young, that is all. I . . . I am one who make you happy. I am woman!" Her hands left her breasts and began traveling down, down her voluptuous body, stroking the soft skin of her waist and belly, then lower, to run her long, tapering fingers along her inner thighs.

Her lips curled into a smile when she saw the effect she was having on Brownlee. But it quickly disappeared when she noticed the lack of interest in the red-coated Corps officer.

Rourke appraised her with a jaundiced eye, his gaze flickering from her dancing breasts to the roundness of her buttocks and thighs. Her silken calves looked strong despite their slenderness. The ankles were trim and delicately boned. She moved as gracefully as she did wantonly, but he detected a trace of weariness in her body, an inner weariness. The kind of weariness that came with selling her body time and time again for nothing more than enough food to stay alive.

Rourke didn't want her. Two months before, he

would have taken her without a second thought. But after having a woman who wasn't a prostitute, anything less was suddenly distasteful to him.

The woman's undulating body misted and faded in his eyes. In its place there was a particularly comely farm girl, a daughter of one of the free settlers. She was a pretty young thing, with shining, clean blonde hair and a coquettish flash in her blue eyes, as well as breasts that were blossoming like ripe, succulent fruit. Two months before, she had flashed those eyes once at Rourke, and he had taken it from there. It was quite convenient, in fact. All the girl seemed to want in return for her favors was a new dress and bright ribbons for her hair.

No whore in Port Jackson could compete.

A sound in the room forced his thoughts back to the present. The whore was speaking.

"Are the two of you men enough to handle such a woman?" she purred.

Rourke pulled his pipe from a pocket in his tunic. "She's yours, Brownlee."

With a roar the sea captain lunged, grasping her around the waist and lifting her like a feather. The woman screamed and kicked and clawed, but to no avail. The momentum of Brownlee's rush carried them forward into one of the cubicles and onto the cot.

With the woman still screaming, Brownlee entered her savagely. Rourke watched for a moment, and then moved to the doorway. He dropped the curtain and stood for a moment longer, listening to Brownlee's rutting. As much as it was distasteful to him, the sounds coming from the tiny cubicle brought a tug to his own groin.

When he turned to leave, his eyes fell on the younger girl. Her eyes were large and luminous as she watched the erotic scene through a crack in the curtain.

Slowly, Rourke moved forward until he stood

directly in front of the girl. When she noticed his presence, her eyes grew even wider and she began to shake her head violently from side to side.

Rourke unfastened the top buttons of his breeches. He replaced the pipe in his pocket, and withdrew a pouch of tobacco, dangling it before the girl's eyes.

"Tonight, around the fires, this will buy you food and rum."

There was only a moment's hesitation, and a quick flick of her eyes once more toward the cubicle, before her hands came up and her head moved forward.

How can we be anything but animals in this heathen place? Rourke thought, as he felt the warmth of her mouth envelop him.

A half hour later, Rourke and Brownlee closed the door behind them and moved down the narrow hallway toward the dining room. At the door to the kitchen, Robbie suddenly appeared.

"Everything to your satisfaction, gentlemen?" he said, a knowing smile splitting his delicate features.

"Interesting," Rourke growled. "An unusual pair, obviously new. Where did they come from?"

"From the Portuguese corsair that landed two weeks ago," Robbie replied. "They're sisters."

Rourke's eyebrows arched at the revelation. That explained the tigercat's protection of the little lamb.

He shrugged and was about to suggest a more experienced replacement, when suddenly a ruckus of male shouts and female screams sounded from the street outside.

Rourke and Brownlee moved quickly into the dining room. They shouldered their way through members of the Corps who were blocking the door, curious themselves as to the source of the melee.

On the street outside, all was bedlam. Everywhere men were fighting, their shouts mingling with the high-

pitched shrieks of the prostitutes as they encouraged
one bloke or another on to battle.

Brownlee threw back his head and his massive
shoulders rocked with bellowing laughter. "Just ventin'
a little steam, 'tis all, Captain Rourke," he roared. "A
little drinkin' and a little wenchin' after so long at sea
. . . 'tis natural that a little fightin' would follow. 'Tis
only healthy!"

Rourke nodded, but there was an uneasiness in the
pit of his stomach. It did appear to be little more than
a drunken brawl. But what had started it?

Did any of it have to do with the rum . . . his rum?

Then, suddenly, the fire from the blacksmith's shop
glinted off of something to his right, drawing his attention.

There, towering above the rest of the fighting mob in
the middle of the dusty street, was the giant form of
Jack Moran. A large crowd of neutral onlookers made
up of both seamen and convicts formed a circle around
him.

In Moran's hand, high above his head, Rourke could
see the leather belt the giant habitually wore. And at
its end, reflecting the blacksmith's fire, was the deadly
iron buckle.

Steven Rourke's blood ran cold. He knew his aide
was a man to be feared even when sober. If Moran had
had too much rum, it would take little provocation for
him to slit a man's throat wide from ear to ear, or dent
his skull to the brain.

"Moran!" he roared, using his broad shoulders and
jabbing elbows to make a path through the crowd.

He was not prepared for what actually met his eyes
when he finally broke through into the circle.

Moran stood, naked to the waist, sweat gleaming on
his swarthy skin and dripping from the mat of hair on
his broad chest. Behind Moran, Cora Lee crouched
like a cat, her dark hair a tangle around her face and
flashing eyes. The vest-tunic she had been wearing ear-

lier had been torn from her, so she too was naked to the waist. Her pear-shaped, firm breasts were heaving, and one of them dripped blood from a slight cut.

"Kill the bloody bastard, Jack, kill him!" she gasped, moving in the mud to stay behind Moran's huge bulk.

In front of Moran was a growling, snarling seaman from the *Venture*, and in his hand gleamed the curved blade of a ten-inch Moroccan dagger.

"That's Kashfir!" Brownlee whispered at Rourke's ear. "He's a bloody Arab, he is, an' he's a mean one. Saw him kill three blacks in Capetown in less than a minute with that sticker. One of 'em was near as big as your man there, he was."

"Moran, back off!"

Steven Rourke cared little how Jack Moran met his Maker, an Arab's knife or a noose. What he was concerned about was the timing. Right now he couldn't replace the big convict, so he wanted to keep him alive.

But Moran listened no more to Rourke than he seemed to hear Cora Lee's shout to "Kill the bloody bastard!" which she was repeating at intervals in a hoarse whisper.

The Arab was half the size of Moran, but he moved with the stealth and grace of an experienced knife fighter. Whether that would even the odds, Rourke didn't know.

They circled each other uncertainly, each carefully gauging the other. The Arab would feint forward with his ugly knife, only to be brought up short by the whir-ring sound of the belt in Moran's hand, the sharpened buckle coming within inches of his opponent's exposed belly.

Both men were drunk. Or at least they seemed drunk. The Arab weaved precariously, as did Moran, in their efforts to remain upright.

Then Rourke noticed something he had missed earlier when he had crashed through the circle of onlookers. Rourke had seen Jack Moran drunk many times, and this was not one of them.

Moran was acting.

But for whose benefit?

There was another feint with the knife, only to be aborted again by the lethal belt buckle. Around and around they continued, as they traded slurred insults.

The scene would have been comic were it not for the presence of the equally deadly weapons both men held.

Moran's face was livid and his eyes were blazing, the mouth twitching as he glowered at his enemy. "You scurvy dog!" he snarled. "I'll teach you to leave a man's woman alone!"

"Woman?" the Arab hissed. "She's a whore . . . an' yer a whore's son!"

"Stand and fight, weasel. I'll crack yer skull like an egg!"

"You go to the devil!" came the bellowing reply. "An' join yer mother there!"

"Arrrgghh!" Moran's hand flashed forward. The belt sang, and then the buckle struck.

Blood gushed from a weal in the Arab's face from his ear to his mouth. Moran made for another swing with the belt, but the Arab, screaming out his pain and fury in his native tongue, drove under the flying buckle.

The curved blade missed its intended target, Jack Moran's belly, but its sharp edge slid down his thigh, opening a six inch gash.

In his lunge, the Arab tripped. Moran was on him in an instant, his massive body propelling them both into the mud.

The smaller man struggled to draw his knees up between their bodies, then heaved with all his strength, raising Moran up off him for an instant. Quickly he rolled free and sprang up to his feet like a cat, whirling to face Moran once more.

"Come on, ye thievin' scum!" he panted. "I can take ye an' yer whole thievin' bunch!"

He crouched into a tight ball and lunged for the spot where Moran lay on the ground. But, for all his size, the giant was lightning-quick. He spun like a top in the soft mud, his powerful legs meeting the smaller man's at the knees.

As the Arab went down he tried for one last plunge of the curved blade. But Moran had already rolled clear and come up on one knee.

Twice the belt spun above his head, and then his arm flashed forward and down. The sound of the buckle slicing through the Arab's forehead was like that of an axe entering a tree in the now still air.

"Jesus gawd almighty," Brownlee whispered.

"Brownlee," Rourke hissed, his mind already whirling with possible conclusions to the affair. "Will you press charges?"

Brownlee shrugged. " 'Twas a fair fight. And if the truth be known, Kashfir was a damn trouble-maker anyway."

"Good. See to your man."

In the middle of the circle, Moran stood astride the groaning, bleeding man like a gladiator, wiping the blood from his belt.

Rourke grabbed him by the elbow and propelled him through the crowd until they were far enough away not to be overheard. There, he pushed the big man to the ground and began packing mud on the gaping and bleeding wound.

"You fool," Rourke hissed. "If the bloody bastard dies I'll have to put you back in irons . . . at least for a while."

"Oh, he'll die, Cap'n, you can be sure o' that," Moran said, his laughter whistling through the gap in his teeth. "I already made sure of it. A wound like that's a painful thing, an' believe me when I say he's a dead man."

Rourke stopped applying mud to the wound and shifted his concentration to Moran's stupid, grinning face. "You mean you meant to kill him?"

"Aye, Cap'n, that I did. An' that's why I got Cora Lee to wiggle fer him an' play him along. So's I'd have an excuse to cleave his skull."

This was another side of Jack Moran, the side that had killed on dark London streets and dumped bodies in the Thames. It was a side of the man that Rourke knew existed, but hadn't seen before.

"Why, Jack?"

"I see'd him talkin' about the rum to a couple o' free settlers. I snecked me up and listened to 'em."

"And?"

"The free settlers passed a lot of coin to the Arab."

"What did they want?"

"They wanted a count o' the rum kegs. The Arab was takin' 'em the count, an' goin' on to tell the Gov'ner his tale, when I set Cora Lee on 'im!"

Suddenly Rourke's smile matched that of the man before him. "A good day's work, Jack. There'll be a few kegs in your kip for tradin' tonight."

"I figured there would be, Cap'n."

"And tell Cora Lee to stop by in a few days for a few sovereigns."

"I'll do that, Cap'n."

Then Rourke's face clouded again.

"Are you sure he'll die, Jack?"

"Cap'n, I'll wager a keg he's already dead."

5

THE wagon ride back to the Hawkesbury from Port Jackson for the Hollister family was not a happy one. Tom sat on the rear of the wagon, red-faced and angry, muttering to himself. Ben Hollister drove the mare listlessly, leaving the reins slack in his fingers, allowing the old horse to pick her own way.

Beside her husband Mary Hollister sat white-faced, her hands clutched together in her lap. She had heard tales of native atrocities, of the wild and drunken orgies of the convicts. She knew that life was cheap in this rugged new frontier.

But she had never actually seen a man killed, literally murdered before her eyes.

It had sickened her, nearly making her swoon, as Ben and Tom helped her up into the wagon. The stark, white-faced fear came later, a mile or so outside Port Jackson, when Ben told her. He had relayed his suspicions about rum replacing the original goods in the *Venture*'s manifest. He told her about bribing the Arab to count the kegs, and then accompanying him and Tom to the Governor with their proof.

It was difficult for Mary Hollister, with her honest and open God-fearing English midlands thinking, to believe so ill of her fellow human beings.

At the conclusion of Ben's story, she had told him so.

"But, Ben, you can't be sure that it was premeditated. It could have been just a brawl. So many of the convicts are bent on violence."

"Aye, they are," he had replied, not meeting her eyes with his. "But you saw the way it happened, the way that little tart egged the man on. Nay, Mary, I do believe the big convict was a part of the rum scheme and was protecting his interests the only way he knew how. A'course, I'll never be able to prove it, any more than I could prove the officers of the Corps are behind it."

"Dear God," Mary had then murmured to herself, "what will we do when we lose Governor Phillip?"

"We'll fight back, that's what we'll do," Tom hissed from the rear of the wagon.

"Aye, lad, mayhap we'll have to start fightin' back . . . somehow."

"No, Ben!" Mary had suddenly cried out. "Before that I'd have us all back in England!"

Ben shot her a withering glance. "Ye know me thoughts on that, woman. We're not but tenants there. Damme, near slaves with nothing to call our own. Here, at least we have the land. I'll hear no more of it!"

And Mary Hollister had said no more. Her husband raised his voice rarely, but when he did, she knew not to raise his anger further.

Ben Hollister was not a violent man, but he was headstrong and set in his ways. He also had a streak of independence that would not let him live under the yoke of another man.

This Mary accepted, because she loved him more than life itself.

So there were no more words on the subject, and that's the way it remained when the wagon rolled into the cleared area in front of the Hollister house.

Annie met them with a smile on her face, but it quickly disappeared. There were no words of greeting from her father as he unhitched the mare and solemnly

led her toward the little shack that served as a stall.
From there he headed directly for the river bank,
where he always went when he had to think out a
problem.

There were mumbled words from her mother that
Annie couldn't understand as the woman walked right
past her and into the bedroom.

If such a sour greeting didn't tell her that they had
returned empty-handed, one look inside the wagon bed
did.

"This is all?"

"Aye," Tom glowered, hoisting a sack of seed to his
shoulder, "this is the lot. We've a pocketful of credits,
but no goods to show for 'em."

Annie's heart fell. She had set her hopes on a new
dress, and maybe even a bonnet.

And then she realized the full significance of this
development, and felt guilty with such thoughts.

Dresses weren't what they needed. They needed livestock, a plow and other equipment for the farm that
would help in the struggle to eke out a subsistence
from this alien soil.

She felt like sitting right down beside the wagon and
weeping. But she held her emotions in check. Spilling
her tears in the dust would do little to help their situation.

Instead, she helped Tom unload the wagon, and
then queried him about what had happened.

With his face still flushed with anger, he told her the
whole story. He left nothing out, including his and
Ben's suspicions. By the time he finished, the anger
was gone, replaced by a tone of anguish and disap-
pointment.

"Those bloody bastards of the Corps control everything."

"So it would seem," Annie agreed. "And if not
now, it appears that they soon will." And then the full

brunt of Tom's story struck her. "Dear God, we are living among savages!"

"Aye, we are . . . warden and prisoner alike!"

Supper that night was eaten in silence, the delicious and lovingly prepared stew tasteless in all their mouths. When the table was cleared and Billy placed in the trundle at the foot of his parents' bed, the family sat down around the fire. This was a time when the events of the day and the hopes of the morrow were usually discussed.

This night they all sat silently, each lost in his or her own quiet depression as they watched the embers crackle and slowly die in the hearth.

At last Tom could hold back no longer.

"Even if there had been enough livestock and supplies from the *Venture* to go around, the bloody bastards would set the price so high that none of us farmers would have enough barter chits to afford what we need!"

"Please do not swear, son," Mary Hollister said in a soft voice.

"But you know 'tis true, Ma!" Tom insisted, jumping from his chair and pacing back and forth in front of the fire. "They keep everything for themselves, lining their own pockets at our expense. It matters not a whit to them if we all starve out here on the Hawkesbury!"

"We'll not starve, son," Ben Hollister said in his deep, rumbling voice. "The soil is richer here on the Hawkesbury River than anywhere else in the colony. All we need is the right equipment, and some decent rain, and we'll have food aplenty."

"But we can't get the equipment, Pa," Annie cried.

Ben took a long drag on his pipe and thoughtfully watched the smoke curl in its lazy circles. "I'll be going over to Parramatta tomorrow. Ran into old Jacob Iverson at the dock today, and he says the market's a little freer there . . . the Corps doesn't have quite the stranglehold on Parramatta yet that it does in Port Jackson."

"I'll go with you!" Tom said excitedly.

Ben laughed. "You'll do most anythin' to avoid cuttin' mallee, won't you, son?"

Tom flushed. It was true. Keeping the dense mallee cut back was a muscle-wrenching chore, and the infernal stuff grew right back within weeks.

"Then we best get to bed early." Ben smiled wearily, rising and tapping the tobacco from his pipe into the fireplace. "Parramatta's another eight miles upstream, an' I want to leave by dawn."

Annie extinguished the candles. Both she and Tom undressed and changed into their nightclothes in the darkness. Across the room she could hear Tom crawl into his cot, and with a grunt turn toward the wall.

"Tom?"

"Aye?"

She started to speak, but suddenly the words wouldn't come.

"What is it, Annie?"

"I . . . were there many clothes that came in off the *Venture*?"

"Didn't see none, but there could'a been. Some of the crates didn't go to the commissary store. I seen 'em bein' carried right up to Officers Hill."

Annie lay down and bunched the straw-filled pillow beneath her head. She closed her eyes tightly, trying to will herself to fall asleep.

"Annie?"

"Aye?"

"I'm sorry I couldn't bring you back a new dress."

Suddenly, for no good reason, she felt like giggling. And did. "It doesn't matter. I don't think I want to start looking like Josie Hunnicutt anyway."

There was a moment's silence from Tom's cot, then he said softly, "I wouldn't want you to be like Josie Hunnicutt."

"I said *look* like her," Annie said, still giggling.

"I know what you said," Tom hissed back at her in a quiet whisper. "Go to sleep!"

But something was nagging at Annie that wouldn't let her sleep. It had been bothering her and tugging at the back of her mind since that afternoon.

"Tom, where does Josie get all those new clothes?"

There was a sharp inhalation from across the room, and then another long silence.

"Tom . . . ?"

"I don't know. Her Pa's probably growin' tobaccy."

"That's what I thought, but Josie said no," Annie insisted, and then exhaled in a deep sigh. There was another question that tugged at Annie's mind besides Josie's finery. She didn't know how to say it, so she just blurted it out in a low whisper. "Tom, how come you never go over to see Josie anymore?"

"Don't know. Not interested, I guess," came the curt reply.

"You used to be. She's the only girl our age among the free settlers. 'Tis only normal for you to court her . . ."

"Will you go to sleep?"

"Tom, did you ever do it with Josie?"

"Annie!"

"You can tell me." She paused, filling her lungs with air. "I'd tell you."

"Will you hush? Damme, Ma will hear you!"

"They're both asleep. I can hear their breathin'. Did you, Tom?"

"No."

"Why not? Besides not bein' ringed, I mean."

"Ain't that reason enough?"

"No, not here in New Holland. It isn't the same here as it was back home. I've been wondering lately what I would do myself if there was a free settler around who was single and young and—"

"I don't want to hear anymore!" Tom whispered

harshly, and then fell silent. Annie could hear his breath coming in gulps, and then he spoke again in a low tone that she thought conveyed a touch of biting anger. "I didn't do anything because I was afraid somethin' would happen. An' I don't want to have to marry the likes of Josie Hunnicutt. Now, goodnight."

Annie could almost see the flush of embarrassment that was now flooding her brother's cheeks. She felt a little of it in her own. But she was glad she had asked the questions, even if part of Tom's answers weren't complete.

She felt an urge to carry on the questioning, but the finality and sudden anger in his last words kept her silent.

And then she could hear his heavy, even breathing and knew he had fallen asleep.

But for Annie there was no sleep. No matter how hard she tried to clear her mind, she tossed restlessly. Her thoughts shifted from curiosity about Josie Hunnicutt to concern for her family's future in New South Wales.

And concern for her own future.

What did the future hold for her, Annie Hollister, seventeen, no longer a girl but a woman full grown?

Would she age beyond her years and soon look like her mother did now . . . with the lines of worry and care etched around her eyes and mouth? In England Mary Hollister had been so full of light-hearted gaiety, always ready to laugh. Even though they had been far from rich, her mother always looked pretty and fresh in her brightly colored dresses and bonnets. What a change had come over her since their arrival here. Annie couldn't remember the last time she'd seen her mother smile.

Was that what was in store for her?

The thought forced her from her bed. Being careful not to wake Tom, she drew the coverlet around her shoulders and moved to the window. Quietly she undid the latch and pushed open the shutters.

Instantly the brisk September air swept back the coverlet and her nightgown and teased through her auburn hair with invisible fingers, making her whole body tingle. She closed her eyes and breathed deeply of the fresh, invigorating air, carrying with it the sweet, tangy scent of eucalyptus. From far off in the distance she could swear she heard the bizarre laughing sound of a kookaburra.

Was it laughing at her? At her pathetic plight?

Her eyes snapped open.

"It will not be the same for me," she said aloud, her jaw setting in a determined line. "It will not!"

Early the next morning Ben and Tom hitched the mare and set out for the river where they would meet the hulk boat that would ferry them to Parramatta. Annie watched the lumbering wagon disappear in the swirling dust of the road, then turned back to the kitchen.

"Think there's much hope of them finding what we need in Parramatta, Ma?" she asked dejectedly, slowly clearing away the breakfast porridge bowls and wiping the plank table with a damp cloth.

"There's always hope," Mary Hollister replied, her voice not quite as full of conviction as she wanted it.

Annie shook her head. "Sometimes I think we're only fooling ourselves. We should never have left England. At least there we knew what we had, and there was always plenty to eat. We work so hard, and yet we're worse off now than when we came." She cast a sidelong glance toward the closed door of the tiny bedroom. "It pains me to think of Billy in fifteen or sixteen years with us not bein' any better off than we are now!"

Annie looked at her mother. She wanted to tell her that she, Annie, didn't want to grow up looking like her . . . old before her time, the scars of worry and toil etched into her face and bowing her still youthful body. She wanted to tell her mother that she wanted something more from life . . . happiness, excitement, simple physical comforts. She almost blurted that she would save every halfpence she could until she could return to England and some semblance of civilization.

She also wanted to confide in her mother the overwhelming feelings that had been growing in her body for so long, and now threatened to explode. She wanted to cry out her fears that she would one day be a shriveled-up old maid who had never known love.

Would she ever know the love of a good man if she stayed in New South Wales? Would she ever know the hard insistence of a man's strong, taut body along the length of hers, or the feel of her breasts pressed against his chest as his arms brought her closer and closer to him in willing surrender? Would she ever be swept away by the winds of passion she knew lay smoldering somewhere in her body?

"Annie?"

"What? Oh, yes, Mother."

"There's hoeing to be done."

Annie nodded and moved to the door, then paused and turned.

Now, talk to her! Tell her! Ask her!

But she didn't. Instead, she bit her lip and said, "I love you, Ma."

Mary looked at her daughter, and for a brief moment the lines softened and disappeared, the skin flushed with warm color, the eyes sparkled, and Annie had a glimpse of the loveliness that she remembered.

"And I love you, my little Annie."

6

CAPTAIN Steven Rourke sat his stallion with one leg thrown over the horse's neck, and stared across the flatlands toward River Fork.

He smiled at what he saw, mentally counting the sovereigns that would come his way when the spring crop now being sown was harvested.

It had been three weeks since the bargain had been sealed with Brownlee and the *Venture* had sailed. A few days before sailing, a stroke of luck had come his way.

A free settler family, name of Corbett, had decided to give up their pioneering dream. At first, when word reached Rourke that they needed passage money on the *Venture* as far as Capetown, with enough left over to take them to England, he had paid little attention.

But then he had overheard one of the marine sergeants lament his own inability to buy the land. It was a choice two hundred acres at the fork of two rivers. There was good grazing, and canals could be dug off the river to water the land during the dry season.

The sergeant's tour was up. During it, he had been fool enough to take up with a convict woman. Instead of using her and discarding her like the whore she probably was, he had moved in with her. Nearing the end of his tour, he had let his emotions rule his common sense and decided he didn't want to leave her.

Since she couldn't return to England with him, he

decided to remain and marry her as soon as he was a civilian again, making it legal.

All this was beyond Rourke's comprehension, but he quickly decided that the sergeant's stupidity could be put to his own use.

The sergeant, Duncan by name, didn't have enough credits for the purchase of such a choice piece of land close in to the main camp.

Rourke cared little for farming himself—indeed, he despised it. But with his quick mind he could see ahead. In the months to come, many more prisoners would be landing in the colony. There wouldn't be nearly enough food grown in the communal plot to feed them.

A blind man could see that the convicts who toiled in that plot, by the governor's orders, did so with listless hands. They were the dregs who hadn't the backbone to stake out a garden plot for themselves and work it.

But still they had to be fed or a revolt would break out. To do this, food would have to be purchased from the farms of free settlers.

Sergeant Duncan fairly leapt at Rourke's offer.

"I'm told you were a man of the soil before your enlistment, Sergeant."

"Aye, that I was. An' that's why I'd like to be back on the land now that me duty's up, sar."

"As you know, Sergeant, while active in either the marines or the Corps we cannot own or homestead land."

"Aye," Duncan nodded.

"I want the Corbett property, at least until my tour is up and I leave here. I will finance your purchase, and provide you with all the equipment and convict labor you need to make the land profitable. You run the farm, Duncan, until I leave New South Wales. Then it is yours. In the meantime you take only ten percent of the profits for your own subsistence."

A low whistle escaped the sergeant's lips. " 'Tis a hard bargain ye drive, Cap'n. Come next winter, food will be scarce. If there's more prisoners, they'll be a pretty penny's profit in the yield from two hundred fine acres."

The man wasn't as stupid as Rourke had assumed.

"Aye, Duncan, it is a hard bargain. Do you have a better choice?"

"Nay, I have not. But what's my guarantee that ye'll let me keep the land, free and clear, when yer tour is up?"

"You will already own the title in your name, and you have my word as an officer and a gentleman."

"Aye, that I have, sar, but I'm no officer an' I ain't no gentleman. What makes you think you can trust me?"

"Because, Sergeant, if I find that I cannot, I will kill you . . . very accidentally, of course."

The bargain was consummated and work on River Fork had already begun.

The entire deal had taken only a third of Rourke's illegal rum supply. Another third had been sold off to finance Captain Brownlee's next trip, and the last third remained cached for further investment.

"Good day to you, Cap'n."

"Good day, Duncan."

Rourke watched the hulking man stride toward him through the tall grass, and congratulated himself on his choice. He had proved not only willing but eager at his task, and though Rourke knew little of farming himself, he could see that Duncan had forgotten none of the training of his youth.

"How goes the work?"

"Better an' faster than expected, Cap'n," the man replied, mopping his dripping brow with a forearm and running a calloused hand through his mop of straw-colored hair. "The canals is almost all dug, an' thanks to the horse and plow ya found, we'll start seedin' in maybe two weeks."

"Wheat?"

"Aye, an' barley . . . an' maybe a little maize up there on the higher ground. The hut fer me an' me woman is near done as well."

"Then the convicts are working?"

"Aye, yer prescription works well," Duncan chuckled. "Jest enough food, jest enough rum . . . and jest the gentle suggestion that 'tis back to Port Jackson if they shirk!"

Rourke nodded and patted the ex-soldier's shoulder. "Good man."

Give a man who has nothing a little rum and a woman when the urge strikes, and you've got a slave.

Rourke knew that Governor Phillip would condemn much of this operation morally, but he could do little about it. The thirty-five men and women convicts he had provided Duncan would have to be fed by the King's coin if Rourke didn't feed them.

Phillip would look the other way out of common sense.

Rourke swung his leg down and eased his boot into the stirrup. As he reined around, Duncan laid a hand on the horse's flank.

"Beggin' yer pardon, Cap'n . . ."

"Aye?"

"Well, sar, I don't know how you come by the horse and plow or the rest, but . . ."

"Out with it, man! What's on your mind?"

"There's rumor, sar, that a drover near Parramatta has twenty fine sheep fer sale. If we could get 'em, they'd be the start of a proper herd, they would."

"Aye, that they would." Rourke nodded, weighing the purchase and its possible future profit in his mind. "Go ahead!"

"An' how shall we pay, Cap'n?"

"With rum."

"Rum, sar? I don't rightly know if he'll sell fer rum, Cap'n."

Rourke smiled and then laughed aloud. "Offer him rum, Duncan. Out here, you can buy a man's soul with it."

He touched the big black slightly with his spurs, and galloped off in the direction of Port Jackson.

Casually he squinted up at the sun, and nodded with satisfaction. The return ride would take about a half an hour. He should be just in time to meet his little blonde innocent.

Josie Hunnicutt scrambled up the last few feet of the rocky path to the top of the inland knoll. Here she paused to catch her breath before starting down the other side. Behind her, the motley huts and partially finished buildings of Port Jackson lay gleaming in the midday sun.

Far to her right she could see the chain gangs' living compound, and beyond that the cluster of white that made up Tent City. That was where most of the convicts lived who weren't industrious enough to cultivate garden plots and erect huts of their own.

"God, how ugly and gloomy it all is. I hate it," she said aloud. "Thank heavens for these weekly escapes!"

Narrowing her eyes to a squint, she could just make out her father's wagon in the center of Tent City. Though she couldn't make out their faces, she knew her father was somewhere in the midst of the crowd of prisoners and marines, selling his tobacco. She also knew that he would haggle and barter till his face grew red from the effort to get the last bit of coin or the last ounce of rum for his illegally grown weed.

Josie turned back toward the path with a smile. That bartering would take hours, more than enough time for Josie to indulge herself in total release in her handsome lover's passionate embrace.

She cursed the rocks that bruised her barely slippered feet as she slipped and slid down the path. It would have been much easier to have taken the cart path on the other side of the knoll, but much riskier, with the chance of being seen by some of the officers below.

The perspiration on Josie's back beneath her dress chilled at such a thought. If word ever reached her father that instead of taking long walks on the beach every mid-week afternoon she was lying naked in the arms of a Corps officer, he would flail every inch of skin from her back.

She rounded the last corner, and her heart began to pound. There was his hut. It made any dwelling in Port Jackson other than Government House look like a sty. Its mud walls gleamed with whitewash, and a brand new brick chimney protruded majestically from the shingled roof.

The roof had been put on at her suggestion, and it had proved to be a wonderful one. She loved to lie naked in bed with the rain beating above her and not have one drop leak through. At her own home on the Hawkesbury, she had to crawl beneath the bed when it rained if she didn't want to get soaked through the foliage-thatch roof.

Her heart beat faster with pride, as if this were already hers. And why not? Why couldn't it be? Didn't he admit she pleasured him better than any of the convict whores?

Almost three months now she had been seeing him regularly every week. And each time, Josie felt he weakened a little more.

'Tis only a matter of time now, she thought, an' he'll ask Pa for my hand. And Pa will give it, gladly. He'll be only too happy to see me married off to a rich officer in the Corps. An' he'll be only too happy to take advantage of all the commissary connections a son-in-law in the Corps could give him!

She stretched up on her toes for the latch key, and

then gasped when she couldn't feel it above the door in its usual place.

Had he already arrived?

Quickly she darted to the opposite side of the hut. The big black stallion wasn't beneath the thatched overhang of his stall.

Perhaps the horse was left at the stables near the officers' barracks, she thought, returning to the door. A squeal of surprise came from her lips when the latch lifted beneath her fingers.

He is here, she thought, pushing the door to and leaning the top half of her body into the room. She was about to call out his name, when she heard the splash of a hand on water from the bedroom.

Josie smiled and felt a tingling sensation run through her as she imagined his broad-shouldered, muscular body nude in the wooden tub.

Without a second's hesitation, Josie made the decision to surprise him and join him in the tub. She removed her shoes and stockings and unlaced the stays from her dress. Quickly she removed it and her chemise.

Taking a vial of scent from her reticule, she dabbed a few drops at her neck and between her breasts. Then she moved to the drape in the far wall and, taking a deep breath, threw it aside.

"Surprise!"

"B'gar, I'll say it is."

Josie gasped. She would have screamed but her throat was too constricted at the sight before her.

Standing in the large wooden tub was a girl about Josie's age. She had raven-black hair and dark eyes. Her olive skin gleamed wetly, and lather dripped from the tips of her upturned, jutting breasts.

Josie's first thought was that the girl was beautiful. Her second was how brazen the girl was. She made no effort to hide her nudity from Josie's eyes.

Then the last thought struck her. Was this girl her rival?

"You're not Rourke," Josie said dumbly, forgetting her own nakedness and taking a few steps into the room.

The dark-skinned girl threw her head back with a roar of guttural laughter. "Gawd, I hope not . . . not with *these*, leastwise!" Wantonly she cupped her breasts and squeezed them until the nipples swelled before Josie's gaping eyes.

The blonde girl then realized how stupid her words had sounded. "Who . . . who are you?" she stammered.

"Cora Lee's me name. Ya might say I'm the maid . . . sometimes. Other times. . . ." She let her voice trail off.

"A maid?" Josie choked.

"All the officers has got maids." Cora Lee shrugged.

"You're a naked whore!" Josie cried.

"Aye, that I am. An' yer a naked *lady*, I suppose?" Calmly the girl stepped from the tub. "Was you wantin' to take a bath, m'Lady?" she chuckled.

"Of course I don't . . ."

Suddenly Josie remembered her own nudity. In confusion she looked down at her own quivering, naked breasts, and then back at the other girl where she calmly sat drying her body.

At last the scream came, and with it Josie's exit. She ran to the other room and, as fast as her quivering fingers would allow, tugged her chemise over her body.

She was frantically lacing her bodice when Cora Lee stepped into the room, still naked.

"My God, have you no shame?" Josie cried.

"Nay, I ain't."

At last Josie finished with her dress and angrily began pulling on her stockings.

"I suppose you're Rourke's whore," she hissed.

"I tol' ya, I cleans his quarters fer him, I does."

"I think you lie."

A piercing peal of laughter erupted from Cora Lee's throat as she moved across the room to stand directly before Josie.

"All right then, I'm the Cap'n's whore . . . we's both his whore."

Josie stomped her feet, her face flushed deep crimson, her eyes flashing fury. "*I'm* not his whore!"

"Well then, dearie, I s'pose yer his wife?"

"Of course I ain't."

"Well, ya gotta be one or the other. They ain't a woman in this bleedin' place that ain't a wife or a whore."

"Yer a slut!" Josie screeched, and leaped forward, her hands like talons clawing for Cora Lee's eyes.

But Cora Lee, raised in the streets of London and fighting since birth just to stay alive, was quick. She stepped aside and brought her fists up into Josie's belly. With a whoosh of air and a gagging sound, Josie doubled over in mid-air and hit the hut's plank floor with a dull thud.

"Claw me eyes out will ya, m'Lady!" Cora Lee whooped, and straddled Josie's prostrate form.

With her knees on the other girl's arms and her weight on Josie's breasts, Cora Lee gathered two handfuls of honey blonde hair on each side of Josie's head. Then she began methodically pounding Josie's head up and down on the rough planks.

"Stop! Dear God, stop! You'll kill me!"

Cora Lee's credo in life was 'kill or be killed'. If Steven Rourke hadn't stepped through the door at that moment, she might very well have killed Josie.

"What in thunder . . . ?"

Josie was falling into darkness. Through the mist that had begun to cover her eyes, she saw Rourke's tall form lean over her tormentor. Then the raven-haired girl was high over his head, kicking and screaming.

Even though her head was no longer being pounded

on the floor, there was now an inner pounding in Josie's skull that continued her torment.

She closed her eyes.

She could hear their voices above her, not clearly, but enough to tell her that the girl was explaining to Rourke what had happened.

When she came to the part about Josie bursting into the room naked, the hut was filled with Rourke's laughter.

On the floor, Josie felt a burning flush of both embarrassment and anger suffuse her breasts. It crawled up over her throat and filled her cheeks with its heat.

She opened her eyes and sat up, forcing the room to stand still long enough to allow her to gain her feet. Once there, she found her shoes and reticule and stumbled toward the door.

"Here now, Josie, m'love, where do you think you're off to?"

"Somewhere outta here, that's where!" Josie snapped, tugging her elbow from his grasp and whirling to face him.

"You mean you'll leave without getting what you came for?" Rourke said, his mouth drawing up on one side in an insolent grin.

"An' pray tell me what ya think I might'a come fer?" she replied as haughtily as possible, lifting her chin as high as her neck would allow.

"Well, m'love, I'm sure you didn't climb the hill just to take tea."

Rourke's words brought a gust of sardonic laughter from the opposite side of the room where Cora Lee stood, still brazenly naked, with her hands on her hips.

Burning with embarrassment, Josie's hand whipped in an arc toward Rourke's smirking face. His reflexes were lightning quick as he caught first her left wrist and then her right in his powerful hands.

"Let me go, you bloody bastard, let loose!" Josie wailed.

Wildly she struggled, kicking at his shins and wriggling her whole body in an effort to free her arms from his grip.

Calmly he held her until she was panting with exhaustion and her face was shining with perspiration. Through all her whining and her attempts to escape, Rourke's smile only deepened, creating tiny wrinkles at the corner of his mouth that accented his look of bored recklessness.

"B'gar, Cap'n, she's a live one, ain't she? Does she give ya the same kind o' tussle in bed?" Cora Lee chuckled.

Finally Josie's struggled slowed, and then ceased altogether. She stood, her eyes blazing fire at him as Rourke answered her stare with a lazily arrogant smile playing around his lips.

At last he released her and turned to Cora Lee. "Out!"

Cora Lee shrugged. "*Yer* the one tol' Jack fer me to drop by."

"That's right, I did," Rourke replied, snatching a leather vest. and tattered skirt from a nearby chair. "And my thanks for cleaning the place up."

With one hand Rourke handed the girl her clothes. With the other Josie saw him press two gold sovereigns into her palm. The movement was surreptitious, but the glint of the gold didn't escape Josie's sharp eye.

"The best to ya, Cap'n," Cora Lee grinned. "An' thanks fer the use o' yer tub!"

Rourke escorted her to the door. To Josie's surprise, the girl didn't even pause to put on her clothes. She just walked out into the sunlight stark naked.

"Brazen slut," Josie hissed.

"Aye, she is that," Rourke said with a laugh, planting a gentle slap on Cora Lee's bottom and then closing the door behind her. "But 'tis all the lass knows."

When the door was latched, he calmly turned and

shucked his red uniform jacket, then began unbuttoning the linen shirt beneath it. All the while, his eyes fastened on Josie, stripping her with their clear blue gaze as they swept from her blonde head to her shoeless feet.

"And now, we'll to our business," he said, his voice husky and low.

"And what business would that be, Cap'n Steven Rourke?" Josie snapped.

"Why, bedding you, of course."

"Ye'll not bed me this day," she hissed in reply. "I'm sorry ye paid yer whore fer nothin'."

"Paid?"

"I saw ye give her the gold!"

Rourke blinked. For a second his eyes took on the icy quality that always frightened Josie. But then the grin returned as he pulled the shirt off and moved toward her.

"The lass deserves something for keeping the place tidy."

"Gold? Two sovereigns? That's a lot fer scrubbin'!"

"I'm a generous man," Rourke said. "You of all people should know that, Josie."

Against her will, Josie could feel her resolve dwindling the closer he came. Her eyes flitted over his tall, lithe, half-naked form. They moved from his wide shoulders across the mat of golden hair covering his chest, to the bulging thighs straining against his tight breeches.

She gasped and made one last try for the door.

"Nay, m'love," he growled, grasping a handful of her blonde hair in passing and bringing her to an abrupt halt. "Seeing the two of you on the floor like that has set my blood racing. I would have my fill of you before you go."

"I ain't yer whore!" Josie cried, backing from him.

"Aren't you now?" he said, jerking her face upward until it was just beneath him.

Again his eyes were that icy blue that she couldn't fathom. They frightened her, for in their depths she sensed a cruelty that she had been unaware of.

"Please let me go, Rourke."

"Are you telling me you don't want me to bed you?"

His choice of words irked her. *Not 'make love'*, she thought, *but 'bed'*.

She started to speak, but all sound except the thunder in her ears was stilled by his hot lips crushing hers. His arms gripped her tiny waist, imprisoning her in their vise-like hold and pressing her body tightly to his.

Josie felt all her defenses slowly crumbling, as she knew they would. The sheer reckless magnetism of this man could conquer her in moments. It had before, and it was now as his tongue scorched and prodded her own.

She moaned in surrender and moved her arms up to encircle his neck.

His lips lifted briefly from hers and her eyes opened to look up into his face. His skin was golden brown from the sun, his lips were sensually full, and he was surveying her with yet another grin of insolence.

"Don't you want me to bed you, Josie, m'love?"

"Aye, damn you, hurry!"

Again his mouth descended over hers, kissing her deeply, forcefully. She could dimly feel the movement of his fingers tugging at her dress. In the next instant it had been removed and only the thin material of her chemise separated her breasts from the heated steel of his chest.

"I want you, Josie girl, and I mean to have you . . . now."

Moaning with desire, she felt his hands tugging at the delicate material of her chemise. The sound of rending cloth jarred her back to sudden reality.

"No, no . . . you're tearing it . . ."

"Pay no mind. There are more . . . a trunkful."

And then she was swept into his arms and quickly

deposited on the bed. Somehow he had discarded his breeches and boots and, with a groan of savage passion, threw himself down beside her.

"You want me now, don't you, Josie girl?"

"Yes, yes, damn you!" she cried, tears of rage and embarrassment at her own unbridled desire tumbling down her cheeks.

And then he was over her, his chest crushing her naked breasts. The feel of his crisp hair on her hardened nipples made her shudder with need and passion. His thighs were like steel against her legs as his lips brutally met hers.

His hands seemed to be everywhere, fierce and yet gentle as they possessed her. Then his lips moved down across her throat to toy with the pink tips of her breasts. They became taut and rose to meet his kiss. His tongue moved over them maddeningly, bringing a low moan from Josie's throat and a warmth that spread throughout her young body.

She arched beneath his touch as his hands parted her knees. There was one last tiny burst of anger when she heard his mocking chuckle against her ear. But it passed, all too quickly, as he penetrated her core of feeling.

The warmth of his entrance centered in her belly, bringing yet another moan of pleasure to her lips. She looked up to see his handsome face above her, the eyes grown dark with desire as his hips met hers in ever harder thrusts.

But on his lips she could still see that arrogant, sardonic smile.

Josie closed her eyes and relinquished her mind to the body she couldn't control.

His attack continued unabated as again and again he buried his flesh deeply inside her. The tension began building deep within her belly until she thought she would scream with the need for release. She arched her back, moving her hips, meeting his every movement.

At last it came with a wrenching shudder that locked their bodies as one. Josie screamed out unintelligible words as he continued on with his merciless, powerful lunges, carrying her to yet another peak. Then his own cries mingled with hers, and she felt his warm wetness join hers.

She lay back, the taut muscles in her body relaxing as she moaned in the aftermath of her pleasure. Vaguely she felt his lips and warm breath at the side of her neck. Gently his hands continued to caress her breasts as she drifted into a twilight drowsiness.

She felt him move, and then heard indistinct sounds she couldn't identify. But she refused to stir, letting the drowsiness claim her.

When she awakened, the room was empty, and the sun cast late afternoon shadows from the window across her naked body.

"Rourke?"

There was no answer. She slipped from the bed and looked beyond the drape into the other room.

It too was empty.

Returning to the bed, her eyes suddenly fell on the new silk chemise lying across its foot. It was a delicate, pale pink, with lace at the bodice and a satin sash of a lovely deep rose.

And lying in the garment's center were two gold sovereigns.

Josie picked them up. She lay them in her palm and, as the sun glinted off their shiny surface, she began to weep silently.

The girl, Cora Lee, had been right, she thought. All women in this God-forsaken place who aren't wives are whores.

All except one.

Suddenly, for no reason she could fathom, Josie Hunnicutt hated Annie Hollister.

7

WEEKS passed. The spring rains gave way to the beginnings of blistering summer. And beneath the blinding orange ball that seemed to move so slowly across the sky, the work seemed to never end. Long hours were spent turning the unyielding soil in preparation for seed. And when seeding was done at last, hoeing and cutting back the ever-encroaching mallee took its place.

Nothing had improved. Tom and Ben Hollister had made two trips to Parramatta, and both were futile. The horse and sheep that Ben had wanted to buy had gone to a higher bidder, an ex-marine sergeant named Duncan. The only purchases they had been able to make had been some tea, sugar, and a month's supply of flour. It was better than nothing, but not nearly enough.

They desperately needed a horse and a plow. Without them, plowing, cultivating, and the weeding after planting had to be done by hand with hoes.

And it seemed that each downward chop of the hoe took another hour off their lives.

Annie had little time now to worry about her future. The day to day present was enough to dull her mind and wrack her body. Sleep came easily not long after dusk, and dawn, along with more back-breaking work, came all too quickly.

Her hands and feet became so calloused that it took ten times normal pressure to feel what she held or the

ground where she trod. She had long ago given up trying to get the grime from beneath her nails during the
daily baths she took in the river.

She worked alongside Tom and her father, and often
Mary would join them. Setting Billy beneath a nearby
tree with a few homemade toys to amuse him, the
older woman would take up a hoe and silently join her
family in the field.

For days on end the routine rarely varied. A lunch of
hardtack, sweet tea and bread would be brought to them
at midday. Taking this, they would sprawl beneath a
leafy eucalypt, quickly devour the food, and then doze
for two hours until the sun's blinding heat abated
enough to take to the fields again.

None of them, least of all Annie, paid much heed to
the fact that Tom suddenly began to take his share of
the food and head for the river.

"To cool off," was his excuse for leaving them, and
he would be gone for the two hours.

When he returned, his hair would be soaking and
plastered to his head from his cooling bath.

At least that's what they assumed.

But then Annie began to sense something amiss.
Tom's hair was always wet when he returned; but his
shirt and breeches, other than spots of perspiration,
were dry. If, after swimming, he put his clothes back
on at once, as it seemed he did since his hair was still
wet when he returned, why hadn't his clothes absorbed
the water from his body?

And then two other things struck her that she hadn't
noticed before.

Each day he would depart with his meal in one hand
and his hoe in the other. Why did he take his hoe
along for a swim? Had it become so much a part of
him that he couldn't bear to lay it to rest even while
bathing?

Annie thought not.

And then she began to notice that Tom, rather than

returning refreshed, seemed more lethargic. As the afternoons wore on and they moved down one endless row and up another, Tom would begin lagging behind.

Even her father began to notice this fact.

"Yer idlin', lad. Come along now, 'tis not fit for yer sister to outdo ya so!"

And Tom would increase his efforts, only to fall behind again.

One afternoon, near the end of the rest period, Annie's curiosity got the best of her.

"Think I'll cool off with a little water on my face," she said, and set off toward the river.

She took a seldom-used path rather than the main one, lest she came upon Tom just rising from the water naked and embarrass him. When she reached the bank, she turned upstream toward the little inlet surrounded by rocks where they usually swam.

Once there, she slithered up to the top of the huge boulders as quietly as possible.

She needn't have bothered. There was no Tom.

Could he already have headed back?

She doubted it.

Could he have chosen another place for his midday dip?

No, the current was much too swift and dangerous all along the river here.

She was about to make her way back down the rocks, when the sound of heavy footsteps in the foliage halted her.

She froze, waiting, her eyes riveted to the opening in the heavy vines. The sounds grew louder, and then Tom came crashing through and stumbled down to the water's edge.

Annie barely suppressed a tiny gasp when she saw him. Sweat rolled down his face and dripped steadily from his chin. His eyes were glazed from weariness and, as he knelt, it seemed his arms could hardly bring his cupped hands up to his face.

Indeed, he finally gave up trying, and merely leaned far enough forward to dunk his head, up to his shoulders, in the water. He did this several times, and then fell to his back on the river bank.

Annie watched him for several moments as he lay there, his chest heaving as he took in great gulps of air.

As she hurried back to the field to rejoin her father, she made a vow to find out the very next day just what her brother was up to.

"Where's the lad?"

Annie stopped, her mind whirling. "He'll be coming along shortly, I guess, Pa. I missed him."

Ben Hollister nodded and grunted with the ache in his body as he pulled himself to his feet. "Well, let's be for it, lass. We've another five hours 'til dusk, an' every minute's a valuable one this time'a year."

Five more hours, Annie reflected, trudging after her father, and six already spent that morning.

Dear God, a mule in harness doesn't work this hard!

The following afternoon, Annie tensely awaited Tom's departure.

But today something was different. He looked more worn out than usual, and instead of taking his leave at lunchtime, he fell to the ground and, with his back resting against a eucalypt, closed his eyes.

For several moments Annie sat watching, her teeth grinding on a piece of tasteless hardtack. Even though he was only eighteen, Tom's face had begun to take on the hard lines around the eyes and mouth that had already aged their father. The veins stood out in his thin arms, and his hands were bleeding.

It was a shame, she thought, and unfair, that she had inherited the body and the stamina of their father instead of Tom. While being tall, her brother had none of the raw-boned toughness of Ben Hollister. Instead, he was built smaller, like their mother.

Just when Annie thought he would forgo his swim

this day, he groaningly rolled to his knees. Then, with a sigh, he pulled himself to his feet.

"A bit of the river'll revive me, I think," he said, and moved off down the path.

"Stay outta the current, son."

"Aye."

Annie watched until he had passed the clearing of the field and disappeared in the trees.

"A little cooling off will do me no harm either, Pa."

Ben Hollister lay back with a sigh, and in seconds his eyes were closed.

Annie walked toward the trees until she was sure she was out of her father's sight. Then, even though her back and legs ached, she pulled her skirt to her knees and began to sprint. She entered the grove of trees at the same point as her brother and, sure-footedly, continued to run until she was near the river. There she stopped, her ears tuned to any sound.

Then she heard it, the splashing noise she expected.

Tom was swimming.

She waited with baited breath until the splashing ended. Did he swim and then just go off into the trees to sleep in the cool shade?

Impossible, for why then would he return so exhausted?

The sound of footsteps on the path alerted her to his movement; but it was not coming in her direction. She listened, not daring to breathe, as he turned away and headed upstream. Moving cautiously and slowly to stay quiet, she followed him by sound rather than sight.

It was hard going. The trees grew closer together here, and the mallee and other growth was a thick tangle that clawed at her arms and face.

Dear God, where would he trudge to each day so far upriver? And what did he do there?

Annie guessed she had traveled about two miles, when suddenly she broke through the underbrush into a tilled field. It was about a hundred yards from the river, and surrounded all around by trees. The area was between three and four acres in size, and manicured every bit as carefully as the fields the family was working nearer the house.

Then she spotted Tom about three hundred yards to her right. His head and neck were bowed, the hoe in his hands rising and falling in a regular chopping motion that was three times his normal speed.

Not once did he look up from his labor, so he took no heed of her presence.

Annie stood stock still, her eyes flickering over the entire area. The vastness of what Tom had done struck her with awe and admiration. He had chopped away mallee, felled trees and rooted stumps on nearly four acres, all by himself. And he had done it on his daily two-hour rest period.

But *why?*

Uncaring if he saw her or not now, Annie moved farther into the cleared field. Some fifty yards in front of her she could see the tips of tiny sprouts poking from the earth.

Reaching a well cultivated furrow, she dropped to her knees and with her fingers cleared the soil from one of the sprouting plants.

"Oh, no," she gasped aloud.

Her brother had cleared and planted a whole field of tobacco plants.

She heard Tom's running feet, but didn't look up until his legs came within her line of sight.

"What are you doing here, Annie!"

"I followed you," she said, looking into the mounting turmoil on his glowering face. "Oh, Tom!"

"Go back!"

"Tom, these are tobacco plants!"

"Aye, yer damn right they're tobacco plants!"

"But, Tom, the Governor has proclaimed—"

"Damn the Governor!"

"Tom!"

He lurched forward and grasped Annie by the shoulders. With more strength than she had thought he possessed, Tom yanked her to her feet. He stood spraddle-legged, facing her. His eyes flashed with a wildness she had never seen before, and his jaw was a hard line of determination.

"Old man Hunnicutt grows 'baccy, an' so do some of the others," he said tightly.

"I know," Annie cried. "But one day they'll be caught and fined . . . maybe flogged!"

" 'Tis worth the chance."

"No, Tom, it isn't!" she hissed, wrenching her shoulders from his grasp.

"It is, an' I aim to keep growin' it. Now get back to Pa. An' mind you, Annie, not a word!"

"Pa," she said, her face flushed with anger. "What will he say if he finds out? You know how he feels. Tobacco is a weed, not fit to take up ground that could grow food. He agrees with the Governor!"

"Pa is a fool."

"Tom," she gasped, "how dare you say such a thing?"

Suddenly his composure broke. His face and shoulders sagged, and abruptly he dropped to his knees in the soft dirt.

"Annie, Annie, don't you see? If we're to survive here, we have to do it any way we can. I know how Pa thinks, and I admire him for it. 'Just or unjust, the law is the law, and all men must live by laws.' Well, damme, it was the tax laws that took our land in England, Annie!"

"I know, but—"

"There ain't no buts. Hell, Annie, the Hunnicutts and half the other free settlers got more food on their tables and clothes on their backs with half the work we put in. Look at Abigail Hunnicutt, and then look at Ma. Abigail don't have to work like a man, and two men at that. If Pa and Ma keep goin' like they are, they won't last two more summers. An' then where will we be?"

Annie hung her head and dropped to her knees beside her brother. She knew that he spoke the words of truth, but she still couldn't bring herself to accept them. She had been brought up too strongly to respect the laws of God and man, and to revere the wishes and beliefs of her parents.

"I mean to take the bit between my own teeth, Annie. I mean to get us a plow and another horse, an' I mean to do it jest like John Hunnicutt did: by growin' tobacco."

Here he paused and leaned forward. Lightly and tenderly he brushed his lips across his sister's forehead, then stood.

" 'Tis a choice I'm makin', Annie, an' damn the consequences. This is a raw land that don't give nothin'. What you get out here, you gotta take. Survival, Annie, 'tis the only choice we got other than death. This ain't England. Out here we got to survive any way we can."

Annie stood. Calmly she smoothed her skirt, and then set off toward the place where she had first spotted Tom.

"What you doin'?"

"You take the hatchet," she said over her shoulder. "I'll do the hoeing. Tomorrow I'll tote my own hoe to the river."

"Annie—"

"You'd best be to it, Tom, the sun's movin'. We'll have to be back with Pa in little more than an hour."

8

AT last the planting was done and the work load could be eased. Not much, however, for the mallee constantly edged its way back into the fields, and weeds of every color and description seemed to pop up overnight in the furrows.

But at least there was the respite of Sunday afternoons. Too tired to do anything else, Ben used the time to rest in his rocker. Mary Hollister relaxed with darning and mending that there was no time for during the week.

Tom, using any excuse he could manufacture, slipped off to the tobacco field. The crop was thriving, and it wouldn't be long before he could cut it and ready it for curing. That fact seemed to give him added strength and energy.

Annie offered to go with him, but he steadfastly refused.

"Nay, take one day fer yourself, Annie-o. I don't mind, and there's not that much needs to be done now anyhow."

So Annie spent Sunday afternoons in the shade of the porch, drowsing or giving her mother a break from the care of Billy.

It was on one of these idle Sunday afternoons that the Hunnicutts came to call.

Annie was playing jack-and-ball with Billy. There was a gentle, cooling breeze that felt good on her skin as it wafted across the porch and lightly caressed her newly washed curls.

The days were growing unbearably hot now, and any breeze was welcome. Soon the summer, with its strength-sapping heat, would be at its peak. With that heat came the possibility of droughts that would wither the crops before they were half grown.

Idly, Annie turned her face to catch more of the breeze, and thought, as she had the previous year, how strange it would be to have Christmas during the hottest part of the year. Here in New South Wales there would be no wading in knee-deep snow or bundling up in a warm coat and cozy muffler.

Mary sat in the rocker beside them. Her hands worked deftly at mending one of Ben's two shirts. She hummed softly to herself, lost in her own thoughts.

The sound of hooves and a whinnying horse brought her upright.

"Now who on earth could that be?"

"What?" Annie said, startled by her mother's voice.

She followed Mary's gaze up the road to where a cloud of dust was snaking its way toward the Hollister farm. Annie rose and shielded her eyes with one hand, squinting to spot who was in the wagon.

" 'Tis the Hunnicutts!" she exclaimed as she spotted Josie waving to her.

"I'll put the kettle on for tea," Mary said, quickly stashing her mending into the basket and bustling into the house. " 'Tis glad I am I scoured this house to such a fair-thee-well yesterday. 'Tis more than fit for company, even the proper Mrs. Abigail Hunnicutt!"

It was good to hear her mother laugh, and even though Annie had mixed feelings about Josie lately, it would be a pleasant diversion to have someone her age to talk to. She returned Josie's wave and moved down the steps just as the Hunnicutt's horse snorted to a stop at the front gate.

"Good morning, Annie." John Hunnicutt smiled,

tipping the brim of his cap in her direction. "Yer Pa ta home?"

"Aye. Most likely he's dozin' in his rocker or he'd be out here to give you a hello," she replied.

John Hunnicutt nodded. He was a small, spare man with grizzled features and eyes that constantly watered. His shoulders seemed to habitually sag, and his face had the look of a man who had seen a hundred storms and was surprised that he had weathered them all.

Now, hearing Annie's words, he nodded and mumbled around his pipe, "No need to wake 'im. Like all of us, he's probably most tired. I had nothin' great to speak to him about."

"Is Mary about?" Abigail Hunnicutt asked from beside her husband, cradling the infant Joseph in her arms.

"Aye, she's inside puttin' on tea," Annie said, and then grinned. "She was all excited when she saw you folks coming."

"Well, Mr. Hunnicutt needs to go back into Port Jackson today, so I thought I'd visit with yer mother for a while. If it's convenient, o' course."

"She'll be delighted, Mrs. Hunnicutt," Annie replied, then looked over at Josie. The girl looked as though she had swallowed ten canaries. "Can you stay, too, Josie?"

"No, I'm afraid I can't," the girl said matter-of-factly. Then her excitement bubbled over and the words came tumbling out all at once. "I'm goin' into Port Jackson with Pa, have to run some errands fer Ma so she kin sit a spell with yer Ma!"

"Yer lookin' chipper 'n fit these days, Annie girl," Abigail Hunnicutt said, easing her enormous bulk off the wagon seat.

Chipper, yes, Annie thought, but drab. Her eyes passed over the mother to the daughter where she sat on one of the buckboard's two side seats. Josie was wearing yet another new dress, and a bonnet to match sat perched on her shimmering blonde curls. The dress was a polished cotton in a deep, mossy green shade, with a scoop neck that was cut low and squared, and a double row of ruffles edging it. The elbow-length sleeves were puffed, and a lighter green cotton filled their inserts. A wide sash, matching the color of the sleeve inserts, ran beneath Josie's high breasts and was tied coquettishly in the back.

"Thank ye, Mrs. Hunnicutt, 'tis pleasant not to have to be in the fields for a day." As she spoke, Annie pointedly directed her gaze at Josie. Their eyes met for a brief instant, before Josie dropped her lashes and began fiddling with the reticule in her lap.

Dear God, Annie thought as her gaze fell on Josie's hands, *she hasn't a cracked nail or a single callous!*

"Annie dear?"

She turned back to Mrs. Hunnicutt. "Aye?"

"If ye've an idle afternoon, why don't ye ride into Port Jackson with me husband an' Josie? I'm sure she would love the company. You two girls rarely get to see each other any more."

"Well, I—"

"Oh, Ma, can't ya see Annie's tired? I'm sure she's of no mind fer a long, bumpy an' hot ride into main camp."

There was no edge to Josie's voice. Indeed, her words sounded sincere. But when Annie turned back to look at the girl, there was a decided pout on her lips, and there was no hiding the wide-eyed look of despair she was directing at her mother.

Damme, Annie thought, *there's no doubtin' it . . . the girl doesn't want me along.*

"B'gar, Josie," Abigail Hunnicutt said good-naturedly, obviously not detecting the look in her daughter's eyes. "Youngsters like you got all the git up n' go in the world!"

" 'Twould be fun," Annie said, as sweetly as she could, "to get away for a few hours."

" 'Course 'twould," Abigail chirped. "Now you come along and ask her Ma. I'm sure she'll say yes!"

"Ask me what?" came Mary Hollister's voice from beside Annie. She had come from the kitchen and now reached out to take young Joseph from Abigail's arms as the woman laboriously hefted her weight up the front steps.

"Oh, Ma, would it be all right if I went into Port Jackson with Josie and Mr. Hunnicutt while you visit with Mrs. Hunnicutt?" Annie said. "Please?"

A slight frown furrowed Mary's forehead. " 'Tis not exactly a place fer young ladies, particularly not on a Sunday afternoon."

Annie knew what her mother meant. Sunday was the convicts' day off. The narrow mud streets of Port Jackson would be full to overflowing with them. They would be either drinking the rum they had been able to get during the week, or bartering for more. And because the male prisoners would be out in force, so would the prostitutes.

"It'll be all right," John Hunnicutt replied with a smile. "I'll keep a close eye on 'em."

Annie stole another glance at Josie in the back of the wagon. At best the girl's face held a sour look.

It made Annie even more determined to go.

"Ma, please?" Annie whispered.

Mary looked at her daughter and smiled. "Well, perhaps a change of scene will perk up yer spirits a bit. Just be wary of those lecherous sailors 'n convicts . . . they ain't seen anythin' as fresh an' pretty as you in Port Jackson!"

"I'll be careful and besides, I'll be with Josie and Mr. Hunnicutt. Don't ye worry none!" Quickly, Annie vaulted into the wagon beside Josie before her mother could change her mind. As Mr. Hunnicutt urged the mare into action, she turned and waved, but Mary was already clucking over the new baby, with Abigail Hunnicutt looking proudly on.

It wasn't often that Annie got into Port Jackson, so she looked forward to it as an exotic adventure. It was filthy and overcrowded, true, and the streets were overrun with beggars and swarming with the illegitimate children of the women prisoners, but there was an electricity to all the activity and hubbub that was so different from her life on the farm by the Hawkesbury River.

The eight mile ride usually took just over an hour, but on this day it seemed to take an interminably long time. One of the reasons was Josie's pouting silence. Several times Annie had tried to coax the girl into conversation, but to no avail. Josie's answers were always curt and sharp, cutting off any further talk.

"I like your dress, Josie."

"Thank you."

"Your bonnet's very pretty, too."

"Thank you."

Finally Annie gave up and lapsed into her own thoughts, refusing to let the girl spoil this delightful adventure.

She wondered if there would be a ship in the harbor. She hoped so. There was such a magnificent beauty about the sleek, slender sailing barks that found their way to this continent so far below the equator. Annie could look at them and dream about all the far-away ports they visited, the freedom they represented. If she were a man, she was sure she would join up with one of the crews and happily spend her life sailing to wild and wonderful ports around the world.

Suddenly Josie's high, whining voice brought her back to the wagon.

"But, Pa! Annie, you tell 'im!"

"What?" Annie asked, oblivious to what had been said while she was daydreaming.

"Well, I was jes' tellin' Pa that he might as well drop us at the general store where we can browse a bit while

he goes on down to that smelly ol' harbor. Then we
wouldn't be in his way or nothin' while he tends to his
business." Her voice took on a wheedling tone as she
smiled coyly up at her father. Annie was sure Josie
usually got her way when she used it.

But John Hunnicutt shook his head firmly. "No. I
promised yer Mamas I'd keep a sharp eye on ye girls,
an' that's exactly what I intend to do. There's enough
mischief already afoot in Port Jackson without lettin'
you two pretties loose!" he chuckled. " 'Sides, they's a
rumor there's a Dutch Merchantman in port takin' on
fresh water. If that's true, they'll be a glut'a carousin'
seamen in the streets as well as the drunken convicts."

"Pa—"

"Quiet, girl! There'll be no walkin' on the beach this
day like you do every Wednesday when we go in."

Annie's brows looked puzzled in a frown. Josie went
into Port Jackson every Wednesday? And she walked
the beach . . . alone?

She started to swivel her head to look at the girl,
when Josie's high-pitched whine again filled the air.

"I won't, Pa! I won't jest sit!"

"An' I say you will, girl."

"Damme if I will! Who wants to sit around all of an
afternoon watchin' you barter 'baccy fer rum! I want
ta—"

Josie never finished speaking. John Hunnicutt's arm
came around in an arc with the speed of a striking serpent. The flat of his palm struck Josie's cheek like the
crack of a musket. Her head rolled to the side and a
piercing wail erupted from her lips, that ended in a
whimper.

"I've tol' ya often enough, girl, about that tongue o'
yours!"

"I'm sorry, Pa, but—"

John Hunnicutt's arm came up again and Josie
recoiled as if she had already been struck a second

time. From her reticule she produced a kerchief and, hiding her eyes from Annie, began whimpering into it.

Annie's eyes moved to the bed of the buckboard where she saw three large canvas sacks. She had wondered earlier what they contained.

Now she knew. And with the knowledge, Tom's words of a few weeks before came flooding over her.

"Annie, girl?"

She turned on the seat and looked into John Hunnicutt's darting eyes and wizened face. "Aye, sir?"

"I knows how yer Pa feels about 'baccy."

" 'Tis all right, Mr. Hunnicutt."

He seemed not to hear her. "I'd like yer word that ye'll not repeat what ye just heard here." His voice lowered. "I cain't work like I used ta, ya know. This way here, well, it makes it a little easier. We all jest got to do what we can. . . ."

"Mr. Hunnicutt?"

"Aye?"

"Ye have my word I'll say nothing about the tobacco."

He nodded and returned his concentration to the horse's rump before he spoke again.

" 'Tis no crime, I say, fer a man to do what he sees he's got to do. The bloody Corps officers is takin' over Port Jackson. They'll soon be able to own almost the whole cargo of every ship that comes in here, an' they'll set what price they want on everything. I'll tell ya, Annie child, there's liable to be a mutiny one o' these days if all us farmers get our backs up. We won't stand for no bunch o' rascals starvin' out our families!"

Out of the corner of her eye, Annie noticed that Josie's annoying whimpering had stopped. Now she was nervously twisting her handkerchief between her fingers where they lay in her lap. When she looked up, her face was strangely pale.

"You all right, Josie?" Annie asked, looking at the girl's ashen features.

"Wha . . . ?"

"I asked if you were all right."

"Oh, yes . . . I'm fine," she stammered. Then suddenly she brightened and pointed a long, slender finger. "Look, we're there!"

Annie followed her gaze, and felt her heart quicken in her breast as they rounded the crest of the hill and saw Port Jackson sprawled before them.

John Hunnicutt clucked the horse into a trot and guided it down the hill and onto the main street leading to the harbor.

It was difficult nagivating the cumbersome wagon through the milling crowds of people, and they frequently had to stop for laughing, screeching children who had strayed from their mothers' sides. Belching black smoke and the sound of steel clanging on steel came from the blacksmith's shop. Peering inside as they passed, Annie could see the huge man in his leather apron, the sleeves of his shirt rolled up to reveal hard, rippling muscles as he pumped the bellows and brought the heavy hammer down on red-hot metal. All the sights and sounds and smells were thrilling to Annie, and she found herself squirming with eager excitement.

"Look, there's the general store!" Josie suddenly cried, pointing and bouncing up and down on the wagon seat. "Oh, Pa, couldn't we stop in there for a biscuit or somethin'?"

"Perhaps later, girl," John replied. "I have business to attend to first, remember?" He gave the mare a light flick with the reins and they trotted on around the Tank Stream, past the gardens leading to the Provost Marshal's cottage, and then approached the wharf.

A tiny gasp escaped Annie's throat as she caught a first glimpse of the Dutch Merchantman. She was a wide-bellied, three-masted ship, with a sharp, jutting prow and gleaming white sides. Even from a distance

Annie could see the sun glinting off her polished teak decks.

Where had the beautiful ship been, Annie wondered, and where was she bound from Port Jackson?

Nervously she rubbed her hands together as she closed her eyes and tried to imagine all the exotic ports the ship would call on in the months to come.

But rubbing her work-hardened, calloused hands together was the wrong thing to do while dreaming of romantic, far-away places. Her eyes snapped open and down to her lap. She almost wept when she saw how coarse and rough her hands were, and thought how many more years they would remain so if she stayed in New South Wales.

"A beauty, isn't she?" John Hunnicutt said, spotting the obvious delight on the girl's face.

Annie nodded. "Imagine what it would be like to sail around the world on her," she said, a wistful sadness in her voice.

Hunnicutt laughed. "I don't think ye'd enjoy it that much, girl. She's sleek and lovely on the outside, but full of rot and scurvy on the inside from all the poor diseased wretches she's been carryin'. Now, you two stay put in the wagon and keep an eye on the 'baccy while I scout around for a bit."

He slid from his perch and moved around to the rear of the wagon. With considerable effort he hefted one of the sacks to his shoulder, and then regarded his daughter.

"Josie."

"Aye, Pa?"

"I'll not be long with what I'm about. Keep yer eyes close on those other two sacks among this thievin' lot, ya hear me?"

Josie nodded and he ambled away, soon disappearing in the crowd of people around the wharf.

The girls sat, watching the bustling activity dockside. Sailors leaned over the ship's rail, trading laughter and sneering remarks with prostitutes. Others were bent with their heads close to men like John Hunnicutt who had something to sell that they couldn't get in the main camp store or at sea.

A crane was lowering huge empty water casks to dockside and bringing full ones aboard. The shouting of both the sailors and those ashore was almost a din.

Annie noticed a giant of a man perched atop a wagon, doling out rum from a keg on his shoulder and pocketing the coin he received for it. Now and then he would roar with laughter in a loud, booming voice and squeeze the breast of a darkly attractive girl standing next to him.

As she watched, she felt an involuntary shudder course through her body. The man seemed mean, evil . . . yet she couldn't take her eyes off him.

"Josie?"

"Aye," the girl replied disinterestedly.

"That huge man on the wagon. . . ."

"What about him?"

"He isn't a seaman and he isn't a soldier . . . yet he isn't dressed as a convict. I thought I knew all the free settlers."

"He's a convict, all right," Josie replied, following Annie's pointing finger. "An' the very meanest of the lot, he is. See that buckle on his belt?"

"Aye."

"Killed a sailor from the *Venture*, he did, with that buckle. Happened a few weeks ago."

A chill went up Annie's spine as she remembered Tom's story upon his return that fateful day from Port Jackson. So this huge, evil-looking man was the one who had killed the sailor. The thought repulsed her, making her turn away to stare out to sea.

"His name's Jack Moran, it is . . . an' the slut beside him—"

Suddenly Josie's words ended in a gasp. Annie looked up to see the other girl's body go rigid and her face

drain of color. Her eyes were glassy as they stared
fixedly at some point beyond Annie's left shoulder.

Annie turned, her own eyes searching for the source
of Josie's sudden silence. The only thing she could see
was the huge, evil Goliath that had fascinated her just
moments before. He had stopped his work and lowered
the keg from his shoulder to the bed of the wagon. He
was now in intent discussion with another, younger
man whose back was turned to Annie. Although tall
and obviously strong, with broad shoulders and a powerful build, the second man was almost dwarfed by the
giant who stood nodding at his words. His long blond
hair curled around the edges of his cap, and he appeared to be wearing a uniform of a kind Annie
couldn't identify from this distance, though he was
definitely not a sailor from the Dutch ship.

The discussion apparently ended, the blond man
turned away from his massive friend, and Annie recognized the uniform of a captain in the New South Wales
Corps. Her mind filled with revulsion, and she started
to look away. At that precise instant, he raised his
head and spotted the wagon where the two girls sat.
His eyes narrowed for a brief moment, then Annie sat
bolt upright as he began to stride toward them.

"Josie, he's coming this way!" she cried.

"Aye," Josie whispered.

"But why . . . why would he?" Then something in
Josie's voice brought Annie up short. "Josie, do you
know him?"

"I . . . yes," came the soft reply.

"But . . . *how*?" she stammered, her eyes scanning
Josie's face with concern.

The girl's eyes were bright, and her cheeks full of
color as she gushed out a reply. "And why not? 'Tis
only natural, comin' into main camp every week like I
do. I mean, why wouldn't I run into some o' the officers now and again? I mean, it is their job to protect
us from the scurvy murderers, ain't it? In their eyes all

women are the same . . . jest whores. Damme, Annie, ya don't think I could walk anywhere in Port Jackson safely without the soldiers keepin' an eye on me, do ya? I mean, girls like us, we ain't whores who kin—"

"All right, all right, Josie," Annie replied, stunned by the girl's outburst, and curious as well. "I was just wondering. . . ."

"Well, there's nothin' to wonder about, Annie Hollister, an' you jest remember that!"

Annie was even more confused, and more than a little startled by Josie's sudden agitation and her obvious nervousness. But before she could press it further, the look in Josie's eyes told her that they were no longer alone.

"Good morning, ladies."

Annie whirled at the sound of the deep, resonant voice at her side. He stood, tall and powerful, his icy blue eyes almost on a level with hers where she sat in the wagon seat.

Annie drew in a sudden breath. She felt obliged to speak, but suddenly her lips were frozen. She felt a ripple race through her body, not unlike an incoming wave from the ocean behind her, as she took in the man's blond, curling hair, and the deeply browned skin that seemed to accent the cool blue of his eyes.

Almost unconsciously, she appraised the width of his shoulders in the bright red jacket, and noted the clean, stark whiteness of his cuff in contrast to the long-fingered, finely boned and deeply tanned hands.

For a long moment he held her in his gaze, unsmiling, intent, almost as though he were boring into the very core of her being. Then a slow smile creased his handsome features. It revealed the whiteness of even teeth behind firm, sensual lips.

He made to take her hand, and Annie noted the smooth, panther-like agility of his every move. She flinched as his fingers touched hers, and then yanked them away when she remembered how they looked with their callouses and cracked nails.

He didn't seem to notice.

"Since Miss Hunnicutt has apparently lost her facility for speech and manners, allow me to introduce myself. I am Steven Rourke. And you, lovely lady, are . . . ?"

For an instant Annie thought she also had lost her facility for speech. She opened her mouth, but nothing would come out. In spite of herself, she was struck by the man's easy confidence and supreme assurance. There was an animal-like strength exuding from him, forcing her to meet his mocking blue eyes. She sensed a tigerish ruthlessness in those eyes, as well as intelligence and wit, and it took effort to remember that this man was the enemy, the cause of much of her family's heartache and struggle.

"My name is Annie. Annie Hollister," she said at last, squaring her shoulders and meeting his gaze head-on.

The smile vanished as if wiped away by a striking blow.

"Annie lives near me on the Hawkesbury," came Josie's voice. "She don't git in ta Port Jackson too often."

Steven Rourke didn't seem to hear Josie's words. His eyes left Annie's and brazenly traveled down to her oft-mended dress. Because of many washings and dryings in the sun, the material had shrunk noticeably since it had been made.

Suddenly the thought struck Annie that she wore no chemise. She could almost feel her full breasts thrusting against the tight material. And from Steven Rourke's eyes, she knew that her nipples were clearly evident.

She could feel a flush beginning to build when Rourke's eyes stopped stripping her and moved back up to her face. Gone now was the coldness she had seen in their depths, and again she saw the reckless arrogance she had noticed when he had first approached the wagon.

"The pleasure is mine, Annie Hollister," he said, bringing the heels of his boots together sharply and bowing slightly from the waist. "And how are you, Josie?"

"Oh, I'm fine, Stev . . . Captain Rourke," came the reply from Annie's elbow. She could feel the girl trembling uncontrollably.

"What brings you two alone to such a scurrilous place as the wharf this morning?"

"Pa has business, uh, on the wharf," Josie replied.

"Oh? And what sort of business might that be?" Captain Rourke asked, one eyebrow arching, but a knowing grin again revealing his perfect teeth.

Annie started to tell him that it was none of his bloody business, but Josie, obviously regaining her normal facilities for speech, blurted out a quicker answer.

"He's tradin' fresh vegetables, he is. He figgered the seamen would be wantin' fresh vegetables, they would!"

The little fool, Annie thought, 'tis too early for vegetables, anyone knows that.

But Steven Rourke didn't seem to care. Through all of Josie's prattle, his eyes never left Annie Hollister, his coolly appraising gaze again traveling slowly over her tall, voluptuous form, from her long, shapely legs up to her slender waist, then flickering momentarily on her full, rounded breasts where they strained against the front of her simple dress.

This time Annie flushed angrily, feeling as though he were sizing her up for market.

He saw the defiant sparkle in her eyes, and smiled. "And spirit to match the form and face? You will go far, Annie Hollister," he said softly.

Josie, overhearing the comment, stiffened. "We'll not be stayin' long in town today, Captain Rourke," she said curtly. "Pa will conclude his business soon an' then we'll be returnin' to the Hawkesbury."

"A pity," Rourke replied. "I should have liked to entertain you ladies in a more . . . leisurely . . . style. But another time, perhaps?" he said, looking directly at Annie.

Josie brushed Annie aside and leaned forward, her bosom nearly falling from its precarious roost in her scant neckline. "My Pa will most likely be comin' back in this Wednesday, like he always does."

Rourke's eyes dropped to the rounded swells of Josie's breasts and barely flickered before returning to Annie.

"And what about you, Miss Hollister? Do you come into Port Jackson often?"

"There is no need," Annie replied, her voice full of sarcasm. "You in the New South Wales Corps control everything, and place a price upon our few meager needs far above what we can afford. Each trip here only brings us fresh sorrow."

Rourke's eyes narrowed and for an instant Annie thought he might strike her. But she meant what she said, and would not take the words back, no matter what he did to her.

Then his features softened and he reached out, not to strike her, but again to take her hand. This time he held it in such a grip that Annie was powerless to withdraw it.

Gently he brushed the warmth of his lips over its hardened surface. Then, still holding her hand in a gentle but firm grasp, he looked into her eyes.

"Perhaps you should come into main camp some time with Miss Hunnicutt. We in the Corps are often able to secure goods at, I assure you, a reasonable price. You might find something to your liking."

With that, he released her hand, bowed shortly to both of them, turned on his heel and strode quickly back toward the bustling wharf.

"Damme," Josie hissed at Annie's shoulder, "the man's truly a bastard."

That night was another restless one for Annie as she tossed and turned fitfully in her bed. Josie had not spoken a word on the ride home, and nothing Annie could do or say would bring her out of her sulky mood.

The girl's face had remained florid through the entire ride, and the kerchief in her hands had been in tatters by the time the buckboard had pulled up at the Hollister's gate.

When Josie's parents accepted the invitation for a bite of supper before continuing on their way, the girl had declined. She contended that the heat of the day had given her a headache and that she preferred to go straight home and to her bed.

"You walk part way with her then, Tom," Mary Hollister had said.

"*No!* No, I don't need nobody to walk me!" Josie had cried. "I don't need nothin' from nobody!"

With that she had flounced out of the house, and Annie had noted a look of relief on her brother's face.

Josie Hunnicutt, Annie thought, tossing on her cot that night, had indeed become very strange.

Against her will, her mind swirled back to the events of the afternoon in Port Jackson . . . and Captain Steven Rourke.

Just the name and the memory of his blue eyes as they caressed her body made her bridle with renewed anger. She remembered his arrogant last words just before he gave her a sardonic smile and swaggered away.

The pompous, self-assured bastard! she thought to herself. She detested everything he represented. She closed her eyes and tried to force sleep to come.

But on the backs of her eyelids appeared a tanned, handsome, laughing face . . . the icy blue eyes full of mischief . . . and recklessness . . . and promise.

9

ANNIE straightened and weaved from side to side to relieve the kinks in her back. When the ache had diminished she leaned forward on the handle of her hoe and smiled in satisfaction.

The tobacco was growing tall and healthy, like the weed it was. It grew three times as fast as the other crops, and, Annie knew, had ten times the purchasing power.

No longer did she feel guilty about growing it. The rumors were rife now that Major Grose would soon be the new Governor. It was said that when that happened he planned on changing the laws concerning land grants, so that men of the Corps could obtain grants while still in service.

If that happened, even more of the ships' cargoes would be siphoned off for use on their own lands. The prisoners would suffer, but the free settler who received no support from the Crown would suffer even more.

"Fight fire with fire and greed with greed," her brother had said, and now Annie had to agree with him.

"It won't be long."

Tom, from two furrows away, had noticed Annie pause in her labor and stood now, watching the smile on her face.

"Aye, not long, Tom. Are you sure you know how to cure it?"

"Aye," he chuckled. "I've sneaked over enough to John Hunnicutt's while he was away and studied his process."

Annie nodded.

She had spoken to none of the Hunnicutts since their trip into Port Jackson a month before. But she had seen Josie and her father every Wednesday afternoon go by on the road toward the main camp.

Once Josie had spied Annie in the fields bent over her hoe. Annie hadn't been sure, because of the distance, but she thought she saw a smile of pure satisfaction on the girl's face before turning away under her parasol.

I work like a slave in the fields, Annie had thought with chagrin, while she rides like a queen into Port Jackson!

That very evening she had urged Tom back to their secret field of tobacco for an extra hour's work before dusk.

They had been doing it each day since, and the results were now before her eyes.

She no longer felt a single pang of guilt for growing the weed.

"I'll be goin' into Port Jackson come Friday fer some supplies." Tom moved over to her furrow, and even though there was no one around, lowered his voice to a conspiratorial tone. "An' I'll also make my contact."

"Contact?"

"Aye. We can't sell our weed in bits and pieces like John Hunnicutt. Pa would surely find out. I've the name of a convict who'll buy the whole crop once it's cured."

An involuntary shiver ran up Annie's spine. "Tom, is it safe to deal with the convicts?"

A momentary cloud passed across his eyes. He toed apart a clod of soil with his boot, and then covered his hesitation with a boyish grin.

"Afraid it'll haf'ta be, Annie. We got no choice. But don't you worry, I can take care'a myself."

Annie wasn't so sure, but his confidence was contagious and soon she was going over his plans with him.

"I'll have the smith in Port Jackson make us a plowshare on his forge. I've already started hewing the wood for a plow . . . got it hid down by the river. One o' these days there's gonna be a horse come up for sale that's strong enough to pull a plow. When that day comes, Annie, we're gonna have the money!"

Annie smiled with anticipation. "Just think of it, a horse and a plow."

"And maybe even a few head of sheep," he added. "We're gonna make this ugly old land work, Annie. I swear we are!"

She nodded and raised her hoe. "Then let's to it. We've got an hour of daylight left!"

They worked until the sun hovered just over the horizon, and then made their way through the brush and trees back to the fork in the trail that led to the river and the house.

"You go ahead," Annie said, turning right toward the river. "I think I'll get off a layer or two of this dirt."

"Best hurry, Annie, the sun'll dip outta sight in another twenty minutes."

"Aye," she nodded, and padded down the path.

She barely paused to remove her skirt and blouse before easing her dust-caked body into the water. She swam out of the little inlet toward the main channel, luxuriating in the feel of the cooling water on her bare skin.

When she felt the current begin to grab her, she turned and slowly, hand over hand, swam back to the rocks. Once there she stood, her breasts bobbing just on the surface, and ran her fingers through the tangled mass of her auburn hair.

Should have brought some soap, she thought ruefully, tipping her head back and letting her long tresses dip into the water, then rising again, feeling it cascade over her bare shoulders and breasts.

"Lovely."

Her eyes flew open, flickering fearfully over the rocks.

And then she saw him. He stood lounging idly with his back against a tree and his arms folded over his red uniform jacket.

"Captain Rourke!"

"Good day, Miss Hollister. Or, more appropriately . . . good evening."

His lips were curled in the same sarcastic, almost cruel, smile she remembered, and his eyes seemed to gleam like two clear blue diamonds in the fading light.

Suddenly those eyes traveled down below her face, and Annie's followed.

"Dear God," she gasped, seeing her bare breasts dancing on the water. She buckled her knees until the water rippled around her neck.

His laugh was a rumbling roar that seemed to pound at her ears like sharp claps of thunder. As it continued she could feel a flush of embarrassment fill her cheeks.

"Are all soldiers in the habit of spying on ladies in their bath!" she cried.

His face took on a mock seriousness, and his eyes darted around first his own position, and then to the water where Annie crouched.

"My sincerest apologies, m'lady, but I fail to see any measures for privacy here in your bath chamber, nor high, body-shielding sides on your tub."

His smile deepened but there was no touch of humor in his eyes. As unfamiliar with lust as Annie was, she could still recognize it in Steven Rourke's eyes as they seemed to bore right through the murky waters and find the nakedness of her body.

Had Annie Hollister been able to see beyond those

cold blue eyes into Captain Steven Rourke's mind, she would have been even more fearful of this man than she was.

For Rourke was all too conscious of her soft body, and the quickened rise and fall of her breasts when she had first seen him. Her face enticed him, with its upper portion in shadow and the full, sensual lips and soft chin bathed in late sunlight, bringing a throb of desire to his loins.

Idly in his mind, Rourke compared this earthy beauty to Josie Hunnicutt. There was no comparison. The little blonde tart, with her whining, childish voice and coy falseness, faded into the background like her sisters, the convict whores.

Annie Hollister was different. He sensed the woman in her, warm and passionate, lurking just beneath the surface . . . waiting to be tapped.

"Did you follow me down here, Captain Rourke?"

Another, even more terrifying thought had struck Annie during his thoughtful silence. *Had he seen her come from the tobacco fields?*

"Quite the contrary," he replied. "My men and I are chasing two escapees from the chain gang. They were headed this way. When I heard you swimming. . . ." He shrugged, letting his voice trail off, and Annie breathed an audible sigh of relief.

"I see. Well, sir, since I'm not one of your convicts, I suggest you be on with your tasks and I'll be to mine!"

"Which would be?"

"First, to get dressed!" she replied, tilting her chin defiantly.

Without a word he bent and retrieved her clothes from a rock. Then, with a catlike grace, he stepped forward until he was practically above her. He leaned forward, and for a moment Annie thought he would spring at her.

Instead, he merely handed her the skirt and blouse and returned to lounge against his tree.

"Now will you please leave?" she exclaimed.

"I find, Miss Hollister, that I am suddenly in need of a rest."

As if that were his final word, Rourke settled down on his haunches and again flashed that calculating smile that Annie had already grown to despise.

"You, Captain Rourke, are an insufferable bastard. Will you please turn around!"

"And you, Miss Hollister, are daft to assume that you are still in the safe, cozy confines of the English countryside. I will not turn around."

Annie's whole body quaked with anger. He was as crude as he was handsome, as self-assured as he was reckless and arrogant. The independent streak that had been in Annie her whole life now refused to let her be intimidated and cowed by such a man.

Two could play at this game!

"Very well," she said with a flip of her head, and she calmly stood and emerged from the water.

She was all too conscious of his eyes following every ripple of her golden skin as she daintily stepped through the shallow rocks until she stood directly in front of him not five paces away.

Carrying her defiance one step further, she placed her clothes on a rock beside her and calmly ran her hands over her entire body, removing as much water as she could.

It was with a sense of deep satisfaction that she noted the look in his eyes as they devoured her long, tapering legs, her firm thighs and buttocks, and her breasts that fairly danced with each movement of her arms.

"Are you satisfied now, Captain Rourke?"

"Immensely. You are the most beautiful woman I have ever seen."

"But not, Captain Rourke, one of your convict

whores who falls to her back with the snap of a finger."

To Annie's surprise, he rose to his feet and turned away.

Somehow the animal masculinity of his presence became even stronger with his back to her than it had been with those cold, probing eyes staring openly at her nudity. She tried to sustain her calm, but found it more and more difficult. The buttons on her skirt and blouse seemed determined to confound her. They refused to slip through the eyelets under the direction of her now trembling fingers.

"I shall walk you home. 'Tis near dark," he said suddenly.

"There is no need," Annie said, accomplishing her task at last. "I'm quite able to find my way."

She moved past him with more haste than she intended, but it wasn't fast enough. His hand grasped her elbow almost painfully. She was spun around until both her arms were in the grasp of his powerful hands.

"Captain!"

" 'Tis a sin to waste such beauty by grubbing in this boorish outland."

Annie's mind was screaming for her legs to move, to carry her away from this man who now spoke so gently but retained the look of intense lust in his cruel eyes.

Suddenly his arms molded around her in a powerful grasp. Through her damp blouse she could feel the heat of his body against her breasts, and could feel his heart beating like a triphammer as his face descended toward hers.

She began a startled protest, but her words were stifled by his kiss. His full, sensual lips were insistent and bruising on her own as she struggled feebly against him. She was partially numbed with shock at his affrontry, and yet, in the back of her mind, she knew that she had expected it.

His kiss deepened, became even more insistent, as

he forced her lips apart and took possession of her tongue. Low, animallike sounds rumbled from his chest as his searing tongue explored ever deeper into her mouth, driving, it seemed, into the very depths of her being.

To her surprise, and relief, Annie felt little from his heated kiss beyond a slight sense of dizziness.

Then his lips left hers and moved across her cheeks, down her neck, planting searing kisses on her throat. She felt his hands move upward over her back and then around her body to her breasts. He took their round fullness in his heated palms and hefted them, as though testing their weight in the damply clinging blouse. Then he ran his thumb back and forth over the nipples until they became achingly taut.

Annie stood, immobile, neither rejecting his advances nor accepting them. When his fingers began working the buttons on her blouse, she spoke.

"Captain—"

"Hush!"

Mistaking her lack of flight for acquiescence, he again took her chin in one hand and turned her face up to his. This time he kissed her more gently, but with more of an underlying urgency. When his tongue attempted for a second time to pry her lips apart, Annie kept them sealed.

This, and the evident lack of arousal in her body, stopped him. He lifted his head from hers and questioned her with his probing eyes.

Now his smile was far from charming. It was hard and thin-lipped, and when he spoke it was through clenched teeth.

"You must forgive my impetuousness."

"I don't see why I should."

"Annie—"

"Are you quite through, Captain Rourke?"

He blinked as if her words had been a slap in the face. His eyes were like granite as they stared at her, and his jaw set in a rigid line as he took a step backward.

"Quite through, Miss Hollister," he intoned, bowing slightly and sharply clicking the heels of his boots together.

He moved aside as Annie brushed past him and gathered her hatchet and hoe from the rocks. Then, with as much aplomb as she could muster, she walked calmly away down the path. When she was sure she was out of his sight, she lifted her skirt and began to sprint. The sun had set below the horizon, and she had to pick her way carefully by the light of the rising moon.

By the time she reached the lean-to stable and tool shed behind the house, she was soaked with perspiration and gasping for breath.

As she moved around the mare, her shoulder brushed the horse's side, striking leather.

Odd, she thought, Tom has stabled the mare but not unsaddled her. She made her way to the hangers and shelves where the tools were kept, deposited the hoe and hatchet, and moved back to the mare.

Just as her fingers found the girth, a rustling sound behind her made her whirl.

Out of the darkness into the moonlight came a bearded, shaggy head. Annie opened her mouth to scream, but before any sound could escape a grimy, calloused hand closed like a vise over her lips.

She tried to struggle from his grasp, when a second pair of arms locked her from behind. A hand closed over her breast, squeezing painfully.

"B'gar, we got a lovely one 'ere, Hazer, an' healthy she is too!"

"Never mind 'er, Toby lad. Have ya got the victuals?"

"Aye, in the sack, there in the front!"

The man in front of Annie released his hold and padded on bare feet to the front of the lean-to. Again she started to scream, but the hand moved from her breast and clamped viciously over her mouth.

"Jes' be quiet, lassie," came a gravelly voice in her ear.

"Slit the wench's throat, Toby, an' let's be off!"

"Soon. Ye take the nag and head fer the river. I'll catch up with ye, after I muzzle her good so there's no ruckus to warn 'em in the house."

Annie forced her body and mind to stay calm, weighing the situation. She guessed that these were the two convicts being sought by Captain Rourke. They planned to steal the mare and make for the inland.

And they planned to kill her before they left.

Again she struggled, wriggling her body from left to right. The hand over her mouth clamped tighter, nearly choking off her supply of air.

"Easy there, missy, ye'll live jest a little longer," he chuckled. "Long enough fer a little pleasurin'."

Annie's struggles ceased abruptly when the man's free hand came up with a knife. She saw the moonlight glint off the steel blade before it moved under her chin. Then she felt its sharp edge against her throat.

"Damn ye fer a fool, Toby File. We ain't got time fer such foolery now!"

"Shut yer mouth and do as I say, Hazer! Take the nag and go. I'll catch up jes' as soon as I gives this lovely young wench a little ride."

"Toby!"

"Go! Damme, I ain't had a real young 'un like this since England, an' it'll be a long time afore I sees another with a figger like this!"

The one called Hazer shook his head in disgust, but he obeyed. Quietly he gripped the mare's nostrils and led her out. The sound of horse and man had barely receded when Annie was yanked against the man and dragged unceremoniously to the rear of the lean-to.

"Don't ye make a sound above a whisper, missy, or I'll forgo me pleasure and slit ye from ear to ear."

The hand left her mouth, only to grasp a handful of her wet hair. She was pushed backward on a pile of straw, and his body followed, pinioning her.

"Yer both fools!" she hissed, summoning all her strength and pushing down the fear in her breast. "No convict has ever escaped inland. Even if ye get over the Blue Mountains, the blacks will get ye!"

"Maybe, but 'tis better'n dyin' in the hole we been in."

The knife lowered. Annie could feel its cold tip between her heaving breasts. And then she could hear the material rent clear to the sash of her skirt. Instinctively, as she felt the cool night air pour over her nipples, she brought her hands up to pummel his face.

But her blows brought only a mocking laugh to his lips as his eyes misted with lust at the sight of her lovely breasts dancing with her exertions.

"B'Jesus, I never seen such a pair o' risin' beauties!"

Annie cried out as the stubble of his beard rasped across her soft flesh and his sharp teeth found her nipple. She tried to push his face away, but he only slapped her hands away and returned cruelly to his task.

"I'll have ye, wench!" he growled, tugging her skirt up to her waist and wriggling his coarse body between her thighs.

"Oh, dear God, no!" she cried, when she heard him rip open the front of his breeches.

"Damn ye!" His fist crashed against the side of her face, sending sudden flashes of jagged light across her eyes. She felt his cruel, calloused fingers clawing at the juncture of her thighs and bucked from side to side in a vain attempt to unseat him.

And then she felt his throbbing hardness on her belly moving down, down. . . . The goal of his quest was nearly reached when Annie's throat erupted in an ear-piercing scream.

"Damn ye to hell, wench!" came his ominous voice. "I warned ye, I did!"

Through the mist that covered her eyes, Annie saw the knife rise and begin its descending arc toward her throat.

She screamed again just as a deafening roar filled the air. The man above her seemed to rise, as if an unseen hand had taken him by the hair and yanked him skyward. His face was frozen in shock as he slowly pitched forward.

Just as quickly, Annie felt the weight of his body being jerked from her own. Her eyes swam open, trying to focus. She saw a flash of red, and then her near-naked body was enveloped in warmth.

A face appeared above hers. Slowly the image jelled into focus, and she recognized Captain Steven Rourke.

His lips were moving, and just before darkness swallowed her, she heard the words, "Little fool. . . ."

10————————————————

FOR two days Annie lay like a stone on her parents' bed. She took food only when her mother could force it down her throat, and then only broth.

She slept fitfully, and dreamed often. In those dreams, which were actually vivid nightmares, she could see the convict's ugly face, his eyes filled with crude lust. She imagined him to be Satan himself.

And then she would see the knife, and the terror would force her awake, screaming.

On the morning of the third day, she felt a bit better and could manage solid food. By that evening, she felt well enough to talk, as difficult as it was. The left side of her face was discolored and sore. Her eye was swollen, but not completely shut. Her mother told her that in a few more days' time she would be right as rain. The blow had not broken the skin.

As Mary recounted the tale, Captain Steven Rourke had spotted the man, Hazer Carnes, leading the Hollisters' mare toward the river. He and two other soldiers overpowered him and quickly learned the whereabouts of his confederate, Toby File.

Rourke had ridden his stallion right into the lean-to just in time. The roar Annie had heard was the sound of Rourke's pistol. The shot had killed her attacker instantly.

"And the other man?" Annie asked. "The one called Hazer?"

"They hung 'im yesterday morning in the square in Port Jackson."

Dear God, Annie moaned to herself, *this is an awful place we've chosen to live.*

"Mother?"

"Aye?"

"Did he ... that man ... was he able to ... ?"

"No," Mary replied, shaking her head from side to side. "No, my daughter, he didn't. Nasty bruises to yer lovely face was all the scoundrel had time fer."

"Thank God," Annie breathed, slumping back to the pillow.

"Aye, thank God, and Captain Rourke," her mother said. "Even though your father barely gave him thanks for his deed."

The next day Annie insisted on returning to the fields. She wanted to feel the hot sun on her back and the cleansing exhaustion brought by the hard work of tilling the soil. She toiled with a will, but by midday found her strength sapped.

"To the house with ye, lass," her father urged. " 'Tis enough ye do fer now!"

Annie gratefully returned to the hut, and found her mother on the porch with a package in her hands.

"A soldier brought it this mornin' from Port Jackson," Mary said, her brow wrinkled with curiosity and confusion.

Quickly, Annie laid the bundle on the table and removed its paper wrapping. She gasped when she recognized the contents as a bolt of deep azure blue broadcloth. In its center was a long length of sky blue ribbon, more than enough for trim and a sash.

Alongside the ribbon was a note. With trembing fingers, Annie picked it up and read.

My dear Miss Hollister: I hope this finds you recuperated from your ordeal. I believe the enclosed will sufficiently replace the skirt and blouse

ruined by the convict Toby File. I have told both
my superior, Major Grose, and the Governor of
your ordeal, and both gentlemen have expressed
their sympathies and regrets. They have also
urged me to invite you to Government House for
tea upon your next visit to Port Jackson. I add
my own invitation, and would deem it a great
honor to serve as your escort to such an afternoon
function.

If, at such a time, the enclosed has been trans-
formed into part of your wardrobe, I would
consider it most gracious of you to wear it.

Your humble and obedient servant,
Steven Rourke
Captain, New South Wales Corps

"Would ye believe that," her mother gasped, reading
the letter over Annie's shoulder. "An invitation to
Government House fer tea!"

Annie was silent. Gently and lovingly she ran her
fingers over the fine material. It would make a beautiful dress, perhaps even two, and with bonnets to
match.

But something held her back from accepting such a
gift, particularly from such a man as Captain Steven
Rourke. His reference to her wardrobe was all too
clear. He knew she had no wardrobe. It was his way of
belittling her just a touch further.

And she was sure that Captain Rourke would press
for more than just tea if she were to attend dressed in
the results of his gift!

And yet another thought struck her, angering her
further. Supposedly there was not a new piece of cloth
in all of Port Jackson. How then did Steven Rourke
come by such an exquisite piece of material?

It was just another instance of the deviousness, the
cunning and the thievery of the men of the Corps . . .
the very men who were supposed to uphold the law

and stop the privateering and black marketing of others in the new colony!

Her mother gasped when she began to rewrap the package.

"Girl, what are ye doing?"

"I'm sending it back, Ma. I'll write a note of thanks but regrets."

With a groan of dismay Mary Hollister snatched the package from her daughter's hands. "Ye'll do nothing of the kind!"

"But, Ma, you don't understand—"

"I understand that neither of us have had a new stitch on our backs fer nearly two years!"

"But this Captain Rourke—"

"What about Captain Rourke? You read the note. The Governor himself has suggested this. Why shouldn't we accept it?"

Annie knew differently. The cloth had come from Rourke, not the Governor. And she was positive that the invitation to tea had been suggested by Rourke as an excuse to once again be alone with her.

But how could she tell her mother that? How could she tell her mother that before the convict had attempted to rape her, Rourke himself had practically seduced her?

She couldn't.

So she merely nodded and went about helping her mother with the evening meal.

That night, Mary told Ben Hollister about the gift and gleefully showed him the note. Iron-jawed, Ben read it, with his smoke-billowing pipe clamped between his teeth. When he finished he looked up, first at his wife and then at his daughter.

Then, without a word, his face as dark as a thunder cloud, he stalked from the house.

"He'll get over it," Mary commented. "It will do no good to hate all the Corps for what a few men, a few bad apples in the barrel, do."

Aye, Annie thought, perhaps not. But the leader of those bad apples is most assuredly Captain Steven Rourke!

Annie smiled happily even though she almost staggered under the weight of the feed sacks in each hand. The heavy burlap sacks contained true treasures, fresh vegetables, flour, and other supplies that had been scarce of late. The *Supply*, a tiny ship that ran between Port Jackson and the smaller penal colony on Norfolk Island, had landed that morning. Part of its cargo had been the excess crop from the island.

She thought Norfolk Island must indeed be a farmer's paradise compared to this land they knew around Port Jackson. It seemed that every season the island farms grew more than they needed for their own maintenance, and more than once they had spared the mainlanders from going hungry by sharing their abundance.

She groaned as one of the heavy sacks slipped from her grasp.

"Allow me."

The rumbling voice was so familiar now that Annie didn't have to turn to know its owner. The sacks were spirited from her hands before she could protest.

"I believe that's your wagon there, beneath the trees, isn't it?"

He forced her to look at him by stepping directly in front of her, blocking the way.

"Isn't it?" he repeated.

Her eyes traveled up his tall form, across the broad chest that was now encased in a new red uniform jacket, to his handsome, angular face. The lazy smile was back, as well as the bold insolence in his eyes. A lock of blond hair had tumbled over his brow, suggesting a boyishness Annie knew didn't exist.

It had been two weeks since the affair in the lean-to, and with all the hard work since, it had almost receded from her mind. So much so, that when Tom had urged her to accompany him on his delayed trip to Port Jackson, Annie had agreed.

Now it all came flooding back over her as Rourke spoke again, sharply.

"You haven't answered my note."

"No, I haven't. I saw no reason to."

"Yet you kept the material."

"My mother insisted that I keep it."

"Your mother's common sense has evidently been lost on you."

Annie's eyes flashed and an angry retort formed on her lips. But she wanted to be gone from this man as quickly as possible. "Yes, that is our wagon," she said coolly, stepping around him.

They walked in silence to the wagon. Rourke hefted the sacks into the back and secured them with ties before he turned to face her.

"You've made drapes of the broadcloth?" he asked, his hand lightly running down the sleeve of her mended blouse.

"No," she said, her face flushing. "My mother has cut the dress. We've started the sewing."

"Excellent. Can I expect you a week from tomorrow, then?"

"Expect me?"

"Government House . . . for tea." Here he laughed carelessly, but Annie detected a subtle cynicism in the sound. "I must admit it lacks the grace of high tea at Shift's on the Strand, or even a country house in Surrey, but at least the atmosphere is somewhat cultured and the conversation a cut above the squalid rantings of the rabble here in the streets!"

The tone in his voice brought her gaze up to meet his. "You hate this place, don't you?"

His eyes took on an odd glaze, as if he were looking through or around her. "Aye. I hate it like I'm sure I would hate hell itself." And then they cleared and seemed to burrow into her very soul. "Don't you?"

"Aye, I do. But 'tis all I have, and I mean to make the best of it."

"As do I, Annie Hollister," he growled. "As do I."

Suddenly her hand was tightly encased in his. He propelled her forcefully around the wagon and a few steps into the trees. Once in the shade and shielded from prying eyes on the street, he turned to her.

Annie knew that he was going to kiss her. Deep in her heart she wanted to be repulsed by his intentions. But in spite of herself she found her eyes closing and her face tilting up toward his. She felt almost grateful when his powerful arms closed around her and his clean masculine scent filled her nostrils.

His lips descended and fastened onto hers, molded them, parting them before Annie knew it had happened. She tasted his tongue willingly, letting it explore the heated interior of her mouth.

The kiss seemed to last an eternity, and Annie let it.

Why not, she thought, why not enjoy just a moment of passion? It was good to feel a man's strong arms about her body, his lips against her own, the beating of his heart against her breasts.

Dear God, why not? Just this once?

Rourke feasted on her lips and thrilled to the pliancy of her body as it melted against his.

He had meant the kiss to be brief, just a touch of their lips. But the longer it lasted the more he felt his belly churn with a desire for this girl that left him shaken.

He found the small of her back and pressed her harder against his awakening desire. For a second she rebelled, and then she relaxed against him, returning his kiss.

When he released her, he stood, still holding her close, his chest pressed against the exquisite softness of her breasts. He could sense, nay, *feel*, the excitement that flowed between them, and from the glazed look in her eyes he knew that she had felt it as well.

"Would it be so terrible, lass, my company for an afternoon?"

"No . . . 'tis. . . ."

"What?"

"I'm afraid of you, Captain Rourke. I look into your eyes and what I see there frightens me."

"You see desire," he growled. "And as a woman that should elate you, not frighten you."

"No, 'tis more."

With a groan he bent his head and Annie forgot her words as her lips met him halfway. This time her response was of a kind that threatened to overwhelm him.

Damme for a fool, he thought, I'll be dragging her farther into the trees if this keeps up. And that won't do, not with this one. This one must progress slowly, all in her own time!

He wrenched his lips from hers and held her at arms' length.

"A week from tomorrow?"

"I. . . ." Annie swallowed. Her mind whirled with the turbulent emotions she had only thought about, and never experienced.

Again she began to stammer. She was about to say no, when he spoke, cutting off her reply.

"I'll have two of my men pick you up and escort you to main camp."

And then he was gone, around the wagon and striding up toward Officers Hill.

Annie's body swayed. Her mind was blank and she was sure her legs would no longer support her weight.

A sound in the trees behind her brought her back to reality. She whirled, and a gasp escaped her throat when from behind a tree stepped a pretty raven-haired girl.

"My, my, our Cap'n, he do like variety now, don't

he?" the girl said, a mocking laugh accompanying her words.

"What do you . . . who are you?"

"Nobody, lass, jest a convict," the girl replied, turning away and fading into the brush and trees.

Annie felt a ripple of fear go up her spine. Was this girl Rourke's mistress? She knew all the officers had convict mistresses.

Annie had already had one round with a convict and had experienced their viciousness first hand.

She had no desire for another go. Especially not with a jealous woman.

Annie willingly accepted Rourke's arm as they stepped from the plank veranda of Government House. She was in high spirits for the first time in a long time, and she let herself revel in them.

There had been an unseasonably heavy rain that morning, making the mid-afternoon sun almost welcome and twice as bearable.

"Your face is radiant when you smile."

"I feel rather radiant," Annie laughed, and then remembered that tomorrow would be another day in the fields, another day of back-breaking labor in her tattered clothes.

The thought darkened her mood.

As they walked, the rustle of the deep blue skirt was pleasant to her ears, not unlike the ebbing of a low tide on a quiet, moonlit night. The neck was cut in a low scoop, and the flared sleeves billowed gracefully. The high waistline accentuated her breasts, and for modesty's sake, a whisk of the lighter blue material disguised the upper swells of her bosom.

She wore no cosmetics because there were none to be had. But Annie knew that she needed none. Her face had been tanned a golden bronze by the sun and there was a natural rosy hue to her cheeks. Her auburn hair was sun-streaked from her exposure in the fields.

It was piled high on her head and held in place with a fillet made from the same sky-blue material as the whisk and broad sash beneath her breasts.

Yes, she thought, we must make a handsome couple. Lowering her eyes she could almost imagine that they were strolling Paul's Walk in London, surrounded by the stately church and opulent houses instead of the steamy squalor of Port Jackson.

This fantasy erased thoughts of the next day from her mind. A smile returned to her lips.

"You enjoyed the afternoon?"

"Immensely," she replied, a light lilt in her voice. "The Governor's wife is lovely."

Rourke chuckled. "Aye, but a trifle boring . . . and naive. She honestly believes that this post is a sacred mission for her husband. And like the Governor, she believes the blacks can be tamed, the convicts made into good citizens, and one day this land will be great and prosperous."

"And you do not believe that, Captain Rourke?"

He smiled and peered at her from beneath lowered lids. " 'Tis not that I don't agree with her, 'tis just that I don't think any of her grand illusions will take place in our lifetime . . . or even the lifetime of the generation ahead of us. And that concerns only the land. As to the convicts and the natives? No hope, none whatsoever. The blacks are uncivilized heathens and the convicts are ignorant rabble."

"Surely not all!"

"*All*, Miss Hollister. You, of all people, should know that from first-hand experience."

They walked silently for several more yards, and suddenly Annie realized that they were climbing. At the fork in the path they had taken the upward turn, toward the top of Inland Knoll, instead of turning right and descending to the Officers' Barrack and stables.

Her body tensed and her pace faltered. She made to withdraw her arm from his, but Rourke's hand closed

over hers, drawing it against his tunic as his elbow held
her forearm fast.

"I believe," she stammered, "that you made a wrong
turn."

One eyebrow arched disdainfully and his lips curved
into a crooked smile. "Oh?"

"Aye, shouldn't we—"

"M'lady, I never make wrong turns," Rourke
chuckled.

The length of his stride increased until Annie was
forced to lift her skirts to keep up.

"Please!"

"Oh, dammit, come along. I want to show you
something!"

Minutes later they reached the very top of the knoll
and Rourke helped her even higher to the top of a
clump of boulders. There they paused, Annie leaning
on his arm, slightly out of breath.

Her eyes came up slowly, scanning the buildings and
daub huts of Port Jackson. Then they looked on out
the length of Sydney Cove to the jutting rocks of North
Point and South Point, and even farther beyond, to the
vastness of the green, placid sea.

" 'Tis beautiful from up here," she sighed. "From
this height it truly does look like a paradise."

"Not out there," Rourke growled, gently turning her
by the shoulders until her eyes surveyed rolling
grasslands dotted here and there by clumps of gum and
eucalyptus trees. "There!" he said, gesturing with his
arm.

Annie gazed in the indicated direction. Far, far in
the distance she saw the ground swell up to a lush
plateau. At the top it was about twice as high as their
own position. It had several groves of leafy trees, and
its undergrowth vegetation didn't look as thick and
menacing as that in the lowlands.

"The hill?" she asked.

"Aye," he said as he nodded. "From there you can see for miles in every direction. You can even see the sea."

"I don't understand."

He turned and placed his hands on Annie's shoulders.

"Around the base of that hill are two hundred prime acres nestled in the fork of two rivers. I own those two hundred acres, Annie Hollister. And I'll soon own two hundred more, and, one day, many hundreds more."

Annie searched his eyes for the meaning beyond his words. She couldn't fathom this statement, when comparing it to the disdainful things he had previously said about the future of the colony.

"I . . . I thought the marines and men in the Corps were not allowed to own land until the end of their tour."

"True," he said, nodding and then letting his blond head rear back as a guttural roar of laughter erupted from his throat. "But there are ways to gain any end, if one is wise enough and bold enough to grasp them."

"Wise enough, Captain? Or cunning enough?"

He shrugged. "Aye, call it cunning if you wish. Call it anything you like, I care not. What I do care about is not being like the rest of them down there."

He inclined his head toward Port Jackson, dropped his hands from her shoulders, and turned back toward his land.

"But you said you hated this place, that it would never be anything in your lifetime. If you believe that, why do you invest in land? Why look to this place for a future?"

"Profit," he replied, a husky resonance filling his voice. "My tour here will be a long one. I plan to live well while I'm here, and live like a king after I leave here."

Annie groaned in disbelief. She thought of their farm on the Hawkesbury. It, too, was prime land, but yielded little.

"Profit, Captain? I think there is no profit in land. We barely eke out enough for ourselves on as many acres as you say you have!"

"Aye, I am aware of that," he nodded. "But you do not have the means at your disposal that I have. Believe me, Annie Hollister, there is profit to be had in the land. There is profit in everything, if a man uses his wits to find and obtain it!"

Annie's jaw clamped tightly shut. When she spoke it was through clenched teeth. "By wits, Captain, you mean *power*, do you not? The power of the Corps?"

"That, too. You should have realized by now that in this wild place, far from the laws of civilization as we know them, a man must live by his wits and whatever else he can use . . . including power."

"And a woman, Captain? How should a woman live?"

"By her wits as well," he drawled with a sardonic smile, his eyes traveling down across the ampleness of her bosom beneath the whisk and her bodice. "But a woman, Annie, has a great deal more than her wits to bargain with. She has power of her own."

Annie's face flushed. She had no doubts about his meaning now. "I understand your inference, Captain Rourke. But there are some things a decent woman still retains even in this wilderness."

"For instance?"

"Her self-esteem, her integrity . . . and something I'm sure you know very little of. Her virtue."

Her words were met with another roaring laugh. "Virtue. *Here*?" His arm swung in a wide arc, taking in the vast planes from inland to the sea. "Annie, lass, you are as naive as our good Governor's wife!"

"Good day, Captain Rourke," Annie replied coldly, and began making her way down over the rocks to the path.

"Wait!"

" 'Tis late, Captain."

"I would continue our little debate!"

"No, thank you."

"Dammit, girl, come along! I have something else to show you!"

For some reason, perhaps because he merely walked away rather than physically tugging her along, Annie followed him. He took a few long strides down the main cart path, and then turned right, onto a smaller path which she hadn't noticed on their ascent.

It wasn't long before they emerged in a clearing beneath an overhang of rocks. Annie came up short when she saw the well-made hut, with its brick chimney and shingled roof.

Rourke produced a latch key, used it, and flung the door wide.

"Look, Annie. Step inside, look around, and see what it's like to feel human again!"

Gingerly she approached the door and peered inside.

What she saw brought a tug to her heart and a mist to her eyes. It was like an English cottage, and its cozyness drew her like a magnet into the room.

The plank floors were covered with a real rug. There were drapes and curtains, not of worn and tattered canvas, but broadcloth. The furniture was hand-hewn and rustic, but it was smoothed and polished. There were sturdy caneback chairs around a gate-legged oval table that would seat six without one person's elbow resting in another's food. There were armchairs placed about the room, comfortable and inviting with their padding and covering. An ornate armoire contained not wooden plates, but pewter.

"Yours?" she gasped.

"Aye."

"How did you...."

"There are ways."

"But even the Governor does not live like this!"

"Only because he is a fool and does not wish to." Rourke moved close to her and took her hands. "I told you, Annie, just because we live in this heathen land does not mean we have to live like heathens."

Suddenly this comparative opulence left a raw, rancid taste in Annie's mouth. She yanked her hands from his grasp and stepped backward, her eyes flashing with anger.

"Now I understand what my father is so angry about," she cried. "Because of your rum and your dealings, you have all this. We barely have enough to eat, little or no clothing or boots. We have no livestock, no horse for a plow . . . because of you!"

Rourke's face darkened with anger that matched her own. "You too can have all this, Annie Hollister."

"Aye, I don't doubt it. And lose all else!"

"What else is there?" he hissed, his words uttered with venom. "Self-esteem? Virtue? Words, just words. And they mean nothing here. I tell you, Annie Hollister, don't air your virtue to me on the one hand and bemoan your poverty on the other!"

She tried to exit around him, but found herself locked in his arms. His swarthy face above hers was made even darker by anger, and his eyes glowed like two blue flames.

"Your virtue, along with your maidenhead, would have been in shambles already if it had not been for me."

Annie gasped. Her arms were pinioned to her side, making it impossible for her to move. His hands dug into her back and he seemed to be crushing the life from her.

"Please. . . . you're hurting me!"

"Perhaps a little pain will bring you to your senses."

Before Annie could utter another word of protest, his lips descended brutally upon hers. There was no gentleness or warmth in the kiss as he bent her backward like a young sapling. As his tongue invaded her mouth, a shudder of stark fear coursed through her body.

The kiss ended as suddenly as it began. Rourke loosened his hold, but didn't release her. Then one hand came to her front and, with a flick, removed the whisk that hid her breasts from bodice to throat.

"Look at yourself. You're ripe for bedding, lass . . . and, by God, I'll be the one to do it!"

He let his eyes roam over the youthful swell of her breasts as they rose and fell with her heavy breathing.

"How dare you . . ."

"I am a man who dares anything. I want you, Annie girl, and I mean to have you."

"Never!" she hissed.

His eyes were like blue glaciers now and he continued speaking as if he were commanding a child.

"I told you that as long as I am forced to live in this place, I plan on living well. On that knoll I showed you I plan to build a house. Not a hut like this, with merely two rooms, but a fine house, with many rooms and fireplaces."

Slowly Annie felt herself mesmerized, not only by his words, but also by the intensity in his eyes as they bored into hers. But she was not prepared for what she heard next.

"Look around you here, and then think what comfort I can create in a house of ten rooms. I want you to share it with me, Annie. Come, be my mistress at River Forks."

Annie was stunned. The impact of his words struck her like a bolt of lightning. He not only wanted to use her, violate her, he wanted her to be his mistress . . . his chattel!

"You must be insane!" she cried.

"Aye, there have been times since I first saw you that I've thought I was mad," he said, his voice husky and low. "I see your face when I sleep, and you fill my thoughts when I awake."

She was struck dumb. "Are you saying, Steven Rourke, that you love me?"

"Love? Love, my dear, is for poets and dewy-eyed young girls who haven't the capacity for lust. We . . . you and I . . . have passion, nay, lust, if you will!"

His lips went to her breasts as his hands tugged at her bodice until one breast leapt free of its confinement. Quickly he captured it with his lips and began to worry the taut nipple with his tongue.

"*This* is lust, Annie Hollister," he murmured. "The feeling a man has for a woman when he knows he must have her!"

At last her arms were free. With her hands, she jerked his mouth from her breast and brought his head upright. Then, in the same motion, she brought her palm across his cheek with all the force in her body.

At first he was startled, and then his anger returned. Annie found herself paralyzed with fear as she stared into the cold steel of his eyes. For a moment she was sure he would strike her back, and she shuddered at the thought of what one of those powerful hands could do to her face.

Then he amazed her with yet another of his mercurial moods. His lips expanded in a grin, and then the room was filled with his harsh laughter.

"No prize so beautiful and desirable should be won without a battle," he said, bowing slightly and rubbing his cheek. "My compliments on your aim."

"You are so damnably sure of yourself, aren't you, Rourke!"

"Aye," he nodded, "I am. There is nothing for you in this God-forsaken place except me. If you don't take my offer, you will never know a man beyond the violence of rape you almost experienced." Suddenly he clutched her hands and thrust them up in front of her face. "Look! Look at those hands, lass! Red, broken, calloused. Why should a woman of your will and beauty, your wit, your . . . passion, be doomed to a life of servitude in an open field?"

His words cut right through to her heart. She could

not deny the truth in what he said. There was nothing and no one for her in New South Wales, and there was nowhere else for her to go.

She stood, tears of fury in her eyes, her breasts rising and falling with her labored breathing. How she hated him, hated him totally, for speaking the truth. At that moment, if there had been a knife in her hand she was sure she could easily have killed him.

Suddenly the beautiful new dress had lost its magic. The afternoon's respite at Government House was far away, as if it hadn't really happened. And she hated him for that, too, for giving her such pleasure, and then yanking it away.

"Sweet Annie, I take what I want. I think one day you will learn to do the same."

"Now I know what frightens me when I look in your eyes, Steven Rourke."

"Aye?"

"You have no heart."

For the first time since they had entered the cottage, Rourke's eyes wavered and then looked away. He handed her the whisk he had ripped off earlier, and moved to the door.

Annie straightened her bodice, replaced the whisk, and made to move around him into the sunlight.

"Perhaps you are right, perhaps I have no heart," he said softly. "But I have a brain and a will. And I'll tell you, Annie, that in the end it is a will you need to survive, and the brain to make it worthwhile."

The tone in his voice was solemn, almost sad.

Annie ignored it. "I'll be going now. You needn't walk me down."

A single finger came up and tilted her chin. This time his kiss was gentle, almost sweet, as his lips brushed softly across hers.

She stepped from the hut, and after a few steps up the path, paused. Without turning, she spoke.

"All you say may be true, Steven. But I will never

become your mistress. I would sooner sell my body on the muddy streets below to all who would pay the price than become a hopeless chattel to one man."

Rourke smiled as he watched her lovely body move away down the path.

"One day," he called out after her.

"Never!" came the shouted retort over her shoulder.

But Steven Rourke knew, he knew with the certainty that he knew there would be dawn tomorrow, that he would win. One day he would possess that body.

But he was also filled with a dread he hated to acknowledge, that even as he possessed Annie Hollister's body, she would never truly be his.

11

THE weeks passed slowly as Christmas approached, and the heat became even more withering. But still they went into the fields.

And as Annie hoed and sweated and cursed the recalcitrant weeds under her breath, she thought of Steven Rourke's words. And no matter how detestable those words and the man's actions had been, she couldn't blot them, or him, from her mind.

And Rourke wouldn't let her. He seemed to appear at least twice a week. He would nonchalantly ride by, with no particular purpose or destination. He would appear at the farm and inquire of her father if he thought there would be enough excess crop to be purchased by Government House, a task that the lowliest of his soldiers could perform.

But never would he speak directly to Annie, at least not in words. Only with his eyes.

They said: *When? . . . When will you tire of this and come to me?*

And when he wasn't there in the flesh, his presence was still felt . . . in Annie's mind. In the midst of the day, under the broiling sun, she would suddenly hear his mocking laughter. In the river, with the water gently running over her naked body, she could feel again the heat of his hands on her flesh and the intensity of his desire as his lips had caressed her nipple.

At night in bed, his handsome, cruel face would

form behind her eyelids, and no matter how hard she tried, she could not will it away.

The questions he had raised in her mind tortured her, draining her and denying her the sleep her body needed so badly.

She was forced to admit to herself that she was ready for love. Her body craved it like it did food. At the same time, she knew that she would get no love from Steven Rourke. He might awaken her body, bring her to a sensual ecstasy, but when it ended there would be no love, only the satiation of her body's desire.

And, like all women, Annie wanted . . . needed . . . more than the arousal of her body and the empty and fleeting fulfillment of her flesh alone.

But would she ever find it? Was Rourke right? Was he her only chance? Was it better to retain her self-esteem, her virtue, her . . . virginity, only to grow old with nothing else?

Would it be better to taste the fruits of desire, and *then* decide if they were bitter?

She was confused, and nightly, lying alone in her bed, she became more confused.

She would silently weep with grief, and then in anger. She would slam her fist into her pillow and toss from side to side on the narrow cot. She would rise and go out into the sultry night air and walk around and around the hut until she was exhausted.

Eventually that would give her blessed sleep, but it wouldn't relieve or erase the hard lump of doubt inside her.

And come the dawn, weary and heartsick or not, it was back to the fields.

The crops seemed to pause in their growing amid the shimmering waves of heat that rose from the dried earth.

All the crops, that is, except the tobacco and the weeds.

The first cutting had been done and laid away for

curing in a secret place Tom had found near the river. Samples of the forbidden tobacco had been taken to his "contact" in Port Jackson and, as a result, a pledge had been given to buy the entire crop.

But the wheat, the barley, the vegetables and, most important of all, the potato crop, were being dried out by lack of rain and run over by the weeds that didn't seem to need moisture to grow.

"We need rain," Ben Hollister said, pushing himself from the supper table and moving to his favorite chair.

"And if rain comes, we'll need a horse to pull the weeder I've rigged," Tom said.

The sudden tenseness in the room could be cut with a knife. Both Annie and her mother's eyes darted from the father to the son and back again as they waited for Ben's answer.

Tom had been working long hours in the evenings on his plow and a weeder he had designed. The plowshare and the teeth for the weeder had been forged by the smithy in Port Jackson, and, a week before, they had been mounted.

Now they sat idle behind the lean-to with no horse to pull them. The mare was too low in the withers and too old for such work. They needed a good strong plow horse, and Tom had found one for sale.

"Heard that a fella name of Downey, Collin Downey, above Parramatta's got a stout Suffolk Punch gelding he's willin' to part with."

"Oh?" Ben growled, lighting his pipe.

"Heard he'll take barter chits or coin, either one."

"Laddie, we've not enough barter chits fer a horse, an' I've not seen any coin fer nearly a year."

Tom persisted. "But ye've finally come to the mind that we've got to have a horse or lose half the crops to weeds?"

"Aye," Ben sighed.

"An' without a horse an' my new plow, we'll never

get the ground turned in time fer a winter wheat crop?"

Ben slammed his hand down on the arm of the chair and swiveled away from his son's stare. "Aye, damme, I agree! But what's the use talkin' on it? We can't afford a horse, lad, an' that's the lot of it!"

Tom stood and, without a word, left the room. In a moment he was back, standing in front of his father, his hand outstretched.

In his palm gleamed eight gold sovereigns.

" 'Tis near enough, I figger," he said. "In England you were a good horse trader, Pa. This an' maybe two chits should buy the Suffolk Punch."

Slowly Ben Hollister's eyes travelled up from the coins to his son's face.

"How?"

Tom averted his eyes from the condemnation he saw in his father's. His face flushed and he suddenly seemed to have trouble breathing.

But at last he spoke.

"Annie and I have grown a stand of 'baccy. This is a pledge to buy the whole crop."

"Tom!" Mary gasped, her hands flying to her throat.

Annie chewed her lip. In her lap her hands worried each other, and beneath her apron her belly churned, waiting for her father's reaction.

Ben Hollister's face clouded. His body tensed and then, with a roar, he lunged from the chair. With his left hand he struck the coins from Tom's palm and then raised his powerful right arm over his son's head.

Tom neither blinked nor moved. "I'm sorry, Pa. But I've only done what had to be done to survive."

Suddenly Ben's red-rimmed, weary eyes misted. The ferocity seemed to leave his body, and, slowly, the menacing arm fell to his side.

With a long sigh he fell back into the chair.

For several moments there was silence, and then Ben spoke, his voice barely a whisper.

"Aye. 'Tis time I realized that we're no longer in England, but still under the Crown's fist." His eyes raised to meet his son's. "We'll leave early for Parramatta."

Tom led the mare down the ramp from the hulk boat into shallow water. The horse snorted and threatened to unfoot him until Ben waded forward to grab the other side of the bridle.

"Easy . . . easy there, girl," came his rumbling, reassuring voice, and she settled immediately.

At last they reached the sandy shore and made their way up to a path that led to the little settlement of Parramatta.

The morning sun was already blazing hot in their faces as they walked the distance, leading the mare.

"What's his name again, son?"

"Downey," Tom replied. "Collin Downey."

"We'll ask someone where we might find him," Ben said.

He mopped the sweat from his brow with his handkerchief and pulled the mare up short, looking around, not sure where to go next. The settlement was fairly new, made up of a few dozen farmers who had despaired of the poor soil around Sydney Cove and had pushed up the estuary for a dozen miles till they found good ground. They had named it Rose Hill, after a species of beautiful scarlet bird that abounded in the area, but most people still referred to it by its native name, Parramatta.

"Old MacGrory would know, wouldn't he?" Tom offered.

"Most likely," Ben nodded. "An' that's his hut right over there."

They moved to the first wattle and daub hut at the outskirts of the tiny settlement. Leaving the mare in Tom's hands, Ben stepped into the compound around the hut and called out, "Hugh . . . Hugh MacGrory?"

A jolly, red-faced woman with mounds of blonde, sun-bleached hair piled on top of her head stepped from the door of the hut. "My man's inland, to the river. The fish are runnin'!" The woman spoke with a decided burr in her lilting voice.

"I'm Ben Hollister from down on the Hawkesbury. This here's my son, Tom."

"Aye, I remember ya, I do."

"We was wonderin' if ya could point us to a place owned by Collin Downey?"

"Aye, fer sure," she nodded. "Collin and his boy keeps to themselves, they do, but I can direct ya right enough."

"We'd appreciate it, missus."

Tom groaned inwardly when he heard the woman's detailed directions. It was a good five miles to the Downey farm, through heavy brush.

"Would ya care fer a bit o' sweet tea afore ya go?" she offered, a wide, toothless smile splitting her friendly face.

"No thank ya, missus," Ben replied. "We'd best get on if we're to be back the Hawkesbury before nightfall." He and Tom left the compound and started down the dusty road.

"Best ya keep an' open eye out fer blacks, Hollister," the woman called after them. "They been raisin' the very devil lately, they have!"

Trading off riding the mare, it still took the better part of two hours before they spotted the cleared fields and the hut of Collin Downey.

Tom's clothes were wringing wet with sweat, and his face and arms were beet red from swatting insects.

"Take heart, lad," Ben chuckled. "With any luck we'll both ride all the way goin' back."

They stopped a few yards short of the hut's porch and called out Downey's name. In response, a whoop of greeting sounded from the interior.

When the door opened, they were greeted by a short,

rotund, jovial-looking man pulling his suspenders up over his shoulders.

"Allo! Welcome, strangers, wherever ye be from!" he called heartily, bounding down the steps with his hand outstretched and pumping first Ben's and then Tom's hand enthusiastically.

"Ben Hollister . . ."

"Sure an' ye're both a sight," the man roared. "Pleased ta meet ya, Ben Hollister!" He continued to pump Ben's hand as if he were greeting a long lost friend. As he moved, his mane of red hair bobbed and his blue eyes twinkled. He clapped Ben on the back and then turned to Tom. "Sure an' this must be yer son, fine, strappin' lad he is, too, spittin' image of his father. Got one of me own just like him! What be yer name, son?"

"Tom," Tom replied, a bit overwhelmed by the zealous welcome.

"Well, Tom and Ben Hollister, what say we get out of this blazin' sun! Saints preserve us if this summer's as hot as the last one. Got so hot that bats and parakeets fell dead right out of the trees, they did! Come in to me house, humble as it is, an' have a spot of tea and some biscuits, an' later on perhaps somethin' a wee bit stronger, eh?" he bellowed, propelling the two men through the front door.

The cottage was similar to the Hollister's, though, if possible, even simpler. Where they at least had rough planks for flooring, here there was a dirt floor, covered with rushes. A single table with four stools was the room's only furniture. A bowl of half-eaten porridge sat on the table. They had apparently interrupted Mr. Downey at his breakfast.

"Is your wife not at home, Mr. Downey?" Tom asked, noting the single bowl.

The merriment suddenly went out of the jovial Irishman's eyes. "No, son, not any more. She was took by the smallpox that hit us eight months back."

"But I thought only natives died from that outburst."

Downey nodded. "Aye, mostly it was the blacks that spread it from one to another. But we were in Port Jackson at the time, an' Bridget—that was me dear wife—Bridget was a nurse of sorts, and determined to do what she could to help the poor ignorant bastards. Long hours she worked, tryin' to save 'em, until . . . until. . . ." He stopped, then took a deep breath and exhaled slowly. "Well, me an' Michael—that's me son—'bout the same age as you, Tom—we picked up and moved as far upriver away from Port Jackson as we could get. Found this spot, an' I've been farmin' it ever since."

"Where is Michael now?" Tom asked, eager to move the subject away from unhappy memories.

The twinkle returned to Downey's blue eyes. "Ah, the lad decided farmin' wasn't fer him—too much hard work tanglin' with the mallee, if ya ask me," he added with a chuckle. Tom shot a sidelong glance at his father, and Ben grinned. "In any event, he loves the sea, he does, so he up and joined the crew of the *Supply.*"

Tom's interest was immediately sparked. The *Supply* was one of the few vessels from the First Fleet that hadn't returned to England. It was a small ship, and Governor Phillip had ordered its crew to begin exploring the areas around New South Wales, in the hopes of discovering new sources of food and areas for settlement.

"Is he off to sea now?" Tom asked eagerly.

Downey chuckled. "Got a bit of wanderlust in yer veins, too, do ya, lad?" He poured boiling water into three tin cups and added a measure of tea to each, then slid two of the cups across the table to Tom and Ben. "Here now, this'll clear some of the dust of the ride from yer gullets. No, they got back about a fortnight ago from Norfolk Island. Ah, the stories Michael can tell ya about that place, sounds like Paradise it does! He went into Port Jackson yesterday to outfit the ship with some new rigging . . . should be back any time now, an' then he can answer all yer questions!" He took a long swallow of the strong tea, then one eyebrow arched. "An' speakin' of curiosity, I've been rattlin' on so about me an' mine that I fergot to ask ye. What is it that brings ye two fine gentlemen so far upriver? Ye thinkin' of settlin' here?"

Ben shook his head. "Nay, we're settled in on the Hawkesbury, and even though times are difficult, we've no mind to moving. At least not yet. Our problem is getting enough livestock and equipment to keep the farm going."

Collin Downey nodded his head in understanding. "Aye, that what's available is at too dear a price."

Ben leaned forward intently. "My son was in Port Jackson a few days ago and heard that you might have a sturdy Suffolk Punch ye're thinkin' of sellin'."

The Irishman's face remained open and jovial, but both Ben and Tom saw the tiny gleam of anticipation enter his eye once the mention of horse-trading came up.

"Aye, three head I've got: two Shire mares and the Suffolk."

Ben nodded. "You wouldn't be fer sellin' one o' the mares, would ya, Collin Downey?"

"I'm afeerd not, Hollister. They're both in foal, and that's the reason I've got 'em."

"Dear God, three head? And two in foal?" Tom exclaimed. "You're rich, Mr. Downey!"

The man cackled heartily. "Nay, lad, not rich, but workin' toward a herd—cattle, horses an' sheep. The land up here is hard. A lot of rock. It don't take too much to crops, but the grass is good."

"Is that why you came up here?" Ben asked. "To grow livestock?"

"Partly. The other reason is I could no longer stomach the thievin' convicts or the soldiers at Port

Jackson. In me own mind one was gettin' as bad as the other!"

Ben nodded. He could see the Irishman's point. If a man had the stock, and the means to get more, especially breeders, it would be far more profitable than crops.

Downey continued. " 'Course, when I got here I found out there's as many or more problems than I had in Port Jackson."

"How so?" Tom asked.

"The bloody blacks."

Ben remembered the warning he and Tom had received from MacGrory's wife in Parramatta. "But I thought the natives had quit raiding."

"They have, generally," Downey replied. "At least down in your part of the country. But up here they're still riled. An, when it comes to it, I'm thinkin' maybe they got a right. They're simple people, they are, huntin' and fishin' fer their food. Damme, I've seen one drop a kangaroo in his tracks at two hundred paces with a boomerang! But they never learned the cultivation of the land, and now that we're encroaching on more and more of their hunting grounds, they're faced with starvation same as we are. So they've taken to raidin' our farms here, stealin' in silent like at night and makin' off with our livestock an' anythin' they can grab from our gardens." Downey's hand slammed down on the table. "Damme, I feel sorry for 'em, but I got all I can handle just to feed meself and Michael when the lad's here."

"We've pretty much tamed 'em around Port Jackson."

Downey chuckled and shook his head. "Ya *think* ya have. Aye, an' maybe ya have down there where the farms are a bit closer together. But up here, where ye have no neighbors an' don't see a face fer weeks. . . ." His voice trailed off and then he suddenly shrugged and again slapped the table with the palm of his hand.

"But let's talk about the Suffolk. Michael's on him now. Soon's he gets back ye can have a look, an' then we'll do a bit of tradin' . . ."

He was interrupted by the sound of horse's hoofs approaching. Immediately, Downey leaped from his stool and hurried to the front door.

" 'Tis Michael, it is!" he grinned. "Now you two just sit yourselves back down there, an' us men'll have ourselves a little party, we will!"

The sun was setting as Ben and Tom finally prepared to take their leave. The time had flown by quickly, even though the haggling over the horse had been tedious, and at times had stretched Ben's patience to the limit. Fortunately, he had had experience doing business before with intractable Irishmen, and in the end a deal had been struck.

The Suffolk Punch was theirs.

Tom and Michael had found an instant camaraderie, Tom listening in fascination as Michael related the tales of his adventures since joining the crew of the *Supply*.

Ben listened with particular interest as the young man told of the ship's thousand-mile journey to Norfolk Island. They had found a better climate there than the one in New South Wales, fish in abundance and vast pines, 180 feet high, which were infinitely superior to the local eucalyptus for masts and building timber. On her last return to Port Jackson, the ship chanced upon another uninhabited island where they discovered large green turtles and myriads of birds that were so tame they could be knocked over with a stick.

It was good to know, Ben thought grimly, that if they couldn't make a go of it on the Hawkesbury there was at least an alternative.

"Pa! Pa, look!" Tom suddenly yelled, his stool tumbling across the dirt floor as he leaped up, pointing to the window.

As one, the other three men whirled in the direction of his pointing finger.

"Saints preserve us!" Collin Downey hissed.

There, staring back at them through the window, was the blackest native Ben Hollister had ever seen. His eyes were wild, his face covered with the grotesque scars they adorned themselves with. His near-naked body was layered all over with multi-colored mud.

Then his face disappeared from the window and all four men scrambled for the door, Collin Downey yelling for his son to grab the musket by the bed.

They tumbled outside and ran around to the side of the house where the black face had been spotted.

There, filling their arms with everything they could pull from Collin Downey's vegetable garden, were five of the natives. A sixth held the reins to the Suffolk Punch in one hand, and in the other he held a long, menacing spear.

Collin started bellowing at them in Gaelic, but they held their ground.

"Perhaps, if we try to reason with them?" Ben said.

His words were greeted by a whoop from Downey. "Aye, man, yer fluent in aborigine, are ye now? An' from the looks o' that one there, they ain't in no mood fer reasonin'."

Ben looked over at the black by the horse. He appeared to be the leader. He returned Ben's stare unflinchingly, and his grip tightened on the spear in his right hand.

"Gives me the shivers, it does," Collin said at Ben's elbow. "Ugly as sin, they are, an' like ghosts from some long ago time." Then he turned toward the house. "Michael, where the deuce is that musket?" he roared.

"Right here, Father." Michael appeared at the corner of the house.

At the sight of the gun, everything seemed to happen at once. When Tom tried to piece it together later, he couldn't recall who moved first.

The black holding the reins to the horse called out to the others in their native tongue, and immediately they dropped their armloads of booty to the ground. When they raised up, however, their hands were not empty. They were each holding a spear identical to the leader's.

Collin Downey, still shouting threats and epithets in Gaelic, began running toward the group hovering in the garden, while Ben and Tom made for their leader.

The man, while not large in stature, was incredibly agile. With an effortless leap he mounted the horse and prepared to turn the animal.

"Yer not goin' anywhere, mate!" Tom cried, his long legs churning in a dead run, closing the gap quickly. "An' particularly not with *that* lovely steed o' mine!"

He reached out and grasped the halter, and with Ben right behind him managed to halt the horse's progress.

And then a deafening roar echoed from the cottage doorway, followed by blood-curdling screams.

At the sound of the shot, the natives in the garden patch dropped their spears and bolted away, disappearing quickly into the darkness.

The black on the horse suddenly went rigid, his eyes wide with hatred and terror as he glared down at Tom and Ben. And then his right arm swung in a wide arc, lifting the spear high above his head.

"Pa, watch out!" Tom yelled, wrenching his body away from the horse's side as the spear whistled through the air toward his body. But he wasn't swift enough. Searing pain wrenched through his left arm, and he fell to his knees, feeling his brain going numb. A sound from behind him made him turn, and the sight that he saw there brought a strangled cry from his throat. "Pa!"

And then all was blackness.

"Well done, Michael, me boy!" Collin called out, following the fleeing thieves far enough to determine they were really gone. Satisfied, he turned back toward the house, cackling with glee. "Ha-ha, 'twasn't sure the old blunderbuss would even fire, 'tis been so long since—"

"Father!"

"Aye? What is it, lad?" he called, trying to locate Michael's voice in the gathering darkness.

"Over here . . . by the horse . . . quickly!"

The tone in his son's voice made Collin Downey's blood suddenly run cold. He raced to Michael, who was crouched low over a dark form on the ground.

"Is it . . ." he began.

" 'Tis both of them," Michael reported in a choked voice. "The spear went clear through Tom's arm, an' his Pa must've been standing directly behind him. The spear went right through his heart. He's dead."

"Jesus, Mary and Joseph!"

"And if we don't get Tom to the hospital in Port Jackson quick, he'll soon be dead, too."

Annie was roused from her restless sleep by the abrupt pounding on the front door of the hut. It must be her Pa and Tom, she thought, but why would they have a need to knock? The front door was rarely latched, and Mary Hollister had intentionally left it open for her husband and son's return.

Confused, Annie slid from the bed. She threw the light coverlet over her nightdress and began groping in the light from the fire's dim embers for a taper. She had just found one, when her mother appeared in the bedroom doorway, a lit candle already in her hand.

"Who is it?"

"I don't know," Annie replied, lighting the taper in her own hand from the one her mother held.

"Oh, dear God, could it be more convicts?" Mary whispered.

"Well, if it is," Annie replied, lifting the musket from its wallpegs, "they'll not have a chance to put a knife to our throats."

Again a pounding on the door thundered ominously through the room. Annie cocked the gun and cradled it in her right arm, with the barrel resting over her left forearm.

"Open it, Ma, and stand to the side."

With the light held high, Mary tugged the door open.

The faces of the two men who stared back at them from the darkness were those of strangers, and both Hollister women knew instantly that the news they brought was not good.

"Be ye Mrs. Hollister, wife of Ben?" the older, more rotund one asked, his blue eyes soft and full of sadness as he looked at Mary.

"Aye, I am," she nodded. "My husband is not here at the . . ."

"Aye, I know, ma'am," came the somber reply. "He is with me . . . or, I should say, he is in the. . . ." He shifted uncomfortably from one foot to the other, obviously searching for his words.

"Out with it, man," Mary cried, her uneasiness now turning to true alarm. "What is it? Has something happened to Ben?"

"Oh, ma'am, there has been a terrible accident. . . ." he began, then was gently brushed aside by the second, younger man.

"Forgive me for being so abrupt, Mrs. Hollister," he said, his voice calm, yet carrying with it a definite urgency. "I fear your husband is dead, slain in a terrible skirmish with natives at our farm in Parramatta. Your son Tom was severely wounded, but still he lives . . . 'tis urgent we get him to the hospital in Port Jackson as quickly as possible. Since your farm is on the way, we thought you would wish to go with us—"

He stepped forward quickly and caught Mary in his arms as she sank to the floor in a swoon.

The pair of them, indeed the entire room, swam before Annie's eyes. She felt as though water had filled her knees and she too would slip to the floor.

Her father was dead?

It couldn't be! Only that morning he had been so full of life, so happy. He had a smile on his face when he had set off with Tom. He had accepted what his son had done as inevitable, and he was actually looking forward to the purchase of a horse.

And now he was dead?

Her body began to sway.

A hand caught her by the shoulder. She looked up into the older, red-haired man's sad eyes.

"Steady, lass! There's much to be done."

He was right. Her father's death was catastrophe, but Tom's as well would be even worse.

She shook herself alert, handed the man beside her the musket she still held, and ran to fetch a water basin. Quickly she filled it and knelt beside her mother who lay, still cradled in the stranger's arms. As she splashed the cool water on her mother's temples and wrists, Annie turned to the young man.

"What is your name, please?" she asked.

"Michael, Michael Downey. And that's me father, Collin Downey."

"Michael, you must help me while I dress my mother, and take her with you into Port Jackson. I must see to my younger brother, Billy. He's not yet two. I can take him to a neighbor's house, and then I'll ride to the hospital to join you."

"Aye, ma'am," he nodded, and carefully lifted Mary into the bedroom, gently spreading her limp figure on the bed. Annie handed him the candle. Michael took it and held it high as he turned his head away from the bed.

Annie quickly stripped the nightdress from her

mother's body. Just as quickly, she managed to pull a dress over the woman's shoulders and arms. But that was as far as she could go. She couldn't manage her mother's weight and tug the dress down at the same time.

"Michael?"

"Aye, miss?"

"Help me!"

He turned, and quickly averted his eyes again. Mary's thighs were fully exposed, and the front of her dress was unlaced, revealing much of her breasts.

"There's no time for modesty now, for any of us. Help me. Lift her!"

He set the candle on a bedside stand and grasped Mary beneath the arms. In moments, with the young man's help, Annie had her completely dressed and presentable.

By this time Mary was stirring. Her eyes flew open, and with a moan they rolled around the room, eventually focusing on her daughter's face.

"Annie . . . Annie!"

And then the full shock of the recent news again struck her. Realization that her husband of so many years was no longer there, and would never be there again, washed over her like a tide. A scream formed in her tortured breast and threatened to erupt from her throat.

Annie grasped her firmly by the shoulders. "Ma, there is no time for grief, not yet. We must save Tom. You must go with these men and see to our son until he gets to the hospital. I will take Billy over to the Hunnicutts, then ride to Port Jackson as fast as I can. Until then, you must be strong." She shook her mother's shoulders gently. "Do you understand me, Ma?"

Mary Hollister had been cut to the bone, stricken with pain beyond any she had ever felt before. But she was from good, hardy stock and now she steeled herself to listen to her daughter's words, and heed them. She looked up through tear-misted and grief-glazed eyes at Annie, and then slowly nodded.

"I . . . I'll be all right."

"I know you will, Ma."

"Let us be about what we must do," she murmured, and painfully rose to her feet without aid.

Annie whirled on Michael. "Is there anything we can do for Tom here?"

Michael shook his head. "The spear came near to takin' his arm off. My father and I bandaged it as best we could, but he's still bleedin' awful bad."

"I'll give you sheets and cloths to make fresh bandages," she said, moving quickly to the chest at the foot of the bed while Michael led her mother to the front door.

Collin Downey gently lifted Mary into the back of the wagon. A sharp cry escaped her lips as she saw for the first time the covered form of her beloved husband.

"Ben!"

Collin kept a firm grip on her shoulders. "You must try to think only of your son, ma'am. He needs you bad."

She looked over to the pale, ghostly white face staring blankly back at her, and immediately rushed to where Tom lay, maneuvering her body until his head was cradleld in her lap. Michael clambered in on the other side of Tom and immediatley began ripping the cloth and sheets into bandages.

Seconds later, Annie crawled into the wagon. She purposefully kept her eyes averted from the covered figure of her father's body and knelt at her brother's side.

"Oh, dear God," she shuddered, seeing Tom's white face and letting her eyes travel down to his mutilated arm. She could see the ugly, raw tear of the wound, steadily oozing blood.

For a moment she thought she would be sick, but forced herself to remain steady.

With Michael's help she managed to arrest most of the bleeding and get the wound properly bound.

"See to it that he isn't jostled any more than is absolutely necessary during the ride," she cautioned, jumping from the wagon.

"Miss Annie—that is yer name, ain't it?"

"Aye."

"You'd best take the Suffolk. He'll last longer than yer mare and he's twice as fast. And he's yer's now anyway."

Annie's eyes went to the rear of the wagon where the big chestnut gelding stood contentedly, now and then shaking his powerful head.

Her eyes misted and a great lump seemed to swell in the middle of her breast and rise on up to clog in her throat.

Dear sweet Pa, she thought. He got his horse.

"We'd best be hurryin', lass," the elder Downey said, his voice at her ear.

She turned and bent forward. "Bless you," she whispered, brushing her lips over his bearded cheek and then looking up at his son where he sat beside her mother. "Bless you both."

"Let's be gone," Michael said to his father.

Collin quickly climbed up onto the wagon's seat and whipped the horse into a gallop.

Annie watched them until they were out of sight, then whirled from the door and quickly dressed herself and her baby brother.

It was hours later, when she had delivered Billy to the Hunnicutts, sputtered out the story to them, and was on her way to Port Jackson, driving the big gelding as hard as the beast would go, that the dam burst and tears flooded in an unending stream down her cheeks.

12————————————————————————

THE *Sovereign*, having passed through a gale east of Tierra del Fuego—a gale which she weathered like the steady old tub she was—rounded Cape Horn and so emerged from tempest into peace, from leaden skies and mountainous seas into a sunny azure calm. It was like a sudden transition from winter into spring, and she ran along now, close hauled to the soft easterly breeze, with a gentle list to port.

Captain Ahab Jones gazed up at the canvas billowing from the Whitby collier's three masts, and nodded. If they could maintain their current speed of eight to ten knots, they should make their destination within a month.

And none too soon, Jones thought, as his eyes darted from the cloudless horizon to the lower decks where his crew was repairing the damage done by the gale.

They were nearly out of stores, and the stench from below decks was nauseating to even the hardiest salts on the crew.

Once they reached New Holland he would have to disinfect the *Sovereign* from stem to stern.

New Holland. He allowed himself a slight smile as he thought of their destination, now so close after the long journey. Had it changed much? he wondered.

He had been a young crewman on the famous voyage of discovery with Captain James Cook and Joseph Banks nearly twenty years before as they searched for the mystical southern continent. He remembered vividly the exhilaration aboard the *Endeavour* as they sighted the massive continent for the first time.

Captain Ahab Jones breathed deeply of the fresh sea air, and wondered silently what he would find waiting for him in New Holland now. It had remained untouched for almost two decades since that original voyage. But then England had lost her war with the American colonies, and Joseph Banks had convinced King George that New Holland was an ideal location for a new penal colony. For the past two years, England had stuffed the holds of many a boat with the abject wretches and shipped them into oblivion thirteen thousand miles away.

The hold of the *Sovereign* was now loaded with almost two hundred of those souls.

The nature of his cargo was distasteful to Jones. But since he was one of the few men alive who had sailed with Captain Cook and knew the south seas as well as any man knew them, he had been commanded to this run.

He was determined to make the best of it. *At least I'll get the poor bastards there alive,* he growled under his breath, then added, *for all the good it'll do 'em!*

His eyes narrowed to two slits as he squinted to the top of the mainmast, where two of the crew were repairing the rigging.

"Double the knots on the mainmast!" he bellowed. "I'll be wantin' full sheets in this wind!"

The men called their "Aye, sar!"s, and Captain Jones moved away from the bridge and down the narrow ladder to his cabin.

Carefully extracting the charts from their protective sheaths, he stretched the parchments out full on the map table and turned up the flame in the overhead lamp. Reaching for the compass, he bent over the charts of the Great South Sea.

To this point he had been following the same course

he had sailed with James Cook twenty years earlier
. . . Plymouth to Rio de Janeiro to Tierra del Fuego,
then around the treacherous Cape Horn. But from this
point, instead of going northward to Tahiti, Jones was
sailing a more southwesterly course, to New Zealand.
He planned on making landfall there within a week,
taking on fresh provisions, then continuing on to New
South Wales, hopefully making Port Jackson within a
fortnight.

He could have chosen to go by way of Tahiti;
indeed, Ahab Jones mused how delightful it would be
to return to that lush, friendly paradise. But following
that particular course would mean approaching New
Holland by way of the Great Barrier Reef, and that he
wanted to avoid at all costs. The Reef had very nearly
cost him his life.

After the *Endeavour* had left Botany Bay, it had
inched slowly northward, nearly always in sight of the
coast but seldom landing. Massive coral reefs began
appearing around the ship, and the tides began rising
and falling by eighteen to twenty feet. Cook felt his
way very gingerly, trying to avoid grounding the ship
on those beautiful but deadly sharp coral antlers. Jones
shuddered at the memory of the grueling ordeal; the
terror of their near-fatal encounter with the Great Barrier Reef had stayed with Ahab Jones until the present
day.

The captain doublechecked the *Sovereign*'s position.
Then, satisfied that they had regained their correct
course after suffering through the gale, he carefully
rolled the charts and replaced them in their sheaths.

With a deep sigh he sank into a chair and reached
for his pipe. Striking a match to the tobacco, he leaned
back and absently watched the smoke curl in lazy rings
over his head.

He was just reaching for a bottle of Nantes he kept
stowed in the small cupboard beneath the table, when
a rapid knock sounded on the cabin door.

"Aye?"

The door burst open and Simpson, the First Mate, rushed in.

"Cap'n, sar. . . ." he began, his face flushed, his breathing coming in gasps.

" 'Aye, Simpson, what is it?"

"Thar's been some trouble, sar."

"Trouble? What sort of trouble?" Jones growled. "Odds blood, man, spit it out!"

"In the hold, sar . . . one of the prisoners . . . a fight, sar. . . ."

Jones sprang immediately to his feet. In the small confines of an old tub like the *Sovereign*, discipline was crucial. Most of the crew needed little excuse for a row under the best of conditions, and dissension among the prisoners could quickly spread chaos throughout the entire ship. He made for the door, but Simpson's hand stopped him.

"No need, sar, I took care of it meself with one swing of me cosh." His beard parted in a toothless smile as he patted the one-foot length of leather-wrapped club he kept perenially at his belt. "Knocked 'im cold, I did!"

"Which one was it?" Jones asked, eyeing the ominous looking weapon.

"The Irish bastard, it was," Simpson replied, the grin disappearing from his face. "Axelrod was just havin' a bit o' fun with one o' the women, an' this paddy bastard takes to defendin' her, he does! Wraps his chains around Axelrod's neck and would'a bloody well strangled him if I hadn't'a cold-cocked 'im!"

"Did you kill him?"

Simpson's gaze shifted nervously to study the toe of his right boot. "Nah. Face is a bit of a mess, though."

"And Axelrod?"

"Got some red marks on his neck an' his voice is kinda high and squeaky," Simpson replied with a scowl. then chuckled. "But Doc says he'll be back to his ol' nasty self 'fore long."

"Send the Irishman to me," Jones growled.

"Aye, sar. Very good, sar," Simpson nodded, and touching the backs of his fingers to the brim of his hat, backed out the door.

Jones moved across the cabin to the shelf where the log was kept, and picked up a long, slender volume next to it.

Slumping back in his chair and relighting his pipe, he opened the cover of the book and began scanning the pages.

The book contained a list of the convicts he carried on this trip. It was a long list, almost two hundred names in all, and beside each name was the prisoner's age and the nature of his or her crime.

Jones shook his head as his gaze followed his finger down the columns. Gerald Colbert, age 15, sheepstealer; Lawrence Peterson, age 17, pick-pocket; James Eric, age 24, forger; Gertie McGruder, age 19, murderer. Young men and women, no more than children, really, who had been caught stealing a loaf of bread or a chicken, thrown in with cut-throats and murderers.

And then his gaze halted as he found the name he was looking for.

Phillip Conroy, age 27, treason and murder.

Phillip Conroy struggled to raise his right hand up to his forehead. Gingerly he dabbed at the gaping gash over his eye with the sleeve of his shirt, and was relieved to see that the flow of blood had ebbed to a trickle. His head pounded, and he fought back the waves of nausea that threatened to separate him from the meager breakfast of cold porridge and tea he'd had hours before.

He leaned back against the rough planks of the wall and closed his eyes. The coldness and dank smells of the overcrowded hold didn't help.

* * *

"Be quick with ye, Irishman: yer slower'n frozen molasses!" First Mate Simpson sneered, jabbing Phillip with the blunt head of his billyclub as Conroy shuffled at an ungainly pace down the gangway, trying not to trip over the manacles that chained his ankles together.

Phillip bit his lip in an effort to hold his temper. His head still throbbed painfully from the blow of Simpson's club, and it wouldn't have taken much provocation for him to whirl on the First Mate and crush him between his powerful arms.

And damn the consequences.

"In here!"

Simpson gave a rapid knock on the door, then jerked it open and roughly shoved Conroy through the entrance, slamming the door behind him.

Conroy blinked in the dimness of the cabin. The quarters were cramped, and even though he was not overly tall, his size was such that it was impossible for him to stand comfortably upright in the low-ceilinged cabin.

Captain Ahab Jones sat perusing a document at a long table, over which a lamp was swinging faintly to the gentle heave of the ship. He was smoking a foul pipe, the smoke hanging heavily in the air of the little chamber, and there was a bottle of Nantes at his elbow.

He looked up as the hatchway slammed behind Conroy.

"Phillip Conroy?" he growled, his eyes narrowing as he regarded the scruffy and foul-smelling prisoner before him. A slight shudder coursed through him as he studied the young Irishman. He was haggard and hollow-eyed, his face nearly hidden from months' worth of beard. His right eye was swollen shut from a deep and bloody gash, apparently Simpson's handiwork. His garments were rumpled and torn from the struggle he had made when taken, and they reeked since he had been compelled to lie in them ever since.

"Aye, I'm Phillip Conroy."

"Sit," Captain Jones said, sliding a stool forward with the toe of his boot, "an' tell me why I should not take the whip to ye."

Phillip eased himself onto the stool, stretching his cramp legs slowly out in front of him. The sunshine filtered through one of the horn windows and beat full on his expressionless face as he gazed levelly back at the captain.

"Ye should." He smiled sourly.

Jones' eyebrow arched. "Ye are impertinent, considering your rather precarious position. Attacking a ship's officer is a serious offense."

"Aye, 'tis."

Jones stared at him, waiting for a flood of apology, or excuse. None came.

"Well? Have ye no defense for yerself, man?" he finally sputtered, frustrated at the man's utter calm.

"None ye would understand," Conroy said quietly.

Jones stiffened. "I am a very understanding man!" he growled. "Ye could have a worse captain than I hearin' yer story . . . one none too concerned about the letter o' the law when it comes to mutinous prisoners!"

Phillip chuckled low in his throat. "You'll end by telling me that I am in your debt."

"You'll end by sayin' so yerself!" the captain bellowed. "D' ye know what I could do with ye by all rights?"

"I neither know nor care," came the answer, wearily delivered.

"I could hang ye by the yardarm and then dump ye overboard!" Jones' hand slammed down on the table as he leaned nose to nose with Conroy, the blood vessels in his neck looking as though they would burst.

Then, suddenly, he expelled the air from his lungs explosively, and crumpled back into his chair.

"I'm not fer likin' this job, movin' prisoners, some not much more than boys and girls."

"I'm fer thinkin' I'd be hatin' it, too, Cap'n."

Again the Captain sighed and reached for the bottle of Nantes. He poured two tankards and pushed one of them across the desk to Conroy.

"Thank ye, Cap'n," the Irishman nodded.

"Yer papers say ye're an educated man, Conroy."

Conroy's fetters clanked as he brought the tankard to his lips. He drank deeply and let a smile creep to his lips as he brought the tankard away.

"Do ye suppose they have special work fer convict scholars where I'm goin', Cap'n?"

Jones disregarded the comment and let his eyes appraise the man across from him. Beneath the grime and the beard he detected the kind of wide, square-jawed face women called ruggedly handsome. Even with the uncombed hair and the filthy beard, Jones could see that the man was still young, only twenty-seven, if the records in the manifest were accurate.

But the eyes looked ancient, as if, like his own, they had seen too much. They stared back at him like two black coals, as if they could cut right into his soul.

Jones' eyes traveled down to the shoulders and huge arms. The man is built like a bull, the Captain thought. From the look of those arms and that chest, Axelrod is a lucky man to be alive!

"It also says in yer papers, yer a rebel."

"Aye," Conroy nodded.

"And a thief."

"Aye."

"And . . . a murderer."

There was a moment's pause, where the eyes flicked away, only to return, darker and slightly more sinister than before. "Aye."

"We've a month to port, Phillip Conroy. I can't have mutiny below."

"Then tell yer men, Cap'n, to leave the female prisoners alone." Conroy's voice was like steel, and in it Jones detected a warning that made him bristle.

"I'll have ta flog ya."

"I expect so."

Captain Jones nodded, returning his concentration to the papers on his desk. "Twenty lashes, come dusk. That'll be all, Irishman."

The clanking of Conroy's fetters as he moved to the hatch made Jones shudder and wish again that he could get a different command.

"Cap'n?"

"Aye?"

"About the lass. . . ."

"What lass?" Jones said, obviously irritated.

"The one Axelrod tried to rape."

"Simpson said it was only a bit of foolery with the girl."

"Perhaps," Conroy shrugged. "But it wasn't foolery with the two of his mates who did rape her on the afterdeck after I was coshed."

"I'll—"

"No ye won't, Cap'n," Conroy hissed. "Because ye can't. There'll be no proof. They'll deny it, an' ye'll not get a prisoner to come forward. They'd end up over the side on a dark night if they did."

Jones' face was pale as he crumpled back into his chair.

"An', Cap'n?"

"Aye."

"The lass. . . ."

"What about her, Conroy?"

"If ye'll look it up in yer papers there, sir, ye'll find out she was only twelve."

Conroy turned and stepped through the hatch, while the Captain dropped his face into his hands.

13

ANNIE sat beside Tom's bed, watching helplessly as the tears welled in his great brown eyes and spilled in rivulets down his pale cheeks.

She had been telling him about the funeral, fighting back her own tears as she related how so many folks had come to pay their respects to Mary and the children, how their father had looked so handsome in his only suit as they readied him for the short trip from the little chapel to the cemetery overlooking Port Jackson, and how fine the minister had prayed as Mary Hollister sprinkled the first handful of earth over her husband's coffin.

That had been a week ago, two days after the wild night ride to save Tom's life. It had taken hours to find a doctor to perform the surgery on Tom's arm, and he had remained delirious most of the time since then. Only yesterday had the fever broken, permitting them cautious hope that he might live. Today for the first time he had opened his eyes and recognized those around him.

But with that recognition had come a flood of memories.

"Pa . . . *Pa*!" he had screamed, as he relived that last terrifying moment when the Aborigine's spear had pierced his arm, and his father's heart.

He had become so delirious that Annie had feared he would do some harm to himself. But he was calmer now, and insisted on knowing everything that had happened since that night in Parramatta.

Annie had filled in the gaps as far as she could, ending with their father's funeral.

But she didn't tell him everything.

She didn't mention that every time she left his side for a hurried cup of sweet tea and a bowl of soup, Captain Steven Rourke would appear all too frequently.

"What will you do now, Annie Hollister?"

"I'll do what has to be done."

"And will that be enough?"

"Do you enjoy gloating, Captain?"

"I care not one whit whether you believe me or not, but I am not gloating. I merely face facts, as you should do."

"And those are?"

"Your farm will go to seed even with your brother back on his feet. His arm, healed, will be near useless."

"And I suppose you have solutions to my problems?" Even as she had said it, she knew his answer.

"You know my solution."

And another time he accosted her on the dusty street. It was just as she rode in from the farm, on her way to the hospital. She was dirty and tired, and bone-weary from riding back and forth each day to Port Jackson.

"How are things on the Hawkesbury?"

"You know how they are," she had retorted. "Ma told me you were there."

"Aye, I was," Rourke nodded. "I looked at the fields. The weeds are higher than the crop, and 'tis near harvest time."

"I'll harvest somehow," Annie said defiantly.

"Will you now?" he said, his cold eyes without feeling and his smile cynical.

And then, as he walked away, she remembered.

"Captain?"

"Aye?"

"Thank you for the ham you brought my mother."

He shrugged. "I could do more."

She exploded at his callousness. "Dear God," she gasped, "you give with one hand and take with the other! Would you blackmail me into becoming your mistress?"

Rourke responded in kind. "A man has to take what he gets. If he does not, another man will!"

"My father always told me—"

"Your father is dead, Annie Hollister, and you are alive. *Take*, Annie, or you'll get nothing!"

His words had fallen like echoes of doom on her weary ears and turned her heart to stone. But nevertheless, as she left him and made her way that day to Tom's bedside, she found herself weeping.

Another thing she didn't impart to Tom was the state of their mother's health. Almost as soon as Mary was sure Tom would live, she had returned to the Hawkesbury. And there she sat, in Ben's old rocker, humming to herself, and doing little else.

She had slipped into a near catatonic state, and nothing Annie could say or do would move her. It had gotten so bad that Annie was often afraid to leave Billy in her care.

All of this preyed hourly upon Annie's mind until she thought she would go mad with worry.

A groaning sigh from Tom brought her thoughts back to the here and now.

"Is the pain back? Can I get you something?" she asked anxiously.

He stared at her for a long moment, and then shook his head, sagging heavily back onto the pillow.

"Looks none too good, does it, dear sister?" he chuckled mirthlessly. "The farm was work enough for six strong arms. Now I've only one." He gingerly touched the massive wrapping of bandages covering his left arm.

The doctor had told her that the major muscles and tendons of Tom's arm had been severed. He had stitched them together as best he could, but they wouldn't know for many months how effective the mending would be. With exercise, the arm might regain all its former strength. Or it might be totally useless.

"Nonsense," Annie replied, her voice carrying more confidence than she felt, "the doctor said you'll be tough as Newcastle steel by Christmas! And, besides"—here she made a wry smile and puffed up the biceps of her own right arm to their absolute limit—"I myself am a demon with a plow!"

Tom's eyes softened as he looked fondly at his sister. "You've spunk, Annie girl, but I fear 'twill take far more than spunk to give us purchase in this new land, now."

Tears welled up in her eyes and her shoulders shook. She was so tired that she found it hard to speak or think clearly.

"There must be a way, there must! We could indenture some convicts. . . ."

"Could we?" Tom replied. "To do that we must house them, feed them."

"The tobacco," she whispered, looking quickly around to make sure the men on the other cots weren't listening. "Shouldn't it be cured enough to market now?"

A faint light of hope shone in Tom's eyes. "Aye, it should. If you could get it in here, to market . . . maybe. . . ."

They fell silent, both thinking their own thoughts.

Yes, the tobacco. Tom had given her the name already. Who was it? A convict. Morgan. No, Moran. Jack Moran. She would contact him . . . arrange. . . .

"Annie . . . Annie!"

"Huh . . . what?"

"Annie, you fell asleep. Dear God, girl, get out of here. I'm fine. Get some rest!"

"Rest . . . aye, a whole night's sleep is what I need."

She kissed her brother on both cheeks and, stumbling along, made her way out of the hospital and across the narrow street to the communal stables.

Dusk had fallen, and with alarm she realized that it would be dark in a few minutes.

Should she attempt the ride to the Hawkesbury in darkness? She had to, for there was no place to stay in Port Jackson.

Groaning and half asleep already, she managed to pull herself into the hide-covered wooden saddle. Pain brought her awake at once. Unaccustomed to so much riding, her inner thighs were raw, and in Tom's saddle she had to ride astride like a man.

Once away from the main camp, she halted. Carefully she pulled her skirts clear to her hips and then bunched them beneath her to do away with the chaffing.

Tomorrow, she thought, kicking the Suffolk into a walk, I will wear Tom's extra pair of breeches under my skirts!

She had barely gone fifty yards when her head began to nod again.

God, she was so sleepy. Perhaps she should rest, just for a few minutes. She could tether the gelding and nap beneath a tree. Just a short nap.

She felt herself slipping, falling, and barely caught herself in time by twisting her fingers in the horse's mane.

Can't be much farther now . . . can it? Been riding for hours. The Suffolk has a nice walk, lulls you to sleep. Which way am I going? Eyes . . . my eyes won't open. . . .

Suddenly she was jerked awake by a strong arm around her middle. Her eyes flew open and struggled to focus.

"Damme, girl, are you trying to kill yourself?"

"Rourke."

Slowly she became oriented. She was sitting side-saddle on Rourke's stallion, with Steven himself on the horse's rump, holding her. The Suffolk was trailing behind them.

"Wha . . . ?"

"I've been following you for an hour, you little fool."

"Should be almost . . . home," she murmured wearily.

"How could you be?" he retorted. "You've been riding around in circles!"

"Oh, no . . . must get home . . ."

"You'll stay in Port Jackson tonight."

"No!" she cried, forcing her eyes open again. She could see his dark face in the moonlight strikingly outlined by his blond hair.

" 'Tis time, Annie. You've no fight left in you."

"I do," she moaned. "I'm just tired . . . so tired . . . can't keep my eyes. . . ."

His arm tugged her until her head rested against his chest. She couldn't even lift her own arms to push herself upright.

"Give up, Annie. Give up."

Aye. Why not? 'Tis all too much. He's right. I can fight no longer.

Annie awoke still feeling weak and disembodied. It was as if she were alert, yet still asleep, floating somewhere outside herself.

Her hands moved over fresh, clean sheets. She found her own, naked flesh, and sighed.

So tired, I forgot to put on my nightdress.

She began to drift off again.

And then she remembered. Her eyes flew open and she sat bolt upright in the bed.

She was in *his* hut, in *his* bedroom, and she was naked!

"Good morning."

Her eyes flew to the doorway connecting the two rooms. His eyes met hers for an instant, and then dropped to her bare breasts hovering just above the coverlet. Quickly she drew the coverlet up to cover herself and slithered backward on the bed.

"I've slept the night here?"

"Of course," Rourke replied, stepping forward and moving to the tub at the foot of the bed. For the first time, Annie noticed steam rising. He tested the water with a finger and nodded. "A little tepid, but warmth enough. As soon as you bathe and dress, you can fix us a spot of breakfast."

The calm assurance of his command nettled her. "No, thank you. If you'll find my clothes I'll just leave."

"I've laid out a chemise and dress there."

He motioned toward a chair in the corner of the room, and then turned toward the door.

"Rourke?"

"Aye?"

"Did you undress me?"

His laugh was instant, full of mockery. "Of course I undressed you. There was no one else to do it, and you were as limp as a sack of potatoes."

His eyes were as arrogant as his smile as they drifted across her body, stripping away the coverlet and feasting on her nudity, as she was sure they had done the night before.

"Rourke . . . did you. . . ."

"What?"

Their eyes held until a flush filled Annie's face, forcing her to look away. She was again frightened by the power she sensed in his body. Her heart seemed to stop for an instant and she could feel her pulse pounding in her throat.

"Did . . . did you take me last night?"

His harsh laughter chilled her to the bone. "Take

you? No, Annie, I didn't take you . . . though I was tempted." Then his expression became almost incredulous. "Dear God, girl, you profess to be a virgin, and you don't know whether you've had a man or not?"

"No, I don't. I. . . ." Suddenly she realized how foolish she sounded, and the flush on her cheeks grew even deeper. "Where did you sleep?"

"There," he said, nodding to where she sat. "Right there, beside you. After all, it is my bed."

Annie gasped. "You slept with me and you didn't. . . ."

"No, I didn't," he replied, his words clipped, his voice like cold steel. "When I take you, Annie Hollister, I want you awake. I want you to know exactly what you're about. Now, bathe and dress!"

"I would prefer my own clothes."

"I've already burned them." He turned and walked through the door, letting the broadcloth curtain fall into place behind him.

"Damn!" she hissed, leaping from the bed. As she passed the tub, she paused. The water looked so inviting. On the floor beside the tub was an open vial. She could smell the fragrant aroma of its perfumed contents.

Biting her lip, Annie felt her shoulders begin to sag. She couldn't resist.

Dear God, it seems I resist less and less each day!

She poured the scent from the vial into the water, and the room was immediately filled with honeysuckle. Gingerly she stepped over the high sides of the tub into the water. It felt glorious, and she couldn't resist easing her still tired body all the way down into it, stretching her aching limbs and letting the weariness soak slowly away.

She spent a full hour in the water, luxuriating in the scented warmth, before finally emerging and drying herself with a large, soft towel.

Such luxury, she thought, pulling the chemise over

her head. And then another thought chilled her as she laced the dress: *What will I have to pay if I keep accepting?*

Even though the dress was not new and it fit too tightly in the bust, she welcomed it over the rags she had worn into Port Jackson.

Two new dresses, she mused, stepping into the other room. It must stop there!

Silently she prepared the meal, reasoning that she did owe Rourke that much. They ate in silence, and at the meal's conclusion, she made to wash the plates and bowls. But his hand on her arm stopped her.

"Don't bother."

"But. . . ."

"I have someone to do that."

"Very well. I must get below now . . . to Tom."

Rourke nodded, and then spoke just as she stepped outside the door. "If you wish, I'll send four or five of my convicts over to help you work the fields this week."

Annie tensed. It would help. If they could just get part of the harvest done. . . .

"I could pay you with part of the harvest—"

"I don't want your money or your crops," he replied coldly.

Annie didn't have to ask his meaning. It was clear in the way his insolent eyes raked her body. A shiver passed through her. As handsome as this man was, as much as he could do for her, Annie still couldn't imagine writhing in passion beneath his body.

It would be so cold, so emotionless . . . so calculated.

But convicts could provide the help she so desperately needed. . . . and then she remembered the tobacco. The tobacco would buy her time!

"Good day, Captain Rourke. Thank you for a night's rest . . . uninterrupted. I shall send the dress back as soon as I can."

"Then you refuse the convicts?"

"Aye. We'll manage. I have other ways."

Rourke shrugged. "Very well. But you can keep the dress. I have plenty more. We take them away from the female prisoners when they arrive and issue them uniforms."

His harsh laughter followed her all the way to the main cart path, stinging her ears and making her even more determined to retain her autonomy.

Halfway down the hill she rounded a bend of rocks and nearly collided with someone coming up.

"Well, well, dearie, ye're gettin' to be a real reg'lar with the Cap'n, ain't ya!"

It was the dark-haired girl Annie had seen in the trees before, and her flashing, darkly lashed eyes still held that same mischievous glint.

"This is not what you think! I—"

"Dearie, ya don't got to explain to me."

"Oh, but I do!" Annie had enough problems facing her. She had no desire to add another. Taking a deep breath, she spoke again. "There is nothing between Captain Rourke and myself. Believe me, the man is all yours, and you're welcome to him!"

The girl's whoop of laughter came so suddenly that Annie took a step backward.

"*Mine?* Dearie, the Cap'n don't belong to no woman, an' he never will! 'Sides, even if I was still beddin' him, I'd share him," she shrugged. " 'Twould make no never mind to me. No, dearie, I just cleans up after him."

The girl moved around Annie, and then paused.

" 'Course, that's not to say that the other one might not be jealous enough to slit yer gullet. . . ."

The other one? Annie thought.

But before she could speak again, the brunette was gone, her hips beneath the tattered skirt moving in a lazy, indolent way.

14

THE *Sovereign* continued its voyage uneventfully for a fortnight, with prisoners and crew alike looking forward to making landfall at the northern tip of New Zealand, where they could replenish their stores and set foot on land, however briefly, before continuing on to Port Jackson.

At last, the lookout in the crow's nest yelled down that he had spotted land, and they made ready to anchor the following day.

"Mr. Simpson?"

"Aye, sar?"

"Bring the prisoners up fer air before the night. It looks like we might have a bit of weather."

"Aye, sar."

Only the men were fettered, and their chains made enough noise to drown out the flapping of the sails and the creaking of the ship's timbers.

Captain Jones' eye fell on Phillip Conroy in the line. "Conroy!"

"Aye?" The Captain made a beckoning sign, and the Irishman stepped from the line. "Cap'n."

"I'm sorry about the girl."

"Are ye, sir?"

"Dammit, man, yes, I am! I plan on preferring charges against the two of them as soon as we reach Port Jackson."

Conroy's smile through the blackness of his beard

was hollow, mirthless. "If the lass could hear ya from her watery grave, I'm sure she'd thank ya, Cap'n."

"Dammit, man, 'tis not my fault she lost her head and threw herself over the side!"

But Conroy had already moved away, aft. Very carefully he settled himself on his haunches and eased his tender, lash-welted back against the rail. His eyes lolled half closed until he appeared to be dozing.

But he was very much alert, the black pupils beneath his hooded lids darting back and forth among the crew, searching.

It was several moments later when Gerald Colbert moved into the space beside him. The lad hunkered down and, without so much as a glance, spoke to Conroy out of the side of his mouth.

"I found out, sar."

"Good," Conroy replied in a low voice. "Which ones?"

"Mason and Yardley's their names."

"Their names mean little to me, lad, but their faces do. Point 'em out!"

"Mason's there in the mainmast rigging, mending sail."

"And the other?"

"Yardley's the one with the red beard, there by the wheel."

Conroy's eyes took in and studied the two men's faces until they were burned into his brain. Then he relaxed and let his eyelids close completely.

"What you gonna do, Mr. Conroy?"

The Irishman's eyes remained closed, but his white teeth gleamed in a smile. "When the chance comes, lad, I'm gonna kill 'em. Both of 'em."

That night the ship began to pitch and yawl, making the old timbers screech and groan eerily. The sea around them became steadily angrier, the waves rising higher and higher over the bow, and the sky turned black as pitch.

And then the squall hit. It came howling out of the skies, to the south of them, and battered the *Sovereign* with winds near hurricane force. Captain Jones was compelled to run before it, heading northward away from its fury.

For two days the tiny ship was buffeted mercilessly in the storm, at times disappearing altogether beneath a black, mountainous wave, only to bob like a cork once more to the surface, her masts and bow shedding streams of seawater.

"We're runnin' far to the north, sar, nowhere near our course!"

"I'm aware of it, Mr. Simpson."

"There'll be hell to pay findin' New Zealand, sar!"

"I'm aware of that as well, Mr. Simpson. There will also be hell to pay jest findin' our location until this storm clears an' there's a star to sight by."

There was an abrupt knock on the door and then a seaman rushed into the cabin without waiting for word.

"Beggin' yer pardon, sar. . . ."

"Aye, what is it, lad?"

" 'Tis Mason, sar."

"What about him?"

"He was directin' a group of the prisoners while they was battenin' down the aft lifeboats, sar."

"I know that, lad. Out with it!"

The young seaman gulped. "He was swept overboard! We'll never find him in this, sar!"

Captain Jones exchanged looks with his First Mate, and then sighed. "Maintain course," he said at last. "May he rest in peace."

Dawn of the storm's third day brought bright skies and calm seas. It also brought confusion, and terror.

Captain Jones and First Mate Simpson spent hours pouring over the charts, trying to determine their position. They had been buffeted so mercilessly by the storm that they now had no idea of their location in the Great South Sea. They took repeated readings with the sextant and carefully charted the course of the sun across the brilliant, cloudless sky.

Making one last calculation on the map before him, Captain Jones suddenly looked up, his face ghostly pale.

"God in heaven," he breathed.

"What is it, Cap'n?" Simpson asked, feeling sudden alarm clutch at his belly as he looked at his superior officer.

"Odds blood, man," Jones hissed. "If our calculations are right, we're damn near right on top of the Great Barrier Reef."

At that precise moment, the lookout in the crow's nest bellowed, "Land ho, Cap'n! Dead ahead!"

Jones shot out of the cabin, with Simpson close on his heels.

On deck knots of shaggy seamen were crowding about, looking out to sea, all staring intently ahead and toward the beautiful and deadly multicolored reefs as they shimmered like a coral necklace in the blue water not five hundred yards away.

"Hard to port!" Captain Jones barked to the mate at the wheel. "Hold 'er steady equidistant from shore!" Then he whirled to the knot of seamen at the rail. "Reef the topsail and mizzen! And all hands keep a sharp eye! This coral is like a lovely woman lyin' in wait to rip a hole in our belly!"

The *Sovereign* heeled to port and began inching her way along the Barrier Reef. Close hauled as she was, and with her topsails and mizzen reefed, she was not making more than one knot.

Jones hurried back to his cabin and searched for his charts on the Reef, charts which he had so meticulously drawn on that fateful trip twenty years earlier with Captain James Cook.

He found them in the bottom of the map drawer, and silently gave his thanks to heaven that he had had the presence of mind to stow them aboard at the last minute, in the unlikely event that just such a catastrophe as this might befall them.

He carefully spread the maps out on the plank table, and stared at the twelve-hundred-fifty-mile-long stretch of coral. The north end was close to shore, no more than ten miles from land. From there the Reef reached out like a tentacle, its southern tip ending over one-hundred-fifty miles out to sea. The shallow waters inside the reef were strewn with coral islets and atolls, as Jones knew very well. Outside the reef, the waters were of great depth, with high tides and tremendous surf on the outer edge.

Jones judged their position to be near the southernmost tip of the Reef, where the tides and surf would be even more treacherous.

Bundling the maps under his arm, he dashed back up on deck, only to see the *Sovereign*'s bow heading straight for an outcropping of coral at the Reef's tip.

"Luff alee!" he bawled, and sprang to the wheel, thrusting the mate aside with a blow of his elbow that sent the man sprawling.

" 'Twas yerself that set the course," the fellow protested.

"Thou lubberly fool," roared the skipper, "I bade thee keep the same distance from shore! If the land comes jutting out to meet us, are we to keep straight on 'til we pile her up?"

He spun the wheel around in his hands and turned her down the wind.

But he was too late.

There was a dull thud, and then a rending, grinding sound resembling that of the teeth of a giant saw gnawing through timber. Both Captain Jones and the helmsman saw the *Sovereign*'s bow surge into the air, teeter precariously for a moment, and then come crashing down over the coral.

"B'gar, sar, we're aground!"

"Damme, man," Jones howled, "don't ya think I know that? Mr. Simpson!"

"Aye, sar!" the First Mate called from main deck.

"Sound all hands! Go below, check the damage!"

"Aye, sar!"

Jones turned back to the white-faced helmsman. "Take the wheel, you bloody fool, and hold her thus to port, against the swells, or the tide'll beat us to death on the rocks!"

The helmsman nodded and gripped the wheel with quivering, white-knuckled fingers. Bellowing orders as he went, Jones moved down the ladderwell to main deck four steps at a time.

Simpson was just emerging from the foredeck hatchway when Jones arrived.

"Well?"

"Ripped twenty feet o' hull out, sar. The bow keel is gone. There's about eight feet o' coral stickin' right into the hold."

"The pumps?"

"All workin', Cap'n, but we're takin' on water four times faster'n we can pump."

"Jesus, Mary and Joseph. What about the prisoners?"

"Ten sliced to ribbons when we hit, maybe another twenty drowned. And, sar . . . ?"

"Aye?"

"The water's startin' to shift aft, sar. It'll go fast, sittin' on the angle we are."

Jones nodded and walked quickly to the rail. Though the sky was clear and there was little or no wind, the water beneath them boiled and churned. Jones knew that just beneath the surface there might as well be a storm.

He turned back. Several members of the crew stood, awaiting further orders.

"Into the ratlines, lads! Furl canvas, all of it! If a wind comes up it'll rip her whole bottom out. And keep men on the pumps. We might be able to buy time. Mr. Simpson!"

"Sar."

"Get the prisoners on deck. Bunch 'em on the bow, maybe the weight will hold us down . . . for a while."

For the next hour the deck was chaos. Everything was done that could be done, and it wasn't enough.

"Cap'n," Simpson said at last, his face an impassive mask. " 'Tis no use. The water's shiftin'. When it does, the tide'll spin us off the rocks and she'll go down like a stone."

Jones nodded. "How long do you suppose, Mr. Simpson?"

"A little over an hour . . . two at the most."

Again Jones moved over the side and peered into the treacherous blue-green water. "Ready the boats and remove the fetters from those prisoners who are manacled."

"Aye, sar." Simpson took a step away, and then turned back. "Cap'n, there's bare enough room in the boats fer the crew . . . an' there'll be no makin' return trips in these waters."

"I know that, Mr. Simpson. Send four men below to my cabin. I'll open the armory. Muskets and side arms for every man. We'll have to keep order when the time comes."

Huddled in the bow amidst the prisoners' milling bodies, Phillip Conroy rubbed his wrists and ankles when the fetters had been removed.

"Why'd they take our chains off, Mr. Conroy?"

The Irishman turned his shaggy head and let his black eyes fall on the boy's pale face. " 'Tis easy to figger, lad. Ye can't swim in chains."

"Dear God in heaven. *Swim*?" young Colbert gasped, standing and peering over the side. "In *that*?"

Conroy nodded grimly, rising to stand beside the boy. "I do believe that's what the Cap'n has in mind. His first duty is to his crew. Can't blame him fer that."

"But . . . but the tide, the rocks, and look there . . . sharks!"

Conroy merely chuckled. "An' big ones they are. Are ye afraid to die, lad?"

The boy swallowed, almost painfully, and rolled his big eyes up to the larger man beside him. "Aye, I'm turrible 'fraid of it. Does that make me a coward, sar?"

Here Conroy laughed openly and clamped a huge hand on the other's shoulder. "Nay, lad, that makes ye a sensible man." Then he grew silent. His heavy black brows lowered as his piercing eyes gazed around the water where it eddied and swirled around the jagged coral. "But there might be a way without swimmin'," he murmured softly.

Captain Ahab Jones emerged from the hatch, followed by four seamen heavily laden with arms.

"Thinkin' of a mutiny, Cap'n?"

Phillip Conroy's bulky body barred his way and the man's coal-black eyes bored into him accusingly.

"Out o' the way, Conroy. There's things to be seen to."

"A word, Cap'n?"

"I said—"

"A word, Cap'n!"

His voice was low and ominous, like steel rasping on steel. Jones could see the tenseness in the wide, powerful body before him, and made to bring up the musket. He could hear hammers click on pistols behind him.

Conroy heard it too and stepped back, but not before he lowered his voice and spoke in a hurried, hushed whisper.

"I know your plan, Cap'n, an' I know why you must do it. But I think there's a way to save the prisoners."

At this point Jones was willing to try anything. He hesitated only a second before replying. "What is it?"

"Over here, skipper, to the rail." Conroy led the way and then pointed to an outcropping of jagged rocks. They were about fifty yards away, and the nearest point of land to the ship. "Those rocks, sir, if we can reach them there's a chance we can walk the rest of the rocks in."

"You're mad, Conroy. The only way the boats can make it is head to sea and then down to that inlet there, then let the breakers take 'em in."

"Aye, the boats might make it that way, but 'tis risky. And, sir, what about the prisoners?"

Now it was said, and both men knew that swimming to any point on shore from the sinking ship was impossible.

Conroy continued quickly, before Jones could speak. "If we could get a line from the bow to those rocks, the lifeboats could guide themselves in by pulling hand over hand. We could ferry them in . . . prisoners and crew alike."

Jones laughed mirthlessly. "And how, lad, do you propose to get a line to the rocks?"

"Think, Cap'n! The *Sovereign*'s an old whaler, isn't she?"

The skipper's eyes grew wide as he whirled on Conroy. "Damme, man, you may have found a way! The harpoon gun is stowed aft!"

"Are the mounts still on the bow?"

"Aye," Jones nodded, fired with hope.

He flew into action, barking orders. In minutes the bulky gun was brought on deck and reassembled. Two of the six bow mounts were rusted out, but four would hold and be enough. The tugging weight of three full lifeboats would be nothing compared to the seventy feet and several tons of a sperm whale.

At last the gun was mounted, the harpoon threaded and the charge laid. Word had spread quickly about the ship, and now seamen and prisoners alike stood in mute silence, praying that the plan would work.

Captain Jones himself stepped behind the gun and swiveled it around, sighting it to Phillip Conroy's instructions. "There, Cap'n, those two jagged peaks that look like a devil woman's splayed thighs. There should be enough jagged edges between 'em for the harpoon to catch."

"Aye, lad. Now pray!"

Jones sighted the gun, allowing for the arc and fall. Then he muttered a prayer himself, and fired.

The harpoon arched into the sky, trailing its life saving line behind it. Breaths were held, fists were clenched, and all eyes strained until they watered.

And then a cheer erupted from every throat as the harpoon and then its trailing line disappeared between the craggy, jutting rocks.

" 'Tis not over yet, lads!" Captain Jones roared. "Lend hands there and play her back gentle!"

Willing hands grapsed the line, gently pulling, tugging the harpoon back across the rocks. The distance was too great to hear the metal grate against stone, but there was a hush among the crowded bodies as if they could.

The wait seemed an eternity as more and more of the line moved back through the men's hands to coil on the deck.

And then it held.

"Thank God," Jones hissed, and his words were met with the sound of many lungfulls of air being exhaled as one.

"An' not a moment too soon," Conroy growled. "Look there!"

The men turned. Ominous gray clouds were rolling in from the sea. Aleady the white caps were rising higher and breaking nearer the swaying vessel.

"Let's get to it," Conroy intoned, climbing up on the rail and grasping the line in his powerful hands. "Keep her taut, lads!"

"May God go with ye, lad," Jones said, his eyes meeting Conroy's for one brief instant.

The Irishman leaned forward and then he was gone, swinging to and fro over the raging sea. Hand over hand he went along the rope. As if they could sense a meal from their watery homes, shark fins broke the surface, circling above the foam.

The heavily corded muscles in his back and arms rippled and bulged with the strain, and sweat gleamed on his skin. Halfway across, he swung his legs up and secured his ankles over the line. A short rest, and then he was off again.

"By the saints," Simpson hissed at Jones' shoulder, "the man's like a monkey."

"Aye," Jones replied. "An' he has the strength of ten, he does."

Twice Conroy lost his grip as he neared the crags where the men aboard the *Sovereign* couldn't keep the line taut. Precariously he swung, with only one hand holding his weight. But each time he managed to swing himself back up and proceed.

"Cap'n?"

"Aye, Mr. Simpson."

"How do we know the prisoner won't reach the rocks an' jest keep goin'?"

"We don't, Mr. Simpson."

And then another chorus of cheers erupted from those who waited on the ship. Conroy had reached the rocks, and with an agile swing he was between them and gone down the other side.

The men holding the line relayed back to Captain Jones Conroy's evident progress as they felt the vibrations of movement in their own hands.

And then the Irishman again appeared, his hands and arms making the motions of a secured knot at his end of the line.

"All right, Mr. Simpson," Jones barked, "let's get those boats into the water!"

The words had barely left his lips when the heavens opened and the rains came down.

* * *

Conroy narrowed his eyes against the stinging rain and watched Captain Ahab Jones climb over the rail and drop into the last boat. Behind Conroy, above the rocks on the flat of the cliff, were the men and women who had already made the fifty-yard journey through the raging sea.

It was near dark now, and the black rain clouds brought night on even faster.

"I don't like ye, Irishman, but I admire ye fer what ye've done. An' I hope they see fit in Port Jackson to reward ye fer it."

Conroy turned slightly until his eyes met the First Mate's. "How can they reward me, Mr. Simpson? An extra ration of water or the like each fer the rest of me life?"

Simpson jerked his eyes away, returning them to the boats crawling toward them.

The rest of his life in this place, Simpson thought. God save the man's soul.

Thunder rumbled above them, and every few seconds the ocean and rocks were eerily illuminated in the orange and yellow glare of lightning.

Suddenly there was a sound like the crack of a whip that rode over the thunder and the ocean's angry roar. It was followed by the unmistakable sound of timbers grinding against the reef.

"Jesus," Simpson gasped, "it can't be!"

"I'm afraid it is," Conroy hissed. "She's breaking up."

And even as he spoke, the *Sovereign* began to list to seaward. Shouts came from the boats as the line grew tauter and lifted higher above them.

"Check the harpoon!" Conroy rasped.

Simpson scurried away, only to be back in seconds. "She's holding. If it goes it'll be the other end."

"Get some men up here fast. If it goes, we'll have to haul 'em in from this end."

Again Simpson hurried away. Minutes later Conroy could hear him returning with others.

And then there was a rending crash, and the *Sovereign* slid from the reef. At the same instant, the rope snapped. All hands in the boats continued to pull. But Conroy could already hear the steel of the harpoon grating on the rocks. Without a steady tension it might well lose its purchase.

And then there were men all around him, with Simpson's voice shouting orders. "Lay on, lads, pull steady now . . . heave . . . heave . . . heave. . . ."

Twenty yards . . . ten . . . then the bow of the first boat struck the rocks. Conroy was there in seconds.

"Get ashore and turn the boat aside! Hurry! Make way for the next!"

They did as they were told, scrambling up onto the rocks, clutching the canvas bag of provisions they had been issued before leaving the ship.

The second boat was emptied, and half of the third, when a huge breaker lifted its stern like a feather. Bodies seemed to fly every which way, their screams lost in the roar of yet another wave.

Conroy flattened himself on a ledge of stone and reached for the clutching hands. He pulled two men and then a gasping woman to safety. When the woman was at last beside him, heaving water from her throat and nostrils, he peered back into the darkness for more.

"Help . . . help me!"

Conroy rolled to the other side of the ledge. The lightning was coming in intermittent flashes only seconds apart. He heard the cry of distress again, partially garbled by water, and strained his eyes toward the sound.

Another orange glow and he saw a hand and a bobbing head. Reaching far out, he grasped a wrist and slowly towed the man closer to get a better purchase.

"Aye . . . thank you . . . my hand, here's my other hand . . . don't let go!"

And then Conroy was holding him directly below the edge of the rock where he lay. It was all he could do to tug the man to the surface against the tide's powerful pull. Slowly the head came clear of the water. It lolled back, and Conroy was staring into the fear-filled, red-bearded face of the seaman, Yardley.

Their eyes met, and Yardley sensed at once the hate and the intent in Conroy's black orbs.

"Conroy . . . no, dear God, man . . . ye wouldn't! Don't, I didn't. . . ."

The rest of his words were gone in the swirling water as Conroy saw the red head bob just once, and then disappear.

"Conroy?"

It was Simpson's voice from the rocks above him.

"Aye? Here."

"Look . . . 'tis Cap'n Jones!"

Conroy scanned the water until he spotted the third lifeboat. Draped half in, half out of the boat was the Captain's body. Evidently he had been knocked unconscious when the swell had nearly capsized the tiny boat.

Conroy stood and arced his body in a long, shallow dive. A few strokes of his powerful arms brought him to the boat and over the side.

"Captain?"

There was no answer, but Conroy could feel life in the pulse at the side of the man's head. Beneath him, Conroy saw an oar, muskets, pistols, and sacks of powder, shot and provisions.

He was about to throw them overboard, when suddenly he smiled. He had spotted an inlet that appeared relatively calm about thirty yards along the shore. Now he took up the oar and paddled toward it. He moved with the lightning, paddling furiously when it struck and using the oar as a rudder in between flashes.

At last the pull of the tide ebbed against the flat surface of the oar. He bore to the right and felt the breakers take him in. The second the boat ground against sand, Conroy was in the water. Straining with every muscle in his big body, he managed to get it beached.

Swiftly he lifted the Captain and placed him high in the sand. Then he unloaded all the bags and guns. Two of the pistols he stuck in his belt. He overloaded a bag of powder and shot, and did the same with a second bag of provisions.

He was just shouldering them when a groan reached his ears from the Captain's direction.

"You'll be all right, sir."

"Conroy?"

"Aye."

The Captain sat up, rubbing the back of his head. "Where are we?"

"A little cove about thirty yards down from the landing spot, sir. They should find you easily come morning."

"Find me?"

A blinding bolt of lightning made day out of night. In the light, Captain Jones' eyes took in the bags and guns slung around the Irishman's body.

"Don't do it, lad. We're a hundred miles north of Port Jackson. No white man's ever been inland from here. There's nothin' but blacks, an' they're killers."

"I'll take my chances, Cap'n."

"Don't be a fool, Conroy. The whole continent is a prison. You're better off in Port Jackson."

" 'Tis open country though, Cap'n, where I can run free."

"The blacks will track you . . . kill you."

"If they do, Cap'n, they'll be killin' a free man runnin', not one in chains, beggin'."

Then he was gone, scrambling toward freedom and the unknown.

"WHAT am I to think? Fer three weeks ye've been too busy. On Wednesdays when I can come up here, ye're gone!"

Steven Rourke sat, his long legs thrust outward, a tankard in his hand. Through rum-fogged eyes, he watched Josie Hunnicutt pace the room. She was dressed in his latest gift, a full skirted dress of muslin dyed a deep saffron yellow, with a bonnet of the same material and shade.

How pretty she is, he thought. She would provide quite an adequate dalliance, if she were not such a shrew!

Her complexion was a healthy pink, her breasts and hips were full and nicely outlined in the dress, and her hair fell in golden ringlets that shone in the sunlight each time she passed before the window.

But, for Rourke, the picture was spoiled when he noticed the tightness about her small, lush mouth, and heard the whining, cloying quality that filled her voice.

He remembered an hour before, when he had first heard her step on the path and thought her slippered tread to be that of Annie Hollister. He had lurched through the door, only to find Josie. The moment he had seen her, bile had started to churn in his stomach.

In recent days, thoughts of the Hollister girl had become an obsession. Thoughts of Josie Hunnicutt had elicited only boredom.

Now, as she paced before him, castigating him with her high-pitched whine, that boredom was turning into outright distaste.

"Rourke!"

His eyes had drooped. Now he rolled them upward and tried to focus them on the fury in her face. "Aye?"

"You haven't heard a word I've said!"

"I've heard enough. Too much, frankly."

"I won't be treated like one of your convict whores!"

"You're not, I assure you, Josie. If you were, I wouldn't tolerate half of what you have already said."

Stung by his tone of exaggerated arrogance, Josie crossed the room until she stood between his wide-spread legs. She leaned forward until her face was inches from his.

"I want more than this . . . more than a once-a-week tryst."

"Do you now?"

"I can no longer hide our liaison from my father. He, and my mother, are beginning to ask too many questions about your gifts."

"Are they? Then I suggest you stop accepting them."

She chose to disregard his sarcastic retorts. "As it is," she railed, "I can only wear them here, in Port Jackson, when I'm with you. I want more!"

"What more?"

"I want to *stay* in Port Jackson. I hate it out on that river . . . the work, the dirt. . . ."

"Then stay," he said, bringing the tankard to his lips.

"With you." Here the sting in her voice abated and again the cloying whine began. "Oh, Rourke, you must know I love you. Marry me, Rourke. Make me an honest woman! Ye'll never regret it. You know how I pleasure you. You know. . . ."

Rourke's harsh laughter was so violent that rum

spilled from the tankard in his hand to stain his white cambric shirt.

"Marry *you?*" he roared. "Surely you jest!"

Josie's scream matched the volume of his laughter as her hand struck the tankard from his hand, sending it crashing against the wall.

"I hate you . . . I hate you!" she shrieked.

Rourke retaliated like a striking snake. The sound of the crashing tankard had barely finished its reverberation in the room when Josie found herself sprawled against the far wall. Her head spun and her cheek burned from his hand's crushing blow.

Tears welled in her eyes and immediately she began whimpering. "How can ye do this to me? Ye know how I love ye. I've done everything for ye! I've—"

"You've shared my bed when I've had a mind to let you."

"Steven!" she wailed, cringing against the wall as he moved over her.

"You needed to use me just as much as I wanted to use you. Now your usefulness has reached an end."

"No! Oh, dear God, no!" she cried, scrambling to her feet and throwing her arms about his waist.

He tried to shake her free, but she was a woman possessed. She adhered to him with the tenacity of a leech.

"Leave off, girl, or I'll crack yer skull!"

"No! I love ya," she whimpered. "I gave myself to ya!"

"You were paid for your services. Now I no longer need those services."

"No, no, ya still want me, I'll be good to ya," she babbled. "I'll do anything. Take me, Rourke, take me now! I can feel ya want me!"

Her hand clutched and caressed his groin. It was true. There was something about her weeping, about her groveling at his feet, that suddenly reawakened his desire for her.

With a growl from deep in his throat he lifted her and moved into the adjoining room, toward the bed.

Outwardly, Josie was still on the verge of hysteria, but inwardly she was smiling.

I've won, she thought. *I've won because none of his other women can give him what I can give him!*

He tore at her clothes like a hungry animal. His hands were rough on her body, but Josie reveled in the treatment because she knew there were times he liked it that way.

"Yes, yes," she moaned, when she felt his naked flesh come against hers.

"Little whore," he rasped.

"Yes, Rourke, I'll be yer whore . . . if that's what ye want, that's what I'll be . . . yer whore, Rourke."

His mouth and tongue attacked her. Her nipples grew taut beneath his lips and her whole body ached with need for him.

I've won, she thought, her mind soaring. *He'll build his house and I'll be its chatelaine! What matter if he doesn't marry me . . . at least I'll be his mistress instead of an unwanted old maid in my father's house!*

Suddenly she felt his body part her thighs. She gasped with pain at the driving, cruel force of his entrance, but arched her body toward his thrusts.

Her arms folded around him, forcing him deeper, willing him to take her. She heard her voice moaning and then screaming out her passion as the room swirled.

She opened her eyes and instantly became mesmerized by his icy, cold stare directed at her.

"Whore!"

"Yes, your whore!" she cried, digging her nails into his back and sinking her teeth into his shoulder.

Rourke cried out in pain but the slamming force of his thrusts didn't diminish. Josie knew he was intent on achieving only his own ends, but she didn't care.

Her ends would be attained later . . . and they would be of much more worth.

As his peak built, he carried her with him. There was release for Josie in just the fact that he was hers. There was no one else for her, only this man that she hated and loved, this male beast who could so satisfy her body and give her the worldly things that were every beautiful woman's right.

If this was being a whore, Josie reveled in it. As he brought her to the peak of frenzy, she became shameless in her need.

Together they reached a soaring culmination and Rourke collapsed, panting, across her body, making no effort to withhold his weight.

Her eyes flew open and searched his face. "Wasn't I good? I was good for ye, wasn't I, Rourke?"

His eyes were inscrutable, vacant, as he stared back at her. Her hands came up, clutching his head, as she brought his lips down to hers.

"Again," she mumbled, "again."

She was about to roll him over and climb over him, when a sound in the other room arrested both their movements.

"Who is it?" Rourke called.

"Me, Cap'n. Moran."

Rourke slid from the bed and pulled on his breeches. Seconds later he was in the other room with Jack Moran.

"Sorry ta interrupt ya . . . uh, in the middle o' business, Cap'n."

"No matter," Rourke replied with a casual wave. "Well?"

"Done, Cap'n. We found the lad's curing racks . . . all eight of 'em."

"And?"

"An' right now eight wagonloads of prime, cured and dried tobacco is stored with the rum cache over ta Botany Bay."

Rourke smiled and nodded. "And the field?"

"All the seeds are chopped. She'll not grow another crop this season."

"You're a reliable man, Jack. You're sure you weren't seen?"

"No chance," the big man replied. "I brought it down the river. They didn't even know I was there."

Again Rourke nodded, his body relaxing with the combination of his recent physical satiation and Moran's good news.

"Have two men start cutting it. We'll trade it off before anyone knows we have it."

"Aye, Cap'n."

The giant moved through the door and Rourke turned back toward the bedroom.

Now let's see what you do, Annie Hollister, he thought, a cruel smile spreading across his face, *without your tobacco to buy the convict help you need!*

"Come back to bed, darlin'," Josie sighed, stretching her body like a sensuous cat and leaving her legs splayed wide.

"Josie."

"Aye?"

"Get dressed."

"But . . . what fer?"

"Get dressed and get out!"

At last the rains came, in torrents. For three days there was no let up. So heavy was the downpour that Annie could barely reach the lean-to and feed the horses without being soaked to the skin. It was impossible to wade through the knee-deep mud in the fields to check on the tobacco, or ride into Port Jackson to arrange for its sale.

So she sat and she waited.

Much of the time she entertained Billy, for her mother hardly acknowledged the child's existence now. Most often, Mary Hollister did nothing but sit in Ben's chair and stare at the hearth.

"Light us a fire, will ya, Annie girl?"

"But Ma, 'tis steaming in here as it is . . ."

"Ben always enjoyed a crackling fire. Light us a fire, will ya, Annie girl?"

Annie lit a fire and then opened all the doors and windows to let the heat escape.

At night, late, she would be awakened by her mother's voice. Mary would be talking to Ben. The first time she heard her, Annie listened to her words. Mary spoke to her dead husband as if he were there, beside her, and they were both still in England.

After that, when she heard her mother's voice at night, Annie would pull the pillow over her head to blot out the words.

It rained again the morning of the fourth day, and then, by noon, it began to clear. Long, glittering beams

to the hut. Still filthy and caked with mud, she fell onto her cot.

Eyes wide, she lay there blanking out her mother's words, until she realized that Mary was calling her name.

"Aye, Ma?"

"It was so much better in England, wasn't it?"

"Aye, Ma."

"Perhaps, when Tom is well, we should go back."

"Aye, Ma."

There will never be enough money for passage back to England, and we would have even less there than we have here.

"In England you might meet a nice young man . . . marry . . . have a place of your own."

"Aye, Ma."

Annie groaned and turned to her side. In England she had met no more men than she had met in New South Wales.

Then, with a sudden gasp, she sat bolt upright on the cot.

Except one.

The memory of that night, his darkly handsome face, his flashing black eyes, swept over her like a warm wave. He had kissed her, and sparked the first passion she had ever known.

Where was he now . . . her handsome Irishman, whose name she had never forgotten.

Where was Phillip Conroy?

"We're nearly out of flour and the tea is gone."

"Aye, Ma."

Annie wasn't sure how many days had passed since she had discovered the loss of the tobacco. It could have been a week, perhaps two.

Time had no meaning for her. She had become nearly as catatonic as her mother.

The days passed in a series of meals, of trying to

care for her mother and Billy, of visits to Tom's hospital bed, of days that blended into sleepless nights, and nights filled with terrors of the dawn.

Her eyes seemed constantly swollen, yet all her tears were gone.

And then Tom came home.

Collin Downey dropped him off on his way to Parramatta. The old man's eyes were red-rimmed and bereft of life when he greeted Annie.

She soon found out why.

"Me son, Michael . . . ?"

"Aye, I remember him well."

"He's gone, the lad is," Downey said. "Swept from the deck of the *Supply* in a storm."

Annie couldn't cry. She had no tears left. "I'm sorry, Mr. Downey."

"Aye, so'm I. Michael loved life. I'm sorry he couldn't ha' lived more of it."

"What will you do?"

"Do? Why, lass, I'll go on . . . I'll survive. That's all any of us can do."

That night she told Tom about the tobacco.

"It was Moran, I know it was! He was the only one who knew we had it . . . he and his whore!" Tom picked the musket from its pegs and began to search for powder and shot.

"What're you going to do?"

"Get the 'baccy back, that's what I'm gonna do. Either that or kill the bastard!"

"Don't swear, Tom," Mary said.

Annie rose and lifted the gun from his arm. "Go outside, Tom. We'll talk."

"Annie!"

"Jack Moran would break you like a twig, Tom. He'd crush you like a clay pot. Go outside!"

They walked, and Annie talked. And as she explained, even in the spare moonlight, she could see her brother's face turn a ghostly white and the tears flow in twin streams down his cheeks.

By the time they had returned to the hut, Annie had told him everything.

Without a word, Tom left her on the porch.

The next morning, Annie carefully folded the blue dress, packed it in a feed sack, and mounted the mare. She rode to the river and stripped all her old, mended clothes from her body.

She swam out to the end of the inlet with the clothes under one arm. Once there, she released them. And as she watched them being carried away by the treacherous, swirling current, she thought how easy it would be to just swim out into the river another twenty feet.

She stayed there a long time, treading water, thinking how easy it would be. . . .

But then she thought about Tom, her mother, and, most of all, about Billy.

Back on shore, she dressed in the chemise and dark blue dress. She fastened the whisk over her breasts and, after brushing her hair to a sheen, she tied it with the blue ribbons that matched the whisk.

Then she mounted the mare and kicked her into a walk toward Port Jackson.

"I'm coming, Rourke. Damn you for the bastard you are, I'm coming."

PART TWO

DECEMBER 1890

17

It was mid-morning. The sun was already high in a cloudless sky, making the air thick and humid. They were in the countryside, with Port Jackson far behind them. The road, no more than a dusty track, wound through tall meadow grass and beneath an occasional arch of eucalyptus trees.

Now and then they passed a thatched hovel with a tiny garden plot grown at its side. These were the plots of married convicts where they scratched out just enough food for their existence.

Inevitably there would be children and a tamed dingo or two playing before the shacks.

"You haven't spoken since Port Jackson."

Annie cast a sidelong glance at Rourke from the shadow of her bonnet. "I have little to say."

"You cannot even comment on the weather?"

"Aye. 'Tis hot."

His jaw clenched, and a ripple of tension appeared beneath the tanned skin. His hands gripped the reins tighter and his shoulders hunched slightly forward. When he spoke it was in a tightly controlled voice.

"One would think, my dear, that you do not enjoy a visit to our new house."

"Quite the contrary," Annie replied evenly. "I enjoy anything that takes me away from the filth of Port Jackson."

They rode in silence for another mile. As it always did, Rourke's anger passed quickly, to be replaced by contrived arrogance and his attempts at cynical humor.

For Annie, this mood was as abhorrent as his wrath was frightening.

"You look very lovely today. But then, you always do." He had turned to face her now, his eyes flicking over her face and then dropping to the front of her dress. He scanned her with a slow, lazy look that seemed to strip the clothes from her body.

Annie flushed slightly. She was all too conscious of how she looked; lovely, yes, but also slightly wanton.

Her dress was green muslin, high-waisted and gathered beneath her bosom by a saffron sash. The bodice was daringly deep cut, displaying her full, rounded breasts almost to the nipples.

Rourke enjoyed dressing her in this fashion, no matter how much it embarrassed her. He reveled in other men's admiring eyes upon her body. It gave him a deep sense of fulfillment to know that her beauty taunted other men, and yet he retained her as his possession.

It was only one of the many quirks in his personality she had grown to hate in the nine months since she had rode the mare into Port Jackson and delivered her body into his keeping.

Her body, but not her soul.

The thought brought a smile to her face.

"Ah, a smile. Does that mean this iceberg I've taken into my house has accepted my compliment?"

The smile remained but turned slightly down at the corners of her lightly rouged lips.

"Of course. Just as I accept the leering glances of all the men you show me off to."

His eyes smoldered on hers for a moment, and then snapped away.

Words. They were her only revenge against him. That, and the fact that, after nine months, Rourke knew that he still did not possess her completely.

But the words she often used to cut him were not always true. She did not enjoy being paraded before other men as his woman.

She constantly felt ill-at-ease when other officers of the Corps, or even Jack Moran, a convict, would be in the hut. He would force her to serve them, always in low-cut dresses, while they talked over affairs of the colony or, in Moran's case, their nefarious business dealings.

During those visits she would tense under the mens' lascivious stares, their eyes darting again and again to the creamy swells above her bodice. She could see how they unconsciously drooled over the coup Rourke had accomplished in snaring her.

Her gowns were custom-made now, sewn by one of the convict women who had been a seamstress, as well as a fence for stolen goods, in England. And the measuring and the cutting was always overseen by Rourke himself.

The gown she now wore particularly enhanced the curve of her back, the swell and flair of her hips, as well as all the other fine lines of her body.

How long, she thought, would her figure remain trim with Rourke constantly at her?

What was it he had said in the beginning, and had repeated often in different phrases since? "I expect from you all the pleasures of marriage without the infernal sanctity of it. I am a very sensual man, Annie Hollister, as I am sure you have already realized. I will expect you to be in my bed when I want you there. And, mark you, girl, it will be often, for you've set a fire in my body and soul."

Every word had proven true.

And now she was afraid. For no matter how many precautions she took, Annie knew that one day the inevitable would happen. She would awaken one morning, wracked with nausea, and find herself with child.

Tears crept into her eyes at the thought.

Oh, dear God, what will I do then? How can I bear

to have his child when, most assuredly, it will be a monster like its father?

"Ah, there!"

Annie's head came up, her eyes following the upward sweep of the land to the top of the hill. The walls were up and already daubed. Three brick chimneys dotted the slate-covered roof, and she could see the convict workmen fitting pane glass into the tiered windows.

Glass. Other than Government House, it would be the only structure on the whole continent with glass windows. When Annie had first learned of them, she had been amazed.

"Where . . . where in the world did you get glass?"

"Capetown," had been Rourke's only reply, in a tone that made it clear she needn't know more.

But, in time, she had learned. It was impossible to shut her ears to all she heard. She discovered that the vast amounts of rum that illegally found their way into Port Jackson came off the *Venture* and two other ships that Rourke and Captain Brownlee had purchased.

With the credits he gleaned from rum sales, Rourke was the largest purchaser of the grain and other foodstuffs that the outlying farmers grew. In turn, he sent his ships back to Capetown full of cheaply bought, high profit cargo.

All this while many of the farmers and convicts alike still hovered at the edge of starvation.

" 'Twill be a fine house," Rourke murmured, bringing Annie's attention back to the hill.

"Aye, it will," she said, and meant it.

For it was the kind of house Annie had long dreamed of having, of living in. But she had dreamed of sharing it with a man she loved, not Captain Steven Rourke.

" 'Allo, Cap'n!"

It was Rourke's overseer, Duncan. He had seen them from the fields down near the fork of the rivers, and had ridden up the other side of the hill to meet them.

"Duncan."

Rourke halted the cart and, in the same movement, slid down.

"Stay here," he said curtly to Annie, and walked on up the hill to meet the man.

Ten minutes later he was back, turning the horse toward a grove of trees. "Duncan has had a bit of trouble with some of the prisoners. He wants me to have a word with them."

"I'll spread the lunch."

"That's what I would have you do."

As it always did, his arrogant tone of command nettled her. "*Have* me . . . *tell* me . . . *direct* me. Damme, Rourke, our lives would be lived much easier if you didn't constantly command me!"

He stopped the wagon beneath the trees and moved around to her side. He helped her down, and then moved his hand up to grip her arm. As his hand moved, his fingers played over the soft surface of her skin.

"You know as well that if you didn't deny me, our lives would be lived much easier . . . and more pleasantly."

"I deny you nothing!"

"Don't you now?" His hand moved up to her throat and his eyes took on an opaque quality like that of a bottomless blue pool. "Fool that I am, I want you, girl . . . all of you. Nothing else will do. Believe me, I'll do anything to make it happen . . . *anything,* do you understand?"

"Aye, Rourke, only too well. How could I help but understand?"

Suddenly his arms went around her waist, yanking her forward, hard against him. His lips came down on hers in a bruising kiss. At the same time, one hand came up to cup and squeeze her breast.

The kiss was long, and Annie didn't fight it. She merely stood, stone-like, enduring his lips on hers and ignoring the heat of his hand on her bosom.

To her surprise, there was a smile on his face when he lifted his lips from hers.

"You know, Annie, if you just once were to let yourself go, you might be surprised to discover you enjoy being with a man."

"Perhaps," she replied coldly. "If I loved that man."

The smile on his lips widened, but there was no laughter in his penetrating eyes. The fingers closed around her throat, just enough to lift her chin, forcing her to look at him.

"Love? You know no more about love than I. Damn you, girl, can't you see we're more alike than you think? Let me, and I'll show you love. Allow me, and I'll make you love me!"

Her laugh was harsh, biting, just as cruel as she knew his to be. "Nay, Rourke, that's what you can't understand, will *never* understand. You cannot force a woman to love you, no matter how much of a hold you have over her!"

"We shall see."

Again he kissed her crushingly, and this time his hand clawed at her breast. She writhed and twisted from his grasp, panting.

Then she noticed that the men in the windows of the house had stopped their work to stare. Even Duncan, on his horse, was watching and enjoying the spectacle.

Furious, she whirled on Rourke. "You knew they were watching!"

"Of course," he shrugged.

"Must you always make me look cheap and ridiculous in front of others?"

"Not always," he replied between clenched teeth. "Perhaps one day I will stop . . . when you stop being a willful bitch."

Stung by what he had done, and even more angry

that he seemed to constantly defeat her with his exaggerated arrogance, Annie drew herself to her full height. She willed the flush of embarrassment to leave her face and made no attempt to hide the contempt she felt for him in her stare.

When she spoke it was in a low, controlled voice. "Just before I came to you, that first night, I bathed in the Hawkesbury. 'Twas in that same inlet where you first came upon me naked. Do you remember the place?"

"Aye," he replied, his brows arched warily.

"The current is strong there . . . very strong. While swimming I thought of how easy it would be to just let myself go with that current."

Again he smiled, the white of his teeth gleaming against his tanned skin. "But you didn't."

"Nay, I did not. But I cannot count the times since then that I wished I had."

He blinked. His eyes widened and the starchy military bearing left his body for an instant. "You wouldn't!"

"Nay, I doubt if I would, now. You see, I love my life, Rourke, even as terrible as it has become. Nay, I don't want to die anymore. I shall live. I shall do everything in my power to remain alive . . . because one day you'll be gone."

"Damn you!" He took a step toward her. For the barest moment she had seen a cloud of concern cross his face. Now it was replaced by deadly anger, and she was sure he would strike her.

But instead he paused, his hand half raised. For the first time since she had known him, Steven Rourke was shaken.

"Damn you, woman. Don't you realize that if you had a little less of the shrew in you and a little more of the wanton, 'tis you who could command me, like a slave."

"That's what you'll never understand, Rourke," she

said, calmly turning from him. "To love is *not* to command!"

There was silence for several moments, and then she heard his booted feet return to the cart. Angrily he whipped the horse into a trot and joined Duncan.

Annie went about emptying the baskets and laying out the meal with a deep sense of satisfaction. It had been a victory. No matter how tenuous and brief, it was still a victory!

And, she thought, as she dropped to the soft grass and leaned her back against a eucalypt, if she could compile enough of them, perhaps he would tire of her.

But even as she dreamed, she knew it would never be. Steven Rourke, in his perverted way, loved her. To him love was command, subservience, possession.

He owned her, therefore he loved her. He loved her, therefore he owned her.

It was all he understood.

So the victory would be hollow. And that night when they returned to Port Jackson, he would redeem it with his hands, his lips, his strong body . . . with the symbol of his masculinity.

He would use her, take her body as he always did when she struck back at him.

Annie shivered, and even though the heat of midday had descended, she felt cold. It was always like that when she looked ahead to the nights.

Because she could never forget that first night. . . .

Not bothering to knock, Annie lifted the latch and entered the cottage. She was just closing the door behind her when he stepped from the bedroom.

His hair was in disarray and he wore only breeches and boots. Light from sconced candles and a low fire cast eerie shadows across his face and highlighted the mat of curling blond hair on his chest.

"An odd hour for a social call, Annie Hollister."

"I—" Annie bit her lip. The white mark of her teeth gleamed against her golden skin.

"Yes?"

"I'll . . . be spending the night."

His eyes grew wide and his lips pursed into a knowing smile. The look of triumph that passed over his features made Annie's stomach churn.

"You will not regret it," he moaned, and stepped forward to embrace her.

"That remains to be seen," she replied, stepping back against the door and throwing her hands up, palms outward. "I think we should discuss our . . . arrangement . . . first."

Rourke started to laugh, and then saw that she was serious. "Very well," he nodded. "But it needn't be such a business-like proposition."

"I think it does."

His jaw clamped tightly shut and he drew himself to his full height. "So be it."

"My brother will need livestock . . . two horses and breeding sheep. I want a guarantee of seed and any supplies needed at the farm. If the coming season is good, I want a guarantee that you will obtain a grant, in Tom's name, for the hundred acres adjoining our land across the Hawkesbury."

"I see you have thought out my part of the bargain in detail," Rourke said, moving to a small, cluttered desk near the hearth.

"Aye, I have. And Tom will need eight convicts, tradesmen and farmers alike."

Rourke returned to stand across the oval table from her. In his hand he held a piece of paper. "I have thought out your part of the bargain as well."

He slid the paper across the table. Annie's eyes flickered down but she couldn't bring her quivering hand forward to pick it up.

"Read it!"

Suddenly there were doubts. The resolve she had

summoned on the ride into Port Jackson began to fade. Had this man any sensibilities at all? And if he did, could she appeal to them?

She felt her body sway and her face drain of all color. She found his face through misty eyes, and saw only a stonelike face.

"Very well. I shall read it to you."

The words, read in a sonorous, unfeeling voice, thundered in her ears. When he finished, the paper was again thrust toward her and a pen laid across it.

"You . . . you can't mean this," she stammered. "This makes me sound like mere property!"

His smile was evil as he shrugged and moved around the table. " 'Tis you who have struck the bargain, Annie. Sign it!"

She leaned forward, her head spinning. Should she dissolve the bargain for any reason before Rourke wished it dissolved, the farm would become his property.

"Even if I do sign, my mother will not. The farm is rightfully hers."

"I think you can convince her. I think, in the woman's present state, she will sign anything you tell her to sign."

He was right and Annie knew it.

Closing her eyes, blotting out the pain she felt, she scrawled her signature across the paper.

"Good," Rourke said, moving his hand across her back. "The paper will never be used, Annie. In time there'll be no need for it. You'll see."

His hand slid down to cup her buttocks and his bare chest moved against her. Suddenly she felt used and cheap.

"Please!"

She tried to pull away from him but he ignored her protest and only squeezed harder, bringing a gasp of pain to her lips.

"Please don't . . . can't you. . . ."

"Why do you sound so surprised, girl? What did you expect?"

"I . . . I don't know. Stop!"

She whirled, her arm in an arc, and then she felt the sting of her palm against his cheek.

"I've agreed to be your whore," she cried out in fury, "but nothing else! You cannot own me!"

"Oh, but I do. You ponder this: your body no longer belongs to you. It belongs to me."

" 'Tis indeed all you want, isn't it? My body?"

"For now," he said, reaching for her. "The rest will come later."

"Never!" She made to strike him again, but his hand easily caught her wrist, the fingers biting into her flesh.

"Watch your temper, girl. If you consider yourself a whore in this matter, so be it. But remember this: whores do not strike their customers."

"You are a monster!"

"I am a man who takes what he wants. And, at the moment, I want you, wild cat that you are."

He moved closer until Annie could see the moisture gleaming on his upper lip. His eyes were empty pits of blue, and his broad chest heaved with what Annie now recognized as desire.

"Rourke!"

"Aye, a wild cat you are," he growled, "but I shall tame you. Take off your clothes!"

"Must you be such a beast?" she cried. "Can there be no gentleness, no—"

"Take them off!"

"I will not!"

"Very well then, leave. The choice is yours."

There it was, clearly stated. There was no choice, and she knew it.

Slowly her hands went to the laces of her dress. Rourke made no offer to touch her. He only stood, rocking on his heels, a smirk of satisfaction on his chisled features.

Slowly the dress slid down her body to puddle at her feet. A flush of rage filled her face clear to her hairline. Her hands trembled so that she had to clasp and rub them together before they would work the buttons on her chemise.

"You look pale, my dear. Do you plan on swooning at just the proper moment?"

"Believe me," she retorted, pulling the chemise off her shoulders, "I would like to, but I won't."

She felt a hot prickling behind her eyelids. But she quickly blinked until the moisture was gone. Then she lifted her chin and stood naked, defiantly facing his smoldering eyes.

His eyes scanned her long-limbed body and rested at last on her full, pink-tipped breasts. "Beautiful. Forgive me, but I have waited so long for this moment that I must make it last . . . savor every second of it."

His voice was gentle now, and there was genuine longing in his eyes. But Annie neither saw nor heard his change of mood. All she could think of was that the inevitable was about to happen.

"Savor?" she cried. "Savor me, as you would a meal . . . or the ownership of a piece of property?"

"Be quiet," he hissed, menace again creeping into his voice. "Do not spoil the moment or I shall strike you."

His hand touched her breast. A finger traced a circle around her nipple.

"You like that, don't you?"

"No."

"To the bedroom."

"No. I can't—"

"Go!"

Stiff-legged, all feeling gone from her body, her mind blank, Annie obeyed. Her heart was pounding so rapidly that she thought it would burst from her chest.

Once on the bed she turned her body slightly away from him and folded her arms over her breasts.

If Rourke noticed her modesty he made no mention of it, as he calmly removed his boots. When his hands moved to the buttons on his breeches, Annie closed her eyes.

She felt his knee depress the bed, and then his flesh against hers. Fear clogged her throat. Suddenly she knew she couldn't go through with it, no matter the consequences.

One second her body lay rigid, and in the next she was springing from the bed.

Rourke was lightning-quick as he moved to seize her wrist. A shuddering sob escaped her, a sob of despair at her attempted escape and its failure.

"To bed, wench," he hissed.

Annie glared at him, her face flushed and defiant. With a shriek she tore at the skin of his bare shoulder with the nails of her free hand, and spat contemptuously into his angry, sneering face.

"Damn you!" he roared, and threw her to the bed like a sack of grain. "I'll have you now, wench, and you'll wish you would have given what I'm about to take!"

His body covered hers, the hair on his chest rasping against her soft breasts. For a second her arms came free. Fierce as a tigercat, she thrust her arms upward and clawed at his face.

With a roar of pain he dropped his weight over her, crushing her into the mattress. His lips ground against hers. Annie clenched her teeth and pulled her mouth away. She balled her fists and pounded on his shoulders and back.

It only brought a laugh, and a victorious, harsh laugh at that, to her ears. She answered it with a scream as his hands seized her breasts.

Again he tried to kiss her. Annie writhed, turning her head to avoid his mouth. But Rourke followed and soon his lips fastened hard to hers.

Her lips felt bruised when, at last, he moved his

mouth to her breasts. She could barely see him now through the tears of pain and fear that misted her eyes. She screamed again when she felt his hands prying her knees apart.

"No, dear God, please!"

"If 'tis rape ye want, wench, 'tis rape ye'll get!"

She tensed her thighs tightly together and tried to ward him off with her pounding fists. But she was no match for his strength. Her legs parted and she could feel his body moving between them.

"I . . . I hate you!" she gasped.

But there was no answer now. Rourke was wholly intent on one thing—the violation of her body.

She refused to let him do this to her. He couldn't. How could any man who truly desired a woman take her like this?

She could feel him now, hotly probing against her, his hands digging into the flesh of her inner thighs. Then his weight was pressing her down. The room echoed with her screams as he pierced deeply inside her.

The pain was unbearable as he started to move. Harder and faster came his body against hers. Her head moved and rolled from side to side. She shrank back, trying to escape him, but it was to no avail.

How long it went on she didn't know. She could feel nothing but pain and shame and fury. She could hear nothing but her own wild screams in her ears.

She only knew it had ended when she felt his weight leave her body. Minutes passed and then she heard his ragged, even breathing.

Asleep, she thought. He could commit such a deed and then immediately fall asleep!

For nearly an hour she lay, coldly naked on the bed, her flesh bruised and throbbing.

Then she raised herself to one elbow. She looked at his relaxed, sleeping form in disgust. Then, slowly, she shifted her gaze down to her own body in the same manner. Her upper arms were already turning blue from his bruising fingers. Red welts had risen on the nipples of both of her breasts from his animal-like love-making.

Love-making?

No, she thought, it had been exactly what Rourke had called it: rape.

Annie bit her lip to keep back the tears and turned her face to the pillow to muffle any sound she might make. For if she cried again, she vowed that he would never hear it. She would never give him the satisfaction of knowing how much he had hurt her, how close he had come to achieving the end he sought; the breaking of her spirit.

No, that would never happen!

Her body quivered as she remembered how his mouth had devoured her like a greedy animal. And the rutting itself when he had forced his entrance was a nightmare, a horrible ordeal that she thought would never end.

But it had ended and now she had some satisfaction.

He hadn't reached her core, hadn't been able to create any pleasure in her body. Once or twice when he had become gentle after the first violent onslaught, she felt her body awakening. But she had been able to stifle any physical passion.

And that she would always do. For she would never let Rourke touch the part of her that really mattered: her heart.

And he never would.

This she vowed to herself. From this day hence she would build a shell around herself that he could never break, no matter if he caressed her body or merely took it. . . .

They took the long route back to Port Jackson, driving directly to the sea and then turning south.

To their left and far below, great rolling breakers

crashed against the rocks. The wind was strong here, blowing Annie's hair from her ribbons and riffling her skirt.

Rourke spoke, but the sound of the breakers drowned his words. She leaned her ear closer to his lips.

"What?"

"I have a leave coming."

"Oh? We should have a holiday then. Perhaps we could go to Botany Bay and count your rum horde!"

His eyes hardened but he made no other sign that he had heard her jibe.

"I sail in a week's time with Brownlee on the *Venture*."

Her heart stopped. Was her contract over? After nine long months of living in this hellish charade, was she at last to be freed?

But he had said, *leave*.

"You're . . . you're leaving?"

His eyes swept her face and a low laugh rippled from his lips. "You needn't look so gleeful, Annie. I'll be back in six or seven weeks. I only go to Capetown to purchase materials and furniture pieces for the house."

"Oh."

"But you needn't fear, my sweet. You will be well cared for by Moran."

"You mean *watched*, don't you?" she hissed.

Rourke shrugged. "Take heart, Annie girl, you may get lucky."

"How so?"

"The *Venture* may go down and I'll be lost at sea!"

Her ears rang with his harsh laughter. Annie turned her face away so he would not be able to read her expression. For if he had, he would see that those were her exact thoughts.

They rode on in silence, soon reaching the communal farm on the outskirts of main camp itself.

Long lines of ragged prisoners chopped disconsolately between the furrows. A few of them had irons forged around their ankles, wrists and waists. Each movement brought a resounding, clanking sound that jarred Annie's nerves.

"Must they be chained?"

"Aye," Rourke replied. "The troublemakers must. 'Tis the only punishment we have for them." Here he chuckled. "Since they are already in gaol, what more could we do to them as a warning?"

To Annie, it was a situation that bordered on lunacy. How could any of them hope to survive in this arid and hostile place unless they forgot their differences, unless all of them, jailers and prisoners alike, turned to work the land with their utmost energy? To survive in this God-forsaken place, every man was vital. But no, it would not do; the punishment had to continue, the artificial conditions established fifteen thousand miles away in England had to persist here in the wilderness. And so they had the grotesque spectacle of the prisoners shackled to one another being marched off to toil on the land, where a warden with a loaded musket stood over them while they worked.

Annie shook her head, her heart filled with hopeless frustration.

Heads lifted as the cart passed by, and brooding eyes revealed their hatred of Rourke, their chief tormentor, and his kept woman.

One man, she noticed, worked with ten times the vigor of his fellows, as if he actually had heart for what he did. He was twice the width of the other men, while not being overly tall. His back and shoulders were broad, with rippling, sinewy muscles that glowed with a sweaty sheen.

As they passed, he glanced up, and Annie found herself staring into the most penetrating black eyes she had ever seen.

When he saw her, his eyes widened and he raised his

shaggy black head higher. So thick and heavy was his beard that only his eyes, and, as he smiled, his even white teeth shone through.

Annie's body tensed and a gasp burst from her throat when she saw that smile.

And then they were past and she felt her whole body shaking uncontrollably.

"Good God, girl, what is it?" Rourke asked. "You're white as a sheet."

"I . . . nothing."

"What is it, girl? Have ye seen a ghost?"

Quickly she composed herself, hiding her face beneath parasol and bonnet.

"Just a bit of stomach," she said weakly, dabbing at her forehead with a kerchief.

" 'Tis the damnable heat," he said.

"Aye."

How stupid, she thought. Now I grasp at straws . . . I try to fantasize what isn't there.

I see a wild, shaggy, half-naked convict, more beast than man, and I think I see Phillip Conroy.

Phillip Conroy. A name . . . a smile . . . from out of the past.

It couldn't be.

She shook her head again to clear it.

Between the heat and Captain Steven Rourke, I most likely will go mad one of these days!

18

PHILLIP Conroy took the proffered bucket of water and dumped it over his head.

"Another?"

"Nay," Conroy said, shaking the water from his shaggy hair, "that'll last me the afternoon."

He retrieved his hoe, and in seconds the air was filled with the sound of his clanking chains as he went to his task with a will.

"Phillip?"

Conroy didn't have to turn. He knew the voice. "Aye, lad."

Gerald Colbert, his own chains rattling, moved up into the furrow beside him. "Ya needn't go to it with such a will, ya know. They don't expect it."

"Aye, I know."

"Then why do ye do it?"

"Time, lad . . . it makes the time go faster." Here he did pause, leaning on his hoe. "Look at 'em. This ground is here to feed 'em an' they work it like they're asleep. An' when they're loosed, they do naught else for themselves but swill rum!"

"Aye," Colbert nodded, and stretched. "Aggg."

"What is it, lad?"

"Nothin'. Jest a stitch in me ribs where the bastard coshed me. 'Twill pass."

Conroy nodded, and his jaw set in a rigid line. He should never have brought the boy into his scheme. It

241

had been too dangerous as it was, much less with the lad involved.

Suddenly he chuckled.

"What?" Colbert asked.

"I was just thinking what a run we gave 'em while it lasted."

"Aye, that we did," Colbert replied, his young face breaking into a wide grin as one eye closed in a wink. "An' when our ninety days of fetters is over next week, maybe we'll do it again."

Both men returned to their chopping, each with their own thoughts.

As he worked, Conroy's mind floated over the Blue Mountains, to the vast, fertile plains he had found after escaping the *Sovereign.*

He had treked inland for two weeks, moving mostly at night to avoid parties of hunting blacks. Tropical forests eventually gave way to grassy valleys and plateaus where they seemed to have turned a bright yellow with blooming wattle.

In the daytime he slept, usually beneath a canopy of foliage cut from the blue-green mallee. He had learned that it reflected the heat of the sun's rays and kept him cool.

He grew to love the vast stillness of the land during the daylight hours, and he learned to co-exist peacefully with the animals . . . wallabies, wombats, and an occasional kangaroo . . . when they emerged at night.

He learned to sense the danger of another human when the shrill night sounds of the cicadas suddenly stopped.

For two full months he eluded the blacks, and, when his supplies dwindled, he learned to live off the land.

It was about that time he had found No-Moonee.

It was by a pool at the base of a tall waterfall. Wild orchids were everywhere, as well as flowering vines to shield him from the sun for the day.

He had crouched by the side of the pool to drink

and dunk his head in the water's coolness. He had just finished when he heard a soft footfall directly behind him.

He whirled and rolled away just in time to avoid being run through by a spear. The weapon was wielded by a young black girl.

Conroy overpowered and disarmed her. It was then that he saw her broken and swollen leg. Hours passed before he could convince her with gestures that he meant her no harm.

In the same way she told him how she had slipped from the precipice above the waterfall.

Once gaining her confidence, Conroy was able to set and splint her leg. But there was no way she could travel back to her tribe. They were nomadic, and by now would have presumed her dead and moved on. Conroy opted to remain and nurse her back to health.

It was one of the wisest decisions he had ever made.

In the weeks that followed, he learned enough words of her guttural, grunted tongue, and she of English, to communicate.

Her name was No-Moonee, and she had lived four-teen summers. She had been taken to wife only a few days before her accident, and knew that her man grieved at her loss as much as she was in grief missing him.

She was a slim, graceful girl with coffee-colored skin and huge brown eyes. When she moved, even with her splinted leg and aided by a makeshift cane, it was with a gracefully sinuous motion that reminded Conroy of a wild creature.

And wild she was. It took him several days to accept the fact that she favored nudity over any makeshift clothing he offered. Once he accepted that, all tension between them disappeared.

In a month No-Moonee was ready to travel. But before she left she taught him how to make and use a spear and a boomerang. She showed him how to slice the mallee leaves and suck moisture from them.

From her he learned how to track the kangaroo, the emu and the possom to their daytime lairs. He became adept with a digging stick, collecting foods such as lily roots, vegetable seeds, grubs and honey-ants.

When she was sure he could survive in this, her wild land, she announced her departure. Her dark eyes grew solemn and reserved when she rubbed her cheek against his and said farewell.

"Friend," she had said, and then she was gone.

Conroy had learned his lessons well, and more times than he could count had given silent thanks to her instruction. Without it, he would have perished.

It was a month later when he was waylaid. He had made his way back to the coast, for it was turtle-mating season and there would be abundant fresh meat and eggs on the beach.

He had just made a good kill when a dozen natives swooped down on him from the cliffs. It was impossible to fight them all, and there was no place to run. His back was to the sea . . . and the sharks.

Why they didn't kill him at once, Conroy never knew. But they didn't. Instead, they herded him back to their makeshift village. It consisted of lean-tos built over the openings of caves in the rocks.

He was tied and thrust into one of these caves for two days. On the morning of the third day he was led into blinding sunlight to stand before the head of the tribe.

The chief's wife sat beside him. It was No-Moonee.

Conroy had lived the remainder of his stay in the wilds near the tribe, yet not a part of them.

And he would have been there still, had not the smallpox hit.

No-Moonee had come to him in the middle of the night, begging his help. He had recognized the disease

at once. And almost at the same time, he made a plan
of action.

Medicines would be needed, and food, for there
were not enough able hunters left untouched by the
smallpox to provide for them all.

Conroy took No-Moonee, two other women and six
men, and trekked south to Port Jackson.

For two full days he surveyed the main camp. On
the third night he struck, stealing all he could carry.
The medicine and food he dispatched with a runner
back to the tribe.

The following night, and the night after that, he
went back again. It was then that he was seen and
recognized by Gerald Colbert.

They talked. Conroy told the lad about the land and
the freedom over the mountains. The boy was en-
thralled. In exchange for his help, Colbert wanted to
return with the Irishman, and Conroy agreed.

Two nights later they were caught.

"Fifty lashes over twenty days, and ninety days in
irons!" Major Grose had intoned as their sentence.

Now the end of the ninety days was nearly up, and
Conroy had already made up his mind.

When the fetters came off, he would run again.

The rumbling of a cart's wheels and the snorting of
a horse brought Conroy's attention back to the present.
Out of the corner of his eye he caught a glimpse of the
cart's occupants. The man he recognized as Captain
Steven Rourke. He'd seen him in the compound pick-
ing convicts to labor on his acres.

Just as the cart drew abreast, the woman turned her
face in his direction.

"Damme . . . it can't be. . . ."

Her eyes widened when they met his. He smiled and
was about to raise his hand in a wave and cry out a
hello, when she abruptly turned away. By then the cart
was past.

Had she recognized him? It had seemed so for a moment when their eyes met.

He had recognized her instantly. There was no doubt of it. On countless nights he would close his eyes in a dank cell of Dublin Castle and see her face.

How many lasses on the highroads of Tyrone and Fermanagh, after his escape, had he leapt from his horse to stop? Each time they had turned their auburn heads to smile up at him with flashing green eyes and dimpled cheeks.

But none of them had been her.

No, Phillip, he thought, ye'll never forget that face.

"Never," he murmured aloud.

"Ye spoke, Phillip?"

"Wha? . . . aye, lad, I did. You know the Corps officer that just went by in the cart?"

"Aye, I know the bastard well. I dug potatoes fer a month on his damnable farm, an' got nothin' fer me trouble but a ration o' rum and a hand across my head when I didn't work hard enough to please him or his overseer, Duncan. He's Cap'n Steven Rourke."

"And the woman . . . do ye know the woman?"

"She's his whore."

Conroy bridled, but held back the retort that bubbled to his lips. The lad wouldn't know.

"What do ya mean, 'his whore', lad?"

"All the officers has their whores. You know that."

"Aye. She's a convict then."

"Nay," Colbert chuckled. "That's where Rourke's different."

"How so?"

"He wouldn't have a convict whore if he could do better."

"Dammit, boy, don't talk in riddles!" To emphasize his words, Conroy slapped a heavy hand to the other's shoulder, nearly knocking him from his feet.

"Hey now . . . what's got you off?"

"Sorry, lad. Just tell me about the woman!"

"She's a free settler's daughter from somewhere up on the Hawkesbury. Don't know her whole name. Seems like her first name is Anna . . ."

"Annie," Conroy said, his eyes drifting back toward the cart, obscured now in a cloud of dust. "Her name is Annie Hollister."

19

" 'TWILL be a fine harvest. Half already in, an' much
more than we need fer ourselves."

Annie nodded as she walked the dusty path beside
her brother. The fields were well tended, fences had
been built from wattle, and across the river she
couldn't count all the milling sheep.

To see all this, what Tom had done with it, made
her hell in Port Jackson bearable. The farm was pros-
pering, even more quickly than she had expected, and
that made Port Jackson worth the price.

"I've put in a good stand of 'baccy, too, Annie, in
our old field."

Annie smiled.

"I figured, why not? I mean, it ain't like any of the
Corps would fine me now. . . ." Annie turned her
green eyes on him and Tom bit his lip. "I . . . I'm
sorry, Annie, I wasn't thinkin'."

She shook her head and sighed. " 'Tis all right,
Tom."

"I mean, I know you come out here to forget. I'm
sorry—"

" 'Tis all right," she repeated, brushing her hair back
from her face. "There's no forgetting, no matter where
I go. He's always there to remind me."

Across the river, on an incline that looked down
over the Hollister cottage and land, they could both see
a ground-tethered horse near a grove of blue mallee
trees. Although they couldn't see the hulking figure of

Jack Moran, they knew he was there, somewhere, watching.

"He's like an ugly, gruesome shadow," Annie sighed, "following me everywhere except to my bed and bath." Here she laughed aloud, a low mirthless laugh that seemed to seethe rather than bubble from between her lips. "And I'm sure he'd love to follow me there, but he doesn't dare. Rourke would kill him."

"I'm saving, Annie . . . every sovereign, every dram of rum I can lay hands on, every leaf of tobacco and extra sack of grain. I'm saving and I'm trading. One day there will be enough money. . . ."

She halted. Turning, she ran her fingers along the lines of his jaw. "Oh, Tom, dear sweet Tom. Sometimes I think this is all harder on you than me. To know your sister is—"

"Annie!"

She smiled. "I was going to say, 'the grand lady of Port Jackson'. At least that's what some of them call me."

She hadn't the heart to tell her brother that there would never be enough money. Somehow her life . . . all their lives . . . would always be controlled by Steven Rourke. Controlled, that is, until he had made all the fortune he lusted for and ended his tour in New South Wales.

Only then would she be free, when Rourke left.

But how many more years would that be? And when he did leave, what would she do? Return to the farm and become Tom's housekeeper?

There would be little else for her. Every man in Port Jackson, including the convicts, knew who and what she was. What man would want Steven Rourke's used merchandise?

And by then Tom would most likely have a wife of his own.

"We'd best be getting back, Tom. 'Tis late and I should sit with Ma a spell before I ride back."

Tom nodded and moved into step beside her. "Why don't you stay the night? 'Twould do Ma good."

"Would it?"

Tom jammed his hands into the wide tool pockets of his breeches and looked away. "It might," he whispered.

"I daren't. I . . . well, shall we say, I have my orders."

But the fact that Rourke had told her to be back in the cottage every night during his absence was not the only reason Annie couldn't stay the night on the Hawkesbury.

The truth was, she didn't want to.

Her mother was almost a non-person now. Except for brief flashes of clarity, she lived almost entirely in the past. There were days when she never arose from her bed at all. When she did, it was only to sit in Ben's old rocker by the fire or on the porch. Once there she would stare off, over the fields, to the horizon and mumble to herself.

She rarely recognized Annie when her daughter would visit the Hawkesbury. And, when she did, it was embarrassing as well as heartrending for Annie.

"Your husband must be a very busy man. He never accompanies you when you visit, Annie."

"Aye, Ma."

"I must go into town one day and see your fine new house."

"Aye, Ma."

"When will we be blessed with a grandchild, Annie? I was just talking the other evening to Ben about it."

Always, during these times of questioning, tears would fill Annie's eyes. She would turn her face away and vainly try to block her mother's voice from her mind. When she couldn't, she would flee to the fields and join Tom, as she had done today, until it was time to leave.

Tom was speaking. "The convict woman you sent out helps with Ma."

"Good. And Billy?"

"She's fine with Billy. Seems she lost her own son to the fever when he was about Billy's age. She took to him, and he to her."

Again Annie only nodded, her eyes glued to the dusty path before her.

"Ma wanders away still, when she's not watched close. We found her down by the river trying to find Pa."

This brought Annie's head jerking up. "The woman must watch her more closely, Tom. She could do harm to herself."

"Aye, I know."

"You'll see to it? You'll tell her?"

He nodded.

And then they were at the newly erected shed that served as a stable.

"You'll not say good-bye to Ma?" Tom asked.

"No, what's the use? An' 'tis near dusk. I must be getting back."

Tom led her horse into the clearing and tightened the girth before handing her up into the saddle. It was a man's rig, but Annie rode it side-saddle, with one knee twisted over the pommel. Then, as she arranged her skirts around her, a question that had been gnawing at the back of her mind came to the fore.

"Tom?"

"Aye?"

"Do you ever see Josie Hunnicutt? I mean, does she ever call?"

A cloud seemed to pass over her brother's face. His eyes flickered on hers for a moment, and then fell to the ground where the toe of one boot dug into the dust.

"She has come by . . . a few times. I'm civil."

"Civil?" Annie tried to break his sudden strange mood with a low, throaty laugh. "You should be more than civil, dear brother. There are few girls available for courting. . . ."

"Don't play the matchmaker, Annie."

She paid no attention. "Josie is a pretty girl, and as she grows older her ways will change."

"She's a tart and you know it."

"Tom, I know no such thing." His eyes were hooded now, glaring at her in a strange way. "Oh, Tom, don't be angry with me. I would just like someone in the family to be happy . . . to be married with a real wedding. . . ."

"Annie. . . ."

"I would like to be friends with Josie. I have no friends. Twice I saw her on the street in Port Jackson. I approached her, and she ran. She wouldn't even speak . . ."

"Dear God!"

"Tom, what is it?"

"You!"

"Tom Hollister, what is wrong with you? You're pale as a ghost."

"You don't know, do you?"

"Know what?" His tone and the blank stare he now fixed on her made Annie stir restlessly in the saddle.

"Dear God, girl, you've never known. All this time and you didn't know. . . ."

"Damme, Tom," Annie cried, exasperated now, "I don't know what you're talking about!"

"Josie!"

"What about her?"

"Before you . . . Josie. . . ." He bit his lip and turned away from her. "I always thought you knew all about it but just never wanted to mention it." Then he looked back at his sister, his eyes full of love and pain. "Annie, before . . . before you, Josie Hunnicutt was Rourke's mistress."

Annie rode in a daze. At times she didn't even try to duck the low-hanging branches that tore at her dress and tugged at her bonnet.

It all seemed so clear now . . . the new dresses and trinkets Josie had received from a secret admirer, the constant visits every Wednesday afternoon with her father to Port Jackson. Even the convict girl, Cora Lee's words that day coming down the slope from Rourke's cottage: 'Not me, but maybe the other one'll slit yer gullet!'

The 'other one' had been Josie Hunnicutt.

What a fool Annie had been not to see it.

And Josie was jealous. Annie had taken her man away. That was why the girl had cut her those times on the street.

It was ironic, and humorous. The more Annie thought about it the louder her sardonic laughter rang in the air.

God, how she would have liked to give Rourke back to Josie. They were two of a kind and deserved each other!

Then she became aware that the steady clip-clop of the horse behind her was growing louder. Over her shoulder she could see the giant hulk of Jack Moran looming larger in the gathering dusk.

Her body grew tense as he broke into a canter and drew abreast of her.

"Ye left late," he said accusingly.

"Aye."

"There's no need riding back alone. We might as well enjoy each other's company, don't ye think?" His last words were accompanied by a booming laugh, and he didn't try to hide the obvious lust in his eyes as he let them linger on the swells of her breasts above the low cut bodice.

Annie drew her light pelerine over her breasts and around her shoulders like a cloak of dignity.

"I do not enjoy your company, Moran."

"Don't ye now? 'Tis a pity, it is!"

Annie shivered. Moran knew she didn't like him, and he also knew that she feared him. And why shouldn't she? If his reputation as a cut-throat wasn't enough, his appearance alone would send chills of fear up anyone's spine.

Often she would catch him staring at her with such an intense look of desire that Annie was sure he was about to rape her. If it weren't for the threat of Rourke, she was sure, beyond a doubt, that he would.

Cora Lee had been assigned to Annie to help with the household duties. When she got to know the girl well, Annie bluntly asked her why she stayed with Moran when she so often said she hated him.

"I eats good," Cora Lee had replied, "an' that's more than most gets. An' if I wander off, he beats me. If I ever wandered off with a thought o' stayin', he'd kill me. That's the way it is."

Annie was patient with the girl and tried to overlook what she was. But she couldn't help despising Cora Lee's acceptance and seemingly placid contentment with her lot.

"Ye're probably lonely at nights now, what with the Cap'n bein' gone near a fortnight." Moran's insinuating tone grated on her nerves.

"Quite the contrary. I believe these have been the happiest two weeks of my life."

Moran roared with laughter and edged his horse closer to hers. "I believe I could make 'em a lot happier, lass."

Suddenly his nearness, his sly hints and his lecherous glances were more than Annie could bear. She neither wanted nor needed a keeper. And, as it was, she would soon need a keeper to watch the keeper!

Her eyes darted forward, along the winding path and then to the heavy undergrowth and trees to the right and left.

She knew every inch of plain and forest between the Hawkesbury farm and Port Jackson.

Moran didn't.

It was dark now, and idle clouds wafted across the moon, obscuring its light for minutes at a time.

Ahead there was a break in the trees to her right. Annie took a stronger purchase with her knees on the saddle and tensed her body.

When the break came, she neck-reined the horse to the right and dug the heel of her stirrupped boot into his side.

The gelding took off like a shot, leaving Jack Moran yelling after her on the path.

It took her a full two hours on the secondary trails to reach Port Jackson. And when she did, there was a smile on her face. It would take Moran another two hours to find his way out of the maze of forest and underbrush into which she had led him.

She handed her horse over to one of the convict grooms at the officers' stable, and started up the inland slope. Then, on impulse, she decided to walk through main camp instead and take the smaller, winding path to the cottage.

The narrow walkways between the huts were dry and dusty. Illumination was spotty, coming from flambeaus resting in sconces on the buildings' walls. Here and there the way was lit by a torch on a single pole erected for that purpose.

Annie had barely entered the maze of main camp when she regretted her decision not to take the main cart path.

The convict prostitutes were everywhere, drawn to the lights like moths. They moved from the glow of one light to another, their breasts nearly bare in low-cut bodices, and their hips undulating provocatively beneath their skirts.

Annie saw one apparently bargaining with a tall,

hawk-faced prisoner, and suddenly the man dragged her screaming into a dim area between two huts. There he lifted her skirts and, with an animal-like growl, pressed her against a wall.

No one paid any attention to her cries.

Annie hurried on.

Many of the women hissed and cursed at Annie as she passed. The male convicts who could afford an evening, or even a few minutes, of their charms, paced the distance between the prostitutes, bargaining.

Every few feet Annie encountered slack-jawed, wide-eyed urchins who tugged at her skirts, begging a bit of tobacco or a coin.

Two of them, a boy and a girl, were particularly persistent. To avoid them she turned into a narrow passageway with wooden steps leading to a higher street.

Halfway up, she encountered a man coming down. Since there was not room to pass, she was forced to retreat. When he drew close, instead of passing her, he moved in front of her, blocking her way.

"Well, damme, what we got here?"

His speech was slurred by rum and beads of sweat glittered on the stubble of his beard. His yellow and blue convict shirt was soaked with a combination of sweat and spilled rum.

"Please, let me pass."

"What fer, darlin'? I got rum an' I got coin. If yer lookin' fer business, I'm yer man!"

He stepped forward until the light fell across his face and shaggy head. Annie could see now that one cheek was swollen with a fat wad of tobacco, and when he smiled there was a wide, dark gap where his front teeth had been.

"Let me pass, you fool. I'm not—"

"Ye're a choice piece, ye are," he leered. Annie took a step backward and found her shoulders against a wall. "Let's have a look at yer tits, darlin'!"

His hands came up and ripped her cloak open.

"Damn you!"

"My, my . . . look'a them. . . ."

His gap-toothed grin was even more menacing as he pressed against her. His hands gripped Annie's arms, bruising them.

"Let me go!" she cried. "Don't you know who I am?"

"Aye, I do!" he cackled. "Yer the dolly that's gonna pleasure me evenin, that's who ye are!" He loosed one of her arms and painfully squeezed a breast. "Big ones they is!" he growled, squeezing harder.

There was a sharp, heavy odor that hung like a cloud over his body. It filled Annie's nostrils, almost making her gag.

She could see the man's eyes now, slitted, dangerous. They stared hungrily at her, as if she were a meal and he a starving man.

"Damn you!" she cried again, struggling in his grasp.

"Ye got no call to be so uppity, darlin', fer one who makes her way on her back."

He bent forward, planning to kiss her with his slobbering lips, when Annie kicked out with her booted foot. Her toe caught him on the knee. He howled in pain and dropped his hands long enough for her to push him away.

As he fell backward, Annie ran past him and up the steps. With a roar he lunged after her. Just as she emerged into the street, he caught her by the shoulders and whirled her around.

"Damn ye, if ye'll not lay fer rum or coin, then I'll have ye fer nothin'!" he bellowed.

Annie opened her mouth to scream again, when over her attacker's shoulder she saw a second figure emerge from the darkness.

"I don't think the lady relishes yer attention, mate."

Still gripping Annie roughly by the shoulders, the

gap-toothed man swiveled his head around to glare at the speaker. "Where ha' ye been, lad," he said, with a roar of ragged laughter. "They ain't no *ladies* in main camp. Now be off about yer business an' I'll to mine!"

"Let her go, friend."

Something about the man's low, rumbling voice struck Annie as familiar, but so engrossed was she in trying to free herself that she could give it no thought. The man's hands grew tense on her shoulders, and then he spoke.

"Ye'll haf'ta wait a bit fer yer pleasurin', lass, 'til I get rid of our friend here."

So saying, he shoved her into a narrow space between two huts and, with a roar, turned on his challenger. He lunged forward, his clenched fist already swinging in a wide arc.

But the other sidestepped easily and, in passing, hammered his two clenched fists into the back of the molester's neck.

The man went down to his hands and knees, but, with a loud grunt, came quickly back to his feet.

Through eyes misted with pain and fear, Annie watched them circle each other warily; the one, her attacker, tall and rangy, the other, a shorter man, but wider, with powerful arms and shoulders.

His back was to her and the light was dim, but Annie could see the lithe muscles of his back ripple with power in the confines of his tight yellow and blue prisoner's shirt.

Then the two met like crashing goliaths in the middle of the street. A knife appeared in the gap-toothed man's hand, and Annie cried out a warning.

She needn't have worried.

The shorter man, emitting a raffish laugh, sidestepped the knife thrust like an agile cat. He caught the wrist with his powerful hands and spun. Annie's attacker crashed against a hut wall, and the crack of his wrist bone breaking was clear in the night air.

There was a howl of pain, and then the sound of clenched fists on flesh. The shorter man's arms seemed to fly back and forth in a blur as his fists pummeled the body before him, holding it against the hut wall.

Then it was over as quickly as it had begun.

The man stood up and stepped back.

Annie's attacker stood against the wall, his eyes glassy, rolling. He leaned slightly forward, poised for an instant in space, and then pitched, face forward, into the street.

Breathing heavily, the man who had saved her turned and moved toward Annie. She recognized him at once as the manacled convict that had given her such a start when she had seen him in the fields.

"Are ye all right, Annie?"

"You . . . you know my name?"

One finger at her chin tilted her face upward.

"I once told you I would never forget your name, Annie Hollister."

She stared at the shaggy beard, and the mane of curly black hair. Her gaze plumbed the depths of his black eyes. And then she smiled.

"Dear God, it is you."

They paused among the rocks at the top of the slope. Below them the flickering torches of Port Jackson seemed far away.

"So that's how I came to be here, in this tropical paradise," Conroy said, smiling with a wry twist of his lips.

Annie couldn't bear to look at him. The few times she had, during their walk up the slope, had made her dizzy. She found herself swimming in the black pools of his eyes. She felt a strange churning deep in her belly when his lips would part and his even, white teeth would flash in that smile that she had never forgotten.

That reckless smile and those dark eyes had been so burned into her brain that, in the years since that night, she had many times awakened from dreaming that he had returned to her.

And now he had.

"Now tell me, Annie lass, what wild winds of fate have blown ye to this place?" His hand touched her arm, and its warmth seemed to flow through her whole body.

"Like you," she said, her voice barely a sound, "my family ran afoul of King George . . . at least his taxman."

She reiterated all the reasons they had decided to come to New South Wales. She told Phillip of her father's death and her mother's current illness. She spoke glowingly of her brother's prowess on the farm.

And there she stopped.

"And you, Annie. What of you?"

Shrugging, she wrapped her arms beneath her breasts and bit down on her lower lip to stem the emotion that threatened to overwhelm her. One night, she thought, one brief encounter so long ago. Why did it weigh so heavily in her heart?

"Then you have nothing to tell me of yourself?"

He was a convict, a thief, perhaps even a murderer. At least Rourke, with all his nefarious dealings, was not a convict.

But then Steven Rourke was not Phillip Conroy, either.

"There is little to tell. I . . . I live here, in Port Jackson."

His hands found her shoulders. Gently he turned her into him.

"Obviously you have not married."

"No, I . . . no, I have not married." She tasted the salty tang of blood inside her lip. She blinked, and tears spilled from her eyes to trickle in a lazy pattern down her flushed cheeks.

She wanted to scream at him to go away, to leave her alone and not bring useless confusion into her life.

But, at the same time, she wanted to throw her arms around that powerful neck and mold her body to his.

"You remembered me, my name . . . just as I always remembered you."

"Phillip, please!"

"You remembered that night . . . as I have."

"Phillip . . . you don't know. . . ."

"I know that your face, the touch of your lips, has haunted me since that night. I know that you are the most beautiful woman I have ever seen. And 'tis not just your beautiful face or your lovely figure, Annie Hollister, 'tis more!"

"I won't listen to you," Annie cried out. "Dear God, I can't!"

She dropped her face into her hands and leaned against his chest. Her shoulders shook as his hands left them to move down her back.

"Ye have an inner quality that I sensed when our eyes first met that night in the moonlight."

Annie could no longer hold back the flood of tears nor the tide of emotion that had built up within her. Sobs wracked her body. She spread her hands and let her cheek fall against the comfort of his chest.

"Say no more . . . please, say no more," she mumbled between great, gasping sobs. "I can stand to hear no more. . . ."

She thought her heart would explode from her breast and her mind would burst. For Phillip Conroy was speaking the exact words that she had always dreamed a man would say, if he truly cared for her.

"Annie!"

"No!" She flattened her palms against his chest and pushed herself free of his arms. "Have mercy! Dear God, can't you see what you are doing to me?"

In answer, he tilted her chin and softly brushed her lips with his. For a moment she hesitated. Her mind reeled with the desire to throw herself into his arms, to feel herself crushed in the strength of his masculine embrace.

Then, with another defiant, "No!" she turned and started to run.

She hadn't covered ten yards when he was upon her again, folding her into his brawny arms in a vise-like embrace.

Then his lips lowered again. They were insistent but gentle, and sweetly warm. Without realizing it, Annie returned his embrace as her arms crept around his neck and a low moan escaped her throat.

In that moment she knew she was alive.

She moved against him, drowning her senses in the taste, the touch, the smell of him. Her fingers found and entwined themselves in the thick, curly hair that lay along the back of his neck.

Then the kiss deepened, became more insistent, and his arms flattened her body so close to his that she could feel the beating of his heart against her breast.

By the time his lips left hers, Annie was locked against him, half in a swoon.

"Annie . . . Annie!"

"Aye."

"Though it sounds impossible, I know 'tis true. I love you. I've loved you since that first kiss so long ago."

"Phillip, no, you—"

"I don't think I really realized it fully until I saw you again . . . that day in the cart. . . ."

She twisted from him, her breasts rising dangerously from her bodice as she gulped great gasps of air. His words had the effect of cold water being dumped over her head.

"You are mad, do you hear me? Mad!" she cried.

"Aye, mad I am—with love for you."

"You cannot love me, Phillip Conroy, you can't!"

"But I do."

"He'll kill you. If he even knew about this . . . this moment, he would kill you!"

"Who?"

Annie wrung her hands together and drew her head down into her shoulders. "You know. You must. The whole colony knows."

"You mean Rourke?"

"Aye. Captain Steven Rourke. I'm his whore."

Not a blink, not even a quiver of his lip to let her know that he had heard her.

"I must be in now." She turned and again sprinted up the hill, only to be stopped this time by his voice.

"I know ye're his mistress."

She didn't turn, but drew her spine as straight as an arrow. When she spoke again, her voice was flat, devoid of emotion. "Whore . . . mistress . . . what difference? 'Tis all the same. Goodnight."

"Annie, do ye love him?"

"Phillip, please, should we meet on the street, do not acknowledge that ye know me, not with a nod or even a look. I shall shun ye as well."

"Do ye love him?"

"We must not meet again, even by accident. Believe me, he would kill us both."

"ANNIE!"

She whirled. His eyes flashed with reflected moonlight as he looked up at her. Even through his beard she could see the set of his jaw and sense the tenseness in his body as well.

"WHAT?"

"Do ye love Rourke."

"NO! No, I do not love him. Damme, Phillip, I hate him. Indeed, I loathe the man. There isn't enough soap in the world to wash his touch from my skin or scent to take the odor of him from my body."

"Good. I shall meet you here, at this same place among the rocks, tomorrow night when the moon is high."

"I won't be here."

He shrugged and she saw the whiteness of his teeth as he grinned. "Then I shall be back the next night, and the next, and the next, until I see you again."

"You are indeed mad. Phillip!"

But he had turned and was now walking briskly down the path. He was even humming.

Again the tears came and the light breeze that rustled her skirts seemed to bring a shiver to her body.

But as she watched his wide back disappear in the darkness, she knew it wasn't the night air that chilled her.

It was the thought of Steven Rourke's return.

"No, Phillip Conroy," she whispered, "I don't love him. How could I, for he's never really touched me. 'Tis you I love. But, I beg you, don't be such a fool to think anything could ever come of this . . . for nothing can."

"Phillip!"

Conroy stopped, moving quickly sideways from the torch's glare. He went into a crouch, his hand gripping the knife in his boot.

In the darkness to his right there was a chuckle, and young Colbert stepped from the shadows.

"Lad, you should give a man warning," Conroy sighed, slipping the knife back into his boot and stepping forward to join his friend.

"We've a gathering . . . about a dozen. More than I would have dreamed."

Conroy nodded, his brows meeting over his eyes. "Where?"

"This way."

Colbert led him along the stream that dissected main camp from tent city about three hundred yards. They came to the end of the tents, and still went on.

"There."

"That's the cook tent."

"Aye," Colbert smiled. "It has thick canvas flaps so it can be blacked out. Besides, the camp cook would go along with us."

"How much do they know?" Conroy asked.

"Damn little. I've just hinted, like ye said."

They entered the tent one at a time, quickly blocking the light in by dropping one of the double flaps behind them before lifting the second.

There were an even dozen, eight men and four women. Conroy introduced himself, and then took them aside, one by one.

He learned their personalities, their feelings about the life that had been forced upon them, and the crime they had committed that had sent them to New South Wales in the first place.

Most importantly, he found out what they had done in their previous lives, and their current job, if any, in the camp.

What he heard was music to his ears. All but one of the men and two of the women were tradespeople. They had worked with their hands, either on the land or as wheelrights, cotters, chandlers, and other skilled workers.

Two of the women were seamstresses. The others were exotically dark and spoke with accents.

"Spanish," the older one explained.

"Why New South Wales?"

"We were shipwrecked, my sister and I," she replied in heavily accented English. "The Portuguese ship that picked us up would have sold us for slaves had we not fled when it landed here."

"So ye're not convicts?"

The woman shrugged. "We might as well be. You hint of leaving this place."

Conroy hesitated, and then nodded. "But we'll not be returning to civilization as you know it."

"Señor, I would not have my little sister grow up to be the whore that I have been forced to become.

Wherever you go is better than this place. We were
born of quality, but we can learn to work on our hands
and knees as quickly as we have learned to work on
our backs."

Conroy liked her.

The one man who wasn't a tradesman was a vicar.
Like the others, he had been convicted of a petty
crime, in his case caused by too much drink.

"An' how odd it is," he laughed. "I've not had a
drop since I've got here!"

Conroy accepted him as well. "I think we'll have
need of the Good Word where we're going," he smiled.

He sat them all down before him in two rows, much
as if they were a class and he the schoolmaster. And
then he told them, very slowly and very carefully,
about the lands and opportunities over the mountains.

He explained that it would be dangerous as well as
difficult, but at least there they could call themselves
free men and women. They could reap the rewards
from their own toil, and one day their children—if they
were lucky enough to survive and have children—
would have better lives than fate had dealt them.

"We won't all go at once. A few will leave with the
first flight, then a few more will be sent for, and so
on."

"What about the savages?" one man asked.

"I am very friendly with a group of them . . . almost their kin."

Conroy explained No-Moonee, and the basis of their
friendship.

"So you see they can help us, and, in turn, we can
teach them better ways to survive."

Here he paused and looked at each of them before
he spoke again.

"You don't have to make your decision now, but we
hope to leave in a month's time, and much work will
have to be done before then."

One and all they pledged their help, whether they would be chosen as the first to go or not.

It was dawn when they emerged, stretching, from the tent.

"Tired, lad?" Conroy asked.

"Aye."

"I've got a trail plotted over the mountains. Are ye too tired to look it over with me?"

"Nay," Colbert said, suddenly wide-eyed and eager. "I'll be back shortly with a horse!"

Conroy laughed. Young Colbert, whether he meant to be or not, was a born thief and fixer. He knew that whatever tools would be needed—harness, horses, clothing—somehow young Colbert would find them.

Five minutes later the lad returned with a big chestnut mare.

"Sorry."

"About what?"

Colbert grinned. "I could only get one on such short notice. We'll have to ride double."

They rode through the gray and orange of dawn until the sun was a quarter high in a clear, blue-domed sky.

At last they reined up and dismounted in the rolling foothills just short of the soaring mountains.

"Here's the key, lad," Conroy said, waving his arm in an arc above the lazily moving stream.

"What's that?"

"This river."

Colbert laughed. "River? Hell, man, 'tis but a stream. I could wade across it on my hands and knees!"

"Aye, and a month ago you could have stepped across it in one stride. But the snows are melting fast up there, lad. A month from now this will be a raging torrent."

Colbert's face paled. "It would take weeks to go around."

"Aye, and wagons wouldn't make it over those peaks. We'll have to make a bridge, upstream there, so we can float it down and secure it on the other side when the time comes for crossing."

Colbert screwed his young, sun-darkened face into a grimace and Conroy could see the wheels turning in the lad's brain. "We'll have to build it in sections and work only at night. Thank God we have a month."

"Can you get the men? Trustworthy ones?"

"I'll get 'em," Colbert said.

"Good lad."

Together they re-mounted and turned the mare back toward main camp.

"An', lad, I might not be going with you and the first group."

"The woman, Annie Hollister?"

"Aye, how did ya know?"

"Because," Colbert grinned, "I see the way ya look at the lass and follow her with yer eyes."

"Don't be so smug, lad. One day the bug will bite you."

Colbert threw back his head and roared with laughter. "It already has."

20

It took all the will and control Annie could summon forth not to meet him the following night.

But it was nearly impossible to sleep. Her body tossed and turned, and soon she was soaked beneath the coverlet. Her lips longed for the taste of his kiss, and her breasts ached for the touch of his hands.

When she did sleep it was fitful. One moment she writhed in terror as Rourke stood glowering over her, his blue eyes spreading fear like an icy cloak around her.

And in the next moment she dreamt of Phillip Conroy. Though she had never known his touch beyond a kiss, the dream was as if real.

In it their naked bodies were pressed together in yearning anticipation. His powerful hands stroked her back, bringing cooing sounds from her throat. She rolled to her back and felt a rain of light, tender kisses on her throat and then down to her breasts.

Her skin was warm velvet and his kisses were a delightful torment. Her sensitive nipples were teased tautly erect by his lips, and his hand gently stroked her inner thighs, bringing her passion to the edge.

As his fingers caressed her, his low, rumbling voice whispered endearments of love.

Trembling and moaning she grasped for him, urging him to make them one. . . .

And then she was drowsily awake, a warm glow suffusing her body, until she realized it was only a dream.

For days she did nothing but sleep and eat. She walked about the cottage in a daze. When Cora Lee came to help with the cleaning, Annie sent her away.

"Are ye sick?"

"Aye, Cora Lee, I am sick. That's why I hide in bed."

"What ails ye?"

"My life."

"Huh?"

"Go away, Cora Lee."

Each time she went down the hill to draw water from the communal well, she felt Jack Moran's eyes watching her every move.

Once he stopped her.

"I'll haf'ta tell the Cap'n ye run off from me t'other night."

"You do that, Moran. And I'll tell him you raped me every night he was gone."

"Damn ye fer a witch!"

"Aye, Moran, a witch I am. Now out of my way or I'll put a curse on ye."

For a week she hadn't gone to the farm or ventured into main camp, for fear of running into Phillip.

But at last she could no longer endure being cooped up like a prisoner in the cottage.

She chose the least revealing of her dresses, a peach-colored muslin with the bodice cut above the swell of her breasts. Just a suggestion of cleavage could be seen above the neckline. The sleeves were full, and they exposed her shoulders. These she covered with a light shawl.

The sky was overcast, and the air was filled with a light mist that threatened rain. She didn't care. The fresh, salt-tinged air felt good on her face, and the scent of it drew her down the hill to the sea.

She skirted the fringes of main camp and headed toward Lookout Point and the rugged cliffs that towered above the bay.

Halfway to the point she stopped and looked around. The area between where she stood and the huts of main camp was open. She could see no sign of Jack Moran.

Good, she thought, the days she had spent isolated in the cottage had blunted his sense of duty.

He was probably rum soaked in his hovel with Cora Lee, or gambling with the convicts in tent city.

It was almost with a light heart that she lifted her skirts and continued on to the point.

"Good day, missus."

"Good day," Annie replied, nodding at the lookout.

" 'Peers we'll get some rain."

"Aye."

"Best not walk clear out on the cliffs, missus. Come the rain they'll be slick as ice."

"I know, thank you."

She walked on, filling her lungs with the tangy salt air and reveling in the powerful sound of the high waves breaking on the rocks far below.

Suddenly she felt a raindrop splash against her cheek. She lifted her face and felt another. The sharp sting as they hit, and then the cooling after-effect as the moisture ran down her cheek, made her shiver deliciously.

She felt a sudden fierceness rise in her breast that matched the rolling of thunder she heard in the distance.

"Oh, to be free," she sighed. "To be free as the wind, and blow wherever one wanted!"

"Every man and woman wants to be free."

Annie gasped and whirled around.

He was beneath a rock overhang, standing on one leg, the other booted foot on a knee-high rock. Casually he leaned forward, resting his elbows on his knees as his black eyes swept over her.

Annie had to tense the muscles in her legs to steady her. He had shaved and trimmed his wild mane. He so looked like he had that night in England that she was taken aback.

But there was one thing different, and that brought a sudden, mirthful giggle to her lips.

"Something wrong?" he asked, his heavy, dark eyebrows arching up.

"Your face . . . 'tis so tanned, except where your beard was!"

"Ah, yes, I suppose it does look rather odd. But in time. . . ."

He flashed the raffish yet boyish grin she remembered, and it nearly melted her heart.

"You shouldn't have followed me."

"I didn't," he replied, broadening the grin. "I've had my urchin spies watching your cottage every hour of the day and night. When I was told you had appeared, I merely waited until I could surmise your direction and run like a bloody deer up the other side of the cliff to meet you."

Annie giggled at this image, but then sudden panic gripped her heart, making her turn and look down the path from whence she'd come.

"Moran?"

"Aye," she said, turning back to him. "He watches me like a hawk."

"I know. I've been watching him. But right now he's besotted with rum and spread between two doxies in tent city. And you, Annie lass, are getting soaked through to the skin."

She looked down. Her skirt had darkened from the rain and she could feel her damp locks clinging to her forehead.

"Here." He held his hand toward her.

Instinctively, Annie reached for it. Their fingers barely touched when she jerked back as if she had touched fire.

"No!"

"What is it? Come, girl, 'tis dry under here."

"I . . . don't dare."

"Because 'tis my hand that offers to pull you in?"

"Aye . . . oh, don't you see? 'Tis foolishness to torture ourselves. . . ."

"I agree."

Without another word he stepped from beneath the ledge and swept her into his arms.

"Damn you."

His laughter matched the rumbling thunder as he carried her back. When they were beneath the ledge she waited, but he didn't set her down.

"Aren't you going to put me down?"

"Why should I?"

Because if you don't, I'll want you to kiss me, she wanted to scream. *And if you kiss me I'll want you to touch me. And if you so much as touch me, we will both be lost.*

Instead of speaking, Annie turned away. She squeezed her eyes tightly shut, but the picture he made remained.

His shirt was unlaced, hanging open over the mat of black hair that covered his bull-like chest. His breeches were tight over the corded muscles of his thighs.

Standing there, holding her like that, his body looked as graceful and as powerful as that of a young stallion. Even in yellow prisoner garb he looked free, full of energy and pride.

Even looking away from him, she could still see the chiseled jaw line, the clefted chin, and the deep-slashed dimple at one corner of his mouth.

The nearness of his breathing, the rise and fall of his chest against the side of her breast, made her body flash between hot and chill.

"Phillip?"

"Aye?"

"Put me down."

He did, but he didn't release her. She opened her

eyes, but she didn't know what to do with them or her hands.

His black eyes, as they stared down at her, seemed to read her mood. The way he looked at her was physical, as if with only his eyes he could actually touch her.

She shivered and twisted from his grasp. Three quick steps brought her to the edge of the overhang where she looked out at the rain and, through its glassy sheets, the mist-shrouded ocean beyond.

The wind was stronger now. It caught her skirts and swirled them around her legs.

"I like to come out here when it's like this. 'Tis peaceful, and yet, with the thunder and the lightning and the rain, 'tis roiling as well."

"Aye," Phillip said, moving to stand just behind her, "like our lives, it is."

His closeness unnerved her. She had to use all her will not to turn into his arms, tell him and shout it to the gray-swept skies that she loved him. She wanted to lean against his brawny chest and tell him that she had always loved the memory of him, cherished it at night in her dreams.

And now that he was here, real flesh and blood. . . .

But instead, she searched her mind for a way to stop this idiocy, to make him see that there was nothing for them. She was property, Rourke's property, bought and paid for, to use as he saw fit until he no longer wanted her.

"In Ireland, on the run, I'd ride the cliffs by the sea. Often I'd climb down among the rocks and look off across George's channel. And there, with the surf crashing around the rocks at my feet, I'd wonder what ever happened to the beautiful green-eyed girl I'd kissed and foolishly left that night."

She felt his hands at her hips, and tensed. Then they

slid on around to meet beneath her breasts and pull her back against him.

"Annie, I love you."

"I am Rourke's mistress."

"But you don't love him."

"Love?" she said hollowly. "Love in this place is for innocent little girls and dewy-eyed poets."

"Ye don't mean that."

"Perhaps not," she said, sagging against him. "But I must believe it. 'Tis the only thing that keeps me sane."

Slowly he turned her body toward his. Annie didn't resist. His hands were warm and firm at her back, and his lips thrilled her as they nuzzled her ear and then traveled down her throat.

"Phillip!"

"Ahh, Annie, me love, 'tis meant to be."

"But it can't be," she moaned, trying to suppress the rush of desire that welled up in her for this man.

A hand moved slowly over the swell of her breast. Its heat seared her skin through the material of her clothing.

So different, she thought, closing her eyes and tilting her face up toward his lips, his touch is so different from Rourke's; questing, not demanding . . . loving, not using.

"I didn't think 'twas possible, but you've become more of a woman. And your hair is lighter. . . ."

"The sun. . . ."

He kissed her, warmly, deeply.

This must stop, she thought, her mind in sudden panic. Oh, dear God, help me think!

But the rising tide of pleasure his lips created fought her rational judgement. His hands came up to caress and hold her cheeks as his lips lifted from hers.

She felt herself descending into the dark depths of his eyes. By slow degrees she felt all fight leave her. Gently, with just the tips of his fingers, he brought her close to him. Their bodies met, and Annie felt herself melt and mold to him.

"As I said, 'tis meant to be," Phillip murmured softly in her ear.

His hands moved to her hips, forcing the lower part of her body tighter to him. Unconsciously, Annie moved her hip and felt him awaken.

"Oh, Phillip!"

Her hands crept to his shoulders, and then lovingly moved over the rippling muscles of his back to clasp behind his neck. When their lips locked this time, it was in a savage kiss of mutual need.

Now a different kind of madness filled her brain. Rourke would return in a month. But a month could be a lifetime in Phillip Conroy's arms.

"I love you," he murmured.

"And, damn me for a fool, I love you, Phillip Conroy."

"Tonight. There will be no moon. Leave the latch lifted."

"But Moran. . . ."

A low chuckle rippled along the strong line of his throat.

"Moran will be busy elsewhere. Say yes, Annie."

Annie closed her eyes tightly. She could feel the beat of his heart against her breast and it seemed like thunder in her ears.

A month.

She would live a lifetime of glorious nights in one month.

"Yes," she sighed. "Yes!"

21

IT was as if Annie had known all along it would happen, from the moment that night in the street when he had vanquished her attacker.

She poured heated water into the high-sided tub with her mind still high on the cliff over the sea.

As she had left him, Phillip had given her a final, long, intimate stare. "Tonight," he had whispered, with a rough tenderness in his voice that had spoken worlds of meaning.

She slipped the clothing from her body and stood naked in the tub. She reveled in the feeling of the warm water caressing her skin as she slowly eased to her knees.

A month, she thought. Not forever, but better than a fleeting moment.

As she applied soap to her body, she caught a glimpse of herself in the narrow, free-standing mirror. Her skin was smooth and a healthy pink. Her breasts were full and lushly rounded, the tips pink and erect from the chill air. Her belly was flat, and her miniscule waist flared out to form the womanly contour of her hips.

Yes, she thought with a smile, I am a woman now. I have had a man, but not love. Tonight I will have it all!

She luxuriated in the bath a while longer, adding scented salts to the warm water until the entire room smelled of fresh-blooming lilacs. Then she rose from the tub and dried her body with a soft, thick towel.

Carefully she donned her best underthings, pushing the fact that Rourke had purchased them from her mind. Of her dresses she picked the green, with its daringly low-cut neckline delicately trimmed in lace.

She noticed how her breasts swelled in the bodice when she reached her hands to the button loops at the back of the dress.

A soft chuckle escaped her lips. *How devilishly sensual and daring I want to be with Phillip, compared to the constant resentment and embarrassment when seen this way by Rourke!*

She brushed her hair to a sheen, and then fluffed it to just the right degree of fullness, allowing the curls to fall loosely behind her ears. She took a vial of scent and dabbed a few drops in the hollow of her neck and then in the cleavage of her gown.

Again she turned to the mirror, appraising herself with one last critical look. Already she had changed. The dull, flat quality was gone from her eyes, and in its place was a glow of barely suppressed excitement and anticipation.

Yes, she thought, this is love!

She left one taper burning in the bedroom and lifted the drape to move into the outer room. One step and she halted, her senses alive.

She wasn't alone.

Her eyes whirled around the room. And then Annie saw her, sitting in the darkness near the hearth.

"Hello, Josie."

"Where is he?"

For an instant, Annie's heart stopped beating. Could the girl possibly know? "You mean . . . Rourke?"

"A'course, Rourke."

Annie breathed again. "He's not here, Josie."

"Ye lie. Where is he? Yer his whore, you know where he is!"

The girl struggled to her feet and lurched toward the table to steady herself.

Annie gasped as the small blonde entered a pool of light cast by the taper on the table.

Her hair hung lank and dirty in matted tangles to her shoulders. Her small, perfect face was battered, one eye nearly closed from swelling. Her skirt was ragged and torn in several places, and a rent in her blouse completely exposed one swaying breast.

"A pretty sight, ain't I?"

"Josie, what happened? Who did this to you?"

"Me father, that's who . . . me loving father! Look at this." She pulled the sleeves of her blouse to expose black and blue bruises on her arms. "And this." She turned, still unsteady on her feet, and yanked the back of her blouse to her neck.

A gasp choked in Annie's throat. Josie's back glowed with angry red welts from her shoulders all the way down to disappear beneath the waistband of her skirt.

"But, Josie . . . why? Why would your father do such a thing?"

"Fer miscarryin' Rourke's bastard, that's why." She turned, dropping her blouse but not bothering to button it. "But he don't know it was Rourke's . . . yet. He waited 'til I was well an' strong, he did. Then he come to me wantin' to know the father. I wouldn't tell him, so he beat me. An' when I still wouldn't tell him, he beat me some more."

"Josie, I didn't even know you were with child."

Her laugh was a high-pitched, hysterical shriek. "No one did, except Rourke! I hid it from everyone else. I cinched me belly up tight an' hid it after Rourke denied it was his and threw me out. That's probably what made me drop it early." Her eyes became narrow slits as they turned on Annie. "I would'a been all right if yer damn brother had an ounce of man in him."

"My . . . Tom?"

"Aye, Tom. I practically took me clothes off tryin' ta seduce him, but he'd have none of it. If he had, yer Tom'd been the brat's father."

A cold chill passed through Annie. She pitied Josie, but she now saw the girl for what she was. Like Rourke, Josie would use anyone and anything for her own ends.

"So now I'm here to get me share from Cap'n Steven Rourke!" She stumbled closer, and Annie recoiled from the stench of rum on her breath. "Either that or I tells me Pa it *was* Rourke what done it to me! Pa will kill 'im, he will."

Annie stepped back, shivering under the gleaming stare of the other girl's good eye.

"But I don't want him dead. I want him alive and in me bed. Look at you, Annie Hollister, jest look! All decked out in them fancy dresses. Well, they're mine, you hear? *Mine!*"

The last words were spoken in an hysterical shriek. Still she advanced, pushing Annie before her.

"Josie, please!"

"An' Rourke's mine, too, damn you! You think you got him, don't ya? You think you love him—"

"Dear God, Josie, I don't love him."

Annie could see now that the girl was mad. She was sure of it when, from somewhere in the folds of her skirt, a knife appeared in her hand.

"Where is he, you witch?"

"In Capetown," Annie said quickly. "He sailed on the *Venture*. He'll be back in a month."

Josie paused. She shook her head several times, as if this would help clear it.

"Gone. . . ."

"Aye, Josie. He's not here, I swear it. Look for yourself."

Josie bolted into the bedroom and in seconds was back.

"Gone! The bloody bastard's gone!"

breeches, rolling them over his hips and down his legs.

Annie found that there was no embarrassing flush creeping over her body as she watched him undress. His chest was even broader exposed and the curling black hair that covered its expanse seemed to accent the darkly tanned skin. His chest tapered to slim, tight hips and heavily muscled thighs.

Ridges of hard muscle rippled along his flat belly as he stood and turned to face her. Below the waist his skin tones were lighter where they hadn't been darkened by the sun.

"You're . . . so powerful, and big. . . ." she whispered, again without embarrassment.

"And you, my Annie, are so beautiful."

A tapering scar, the flesh around it furrowed, gleamed on his left hip. Annie stepped forward and ran her finger along it.

"An Englishman's musket ball. It happened on the night they caught me for good."

Then in a step he drew her to him, pulling her into his arms, pressing her so hard that her breasts flattened across his chest. The feel of the wiry dark hair against her nipples brought a gasp to Annie's lips.

His belly and thighs were hard against her, bending her backward, as he bent his head to kiss her. Together they fell to the bed, his lips demanding, his tongue seeking hers.

Annie heard a soft sigh, and then a whimpering deep in her throat. Her lips burned with the scorching pressure from his, and a wave of dizziness made her lose all sense of time and place.

The feathery touch of his fingers over her breasts brought more moans to her lips. Her hands found his head and her fingers curled in his thick hair. She tugged until she felt his lips at her breast.

Already she sensed that he was a masterful yet gentle lover, and she bit her lip to still her voice from crying out to him to hurry. For she could tell from his touch that he wanted to go slowly, to savor her body and, this, their first time together.

His hands brushed across the taut flesh of her belly to her thighs as his lips continued to draw sweetness from her breasts.

"You are as beautiful to touch as you are to gaze upon," he whispered, the heat of his kisses causing a stir in her deepest core.

"Phillip . . . my darling Phillip, I want you."

"Soon . . . soon."

She parted her thighs in surrender to his probing hands. And then he moved possessively over her body. She felt his narrow hips settle against the soft flesh of her inner thighs.

"Phillip!" she cried, breathless to receive him, rippling her fingers along his back to urge him on.

And then she cried out as she felt the slow, steady throb of him fill her. Far away she heard his voice gasping her name, and her own voice crying out his.

His movements were sure, his thrust deep. He was a man who knew women, who knew how to draw sensual ecstasy from their aroused bodies.

She could feel the passion in her belly spread and suffuse her breasts and thighs. Higher and higher it rose, demanding to be fulfilled.

Gently but demandingly he moved against her, and she answered each of his thrusts with an eagerness she would never have believed she possessed.

And then he slowed his movements, as if to tease her. She replied by digging her nails into his back and arching her body upward.

"Ohhhh, Phillip!"

"Yes, yes!" he gasped against her ear.

Another startled cry escaped her lips, and sudden, exquisite pleasure flooded her body.

And she cried out again, as their passion spilled over and their love for each other culminated.

Her eyes flew open and she gazed up into the rapture she could see in his face above her.

Annie opened her lips to speak, but no sound came forth. She wanted to tell him how wonderful it had been, how soothed and loved she felt.

But then he was kissing away the tears in her eyes, and she knew that no words were needed.

She sighed from the depths of her soul and kissed him back, happy with his weight suspended over her, the press of his flesh on hers so intimate and loving.

Annie awoke wrapped in the cocoon of his strong arms. Her flesh tingled in the candlelight as a lazy finger traced the delicate patterns of the faint blue veins in her breast.

"I should be gone. 'Tis near dawn."

"No," she said, inching nearer his warmth. "Not yet."

Her body glowed with comfortable satisfaction and she couldn't bear to have it end, not yet. Annie now knew the full range of passion in her body. Twice more they had made love, and she could still feel the swollen surfeit of it.

She could feel his breath at her ear. "Tell me . . . about the girl. The one you called Josie."

With the rain steadily pounding on the slate roof overhead, Annie told him the whole story, from the very beginning.

When she finished, there was only the sound of his heavy breathing in the room. For long moments she waited, and then he spoke, his rumbling voice tinged with menace.

"Rourke has given up his right to live."

"What are you saying?" Annie grabbed his hand in fear and covered her breast with its palm. "You wouldn't. . . ."

"Aye, I would, Annie, if he stands in my way."

"Phillip, no! That would make you no better than he!"

"Annie, 'tis a cruel world beyond these shores. And here it is even crueler. Here there is no goodness or honor, there is only survival. And if one does not fight for it, even with violence, if that is necessary, one doesn't survive."

How often she had heard those same words before. But this was too much. No matter how evil she found those around her, Annie refused to be a part of it.

"No, Phillip. I love you, but I don't want you that way. If Rourke has no conscience, indeed if the whole world has none, I do."

"Then come away with me!"

His words drew her bolt upright in the bed.

"Away? Where on earth to?"

He pulled her back and held her to his side. Then, slowly in even tones, he told her of the vast lands beyond the Blue Mountains. He told her of his friendship with the natives, and his months of learning to survive in the wilderness.

"Your Governor Phillip was right, Annie, when he said that one day this would be a great land. Beyond those mountains we could be safe from Rourke, from all of them. And once there, Annie girl, an empire could be built."

"But how? I—"

"Livestock . . . sheep and cattle. There are vast plains of grass there, and fertile soil."

Annie shook her head. "Where would you get the breeding stock?"

Here Phillip raised himself on one elbow and looked down at her. Slowly his lips spread and his teeth gleamed in a wide smile. "Rourke."

"What?"

"At Riverforks he has three hundred head of prime sheep and forty head of beef."

"You mean. . . ." she began, gasping and suppressing a laugh of her own, "you mean, steal Rourke's livestock?"

"Aye. There are others who are tired of this pest-hole. They want to gamble with me. When the time is right we'll go, and we'll take Rourke's sheep and cattle with us."

Suddenly Annie felt weak. Here, in a few seconds, she had found the answer to her prayers.

"We'll have a good life, Annie lass," he whispered, moving his arm across her body. "Annie . . . you're mine."

"I know I want to be. I—"

"Go with me, Annie."

Crazily she threw her arms around his neck, hiding the tears that suddenly welled from her eyes. Her body ached for him and her mind screamed to say yes.

But she couldn't.

Her mother, Tom, Billy . . . they would all be ruined. Rourke would never stop exacting the toll for her defection.

She couldn't say yes.

Instead, she continued to hide her face and whispered, "Love me, Phillip! Love me again!"

22

PHILLIP began the building of the bridge, and then passed the construction on to a ship's carpenter named Markham.

"Can ye finish it in less than a month?"

"I'll try," the man replied, "but I can't guarantee it. I could, if we could get more men and work a shift now and then in the daytime."

"Risky, but I'll try."

Conroy conferred with Gerald. Two days later the lad found an answer.

"Women?"

"Aye, they like their rum as well as a man," Colbert laughed. "An' not all of 'em likes to flatback fer it."

Two afternoons later, Conroy rode out to confer with Markham.

"I'd've never believed it," the man said, shaking his head in wonderment. "They work as hard as the men, and if a Corpsman goes by they can find the damndest ways to distract him away from where the buildin's goin' on!"

"We'll make it then?"

"Aye," Markham replied, "with time to spare."

Phillip managed to get himself and Gerald transferred from main camp to Rourke's farm, River Forks. During each of their rest breaks, they meticulously earmarked and catalogued the prime sheep and cattle they would take with them when the time came.

After a particularly exhausting morning, Conroy begged off for an hour's sleep.

"Ye're pushin' yerself too hard," Colbert said.

"Aye," Conroy replied with a grin. "But I've got a world of convincin' to do on the lass before that bastard Rourke returns. How are we doin' with the horses and wagons?"

"The horses are no problem. I've bribed a lad at the stables. The wagons are another thing, though. We'll have to steal 'em at the last minute, but I think I've got a plan. . . ."

He was about to launch into it, when Conroy's snores assaulted his ears.

The days continued cool, and always there was the rain. For Annie, they slipped past, intermingled with both joy and frustration. There were times when Phillip's ploys, even with the help of his convict comrades, didn't succeed in keeping Jack Moran occupied.

But more often than not they did. And those days were spent almost entirely in joy. Annie and Phillip were together every possible moment. There were long walks on the beach or into the countryside, where they would meet. There were visits to the farm, when Annie would steal away to the river. There, beneath a make-shift canopy of yellow mallee leaves, they would make love.

The time not spent making love was used to fabricate new ruses for their next tryst.

But both of them knew that there were darker, even more ominous clouds above them than those that dropped the gentle moisture on their naked bodies.

There was the cloud of Captain Steven Rourke's return.

Thinking of this, Phillip constantly badgered her for an answer, a decision.

Annie couldn't give him one.

So she distracted him with tenderness and her body.

She was determined that the short time they would have together would be unspoiled. She feared that if she told him everything about the hold Rourke had over her and her family, it would create a breach in their intimacy.

She was also afraid of Phillip's reaction and what he might do. She had learned much more about this Irishman in the past few weeks, and what she learned both thrilled and frightened her.

She had come to realize that, in some ways, Phillip Conroy was not unlike Steven Rourke. He, like Rourke, had an unbridled temper when he was angered. In time she had come to see beneath that flashing, boyish smile. And what she saw was a capacity for danger and violence far greater than Steven Rourke's.

"I would kill for you . . . or die for you."

"I want you to do neither."

Gone was the rash wildness that had overwhelmed their first few times together. Now it was a warm, mellow savoring of each other and their every moment as one.

And at the end of the day, or the evening, or the night, there was never a need for words. Their love was real. This they both knew. It was forged between them in an invisible yet strong bond.

But only Annie would admit, and only to herself, that the bond must one day be broken. And that knowledge filled her heart with dread and despair.

"The master plan is ready, Annie. We know exactly how to steal the livestock, and I have already mapped a way through the mountains."

" 'Tis near dusk, my darling, must we talk of it now?"

"Damme, yes, we must! Rourke will return in a fortnight."

Her hands skimmed over his body as lightly as feathers, manipulating him, bringing the sweetness of his need for her to a peak.

"Annie!" he sighed, but returned her kiss, her touch.

He buried his face in the fragrance of her hair, his hand in the warmth of her thighs. Her breasts swelled against him as they came together, and then he was on his back, tugging her over his body.

With a soft cry she guided him into her, and then she was moving in wild abandon. Inside her a core of ecstacy grew, expanded, until it burst and she lay whimpering against his chest.

"I'll have everything ready in a week's time, Annie lass. And then we'll go."

"Phillip, I—"

"We'll go! If you won't go willingly, I'll play the pirate and tote you off in a sack!"

It was with a heavy heart that Annie made her way back to the cottage that evening. She knew that within the next few days she would have to tell Phillip the truth. She prayed she could soften it somewhat with hope; hope that one day Rourke would tire of his game and, having amassed the wealth he so coveted, would leave New South Wales.

When that day came, she would join Phillip over the mountains.

She prayed that Phillip would accept that, would see the wisdom of it.

She turned off the cart path and, emerging from the rocks, nearly crashed into the looming hulk of Jack Moran.

"Ah, so there ya are, damn ya!"

Annie gasped and flattened herself against a boulder, thinking he meant to attack her. But no attack was forthcoming. Instead he merely stood, glowering down at her from his towering height.

And then she saw his face, his shoulders, and his chest. His shirt had been ripped away, and now hung in bloody tatters. One eye was swollen nearly shut, and blood still gushed from his smashed nose. His shoulders and massive chest displayed a network of red and angry welts.

Her mind whirled in confusion, but before she could ask who could have possibly inflicted such damage on the most feared bully in main camp, he spat at her and stalked away.

"Ye are a witch!" he hissed over his shoulder. "Ye're a bloody witch sent to curse me!"

And then he was gone.

Annie, fearing he might change his mind and return, fled on winged feet to the cottage.

Crashing through the door, she came up short with a scream.

There, naked to the waist, his chest heaving and gleaming with a sweaty sheen, was Steven Rourke.

Annie swayed. Her knees felt as if they had suddenly been filled with water instead of gristle and bone.

The words of his explanation for returning a fortnight early spun through her brain in disjointed sentences.

"Two weeks out of Botany Bay aboard the *Venture* . . . met her sister ship, the *Caroline* . . . her skipper had word from Capetown . . . I'm to return to England and face charges . . . seems our good Governor Phillip has informed the Crown courts of my little escapades here. . . ."

He's leaving, Annie thought, he's being forced to return to England . . .

I'm free!

"You stand there teetering in a swoon, my dear," Rourke said, appraising her with eyes that seemed to penetrate the fabric of her gown. "Is this any way to greet your ardent lover after a long sea voyage?"

His intent and desire were only too clear in his eyes. Moving as best she could to make it appear natural, Annie put the table between them.

"You're . . . you're going back to England?"

"No."

"What?" Her head jerked up. Intently she stared, but she could discern nothing but open desire for her in his eyes and features. "But when the next King's ship arrives here it will bear a written command from the King's courts for you to appear in England."

"And so it will." He moved as quickly as a snake around the table and grasped her arm. "But business later."

Free, almost free. Her mind reeled, now daring to hope. Oh, dear God, maybe these last, blissful, loving days with Phillip would not have to end after all. Maybe. . . .

But now, after those ecstatic, loving days, and with the hope of freedom so near, she could not bear to have Rourke touch her again. Even now she flinched and her skin crawled beneath the bite of his fingers into the flesh of her upper arm.

"Let me go!" she cried, yanking her arm from his grasp.

"Let you go?" His face clouded and the heavy brows came together in a scowl. "Haven't you realized yet, girl, that I will never let you go?"

Annie backed away from him, clamping her hands over her ears. "No! I will not listen to you! I won't hear a word you say!"

"Oh, my dear mistress," he hissed, smiling wickedly, "I am afraid you are indeed obliged to listen to everything I say, and do everything I command."

"You are a devil, indeed *the* devil incarnate, and I hate you!"

"Ah, but you see, I have grown to love you. Much as I hate to admit to such a human weakness, Annie, I fear I have succumbed. I realized it during those long, lonely nights on the *Venture*. Your face was constantly before me, and your body always in my thoughts."

"*Love*? Rourke, you know not the meaning of the word!"

He laughed. "Once true, but no longer. Come now, I

would hear you welcome me home with sweet words."

"We are quit!" she cried, still backing from him. "You said yourself you are forced to leave. Our bargain is at an end."

Her heart beat wildly in triumph. What could he do to her family now? Nothing, for he was a wanted man himself.

Again the cloud passed across his eyes and a line of tension appeared along the edge of his clenched jaw.

"I think, in my absence, you have forgotten that you are my personal possession. You are a woman paid for, a woman who owes me, and I think you are now in arrears."

"I do not belong to you! My spirit and my soul are my own!"

"Perhaps, but what of your body? I am the only person who has rights over that."

"No longer!"

He had been advancing toward her. Now he paused, his icy eyes delving into hers for the meaning of her words.

"How so? Have you taken another lover in my absence?"

Annie bit her lip, wishing she could retract her sudden outburst. "No. I only meant—"

"You are a terrible liar. *Who?*"

"Damn you, no one!" she cried.

"Perhaps you have even now just left him, eh?"

Now he moved like a cat. His old arrogance had returned, and with it his strange, mercurial moods. In this state she knew Rourke was capable of anything.

"You know, Annie, I have often fantasized such a thing. I know 'tis possible, for beneath that stony facade you present to me, I sense passion. 'Tis odd, a coincidence, but when I arrived and found you gone, I wondered. Then, when I found Moran not watching you, the fantasy became real. And while I was beating

Moran, I thought of killing him . . . and perhaps you and your lover."

"Rourke!"

" 'Tis true, you know. You have indeed bewitched me. I would kill any other man who touched you."

"Rourke, there is no man, I swear!"

"You lie!"

His voice was thunder in the room, and before her eyes she saw the change occur that she had witnessed so many times before. The change from man to beast.

"No, no, don't touch me!"

Then he was upon her. His lips met hers in a bruising kiss that forced her against the wall. His fingers tore at the bodice of her dress, ripping the laces and the frail material. Her breasts swelled against the material as she strained to escape him. There was another rending tear and she was bare to the waist.

"Dear God, I want you, Annie. Can't you see that now?" he rasped.

"Yes!" she screamed. "I see!" She clutched her breasts, squeezing them together and upward into two jutting cones. "This! This is what you want, *all* you want, my body!"

"No!"

"Yes. My body is all you see, all you want. That is why there is nothing in your eyes but ice, because you are nothing inside!"

With a roar his hands again flew to her body. She was jerked forward with one hand around her neck and the other at the yoke of her dress.

Before she realized it, the dress was gone and she was swaying in the air above his shoulders. Then she was flung onto the bed, and Rourke, his face a mask of fury, was tearing at his own clothes.

She tensed, preparing to spring free, as she watched.

When he was naked, he placed one knee on the bed and lurched forward to cover her body.

With a scream Annie dug at his eyes with her nails and buried her teeth in the fleshy part of his shoulder.

"Bitch!" he cried, recoiling in pain, blood running down his face and arm. "I'll tame you, bitch!"

He moved like a striking serpent, his hand slapping her across the face. And then again and again, until there was a ringing in her ears and a dizzyness in her head.

She saw him above her, leering, and heard his harsh, inhuman laughter.

And then she felt the pain of his abrupt penetration.

She fought. She cried. She bit and scratched and writhed, trying to unseat him.

But eventually her screams died away to low-pitched sobs as her strength became exhausted.

She lay, tense and drained, her body aching. His cruelty and his lust had known no bounds. Now he stood at the tiny window with his back to her. His upper body was illuminated by a shaft of gray light.

" 'Tis near dawn," he whispered, not turning.

Annie remained silent.

"You should have learned by now. What is mine, I keep. And I keep it no matter the cost or what I have to do to keep it."

Here he turned, his face in shadows as he stared down at her. Annie shivered, for even in the near darkness she could sense the cold glare of those eyes on her naked body.

"I'm not going back to England. 'Tis all over here, but I've made a tidy sum. Not enough for the life I want, but enough to start a new venture. Brownlee and I have three ships, well manned, well armed. We'll leave here, take to the seas as privateers."

"Pirates?" Annie hadn't meant to speak, but the audacity of the man suddenly brought the word to her lips.

"Aye. Before we go I'll sign the papers and register

them. The farm is Tom's, free and clear. We'll never live in our new house, but I'll build a better one somewhere. 'Tis Duncan's now, and he's welcome to it and the rest of New South Wales."

Annie's throat was so dry she could barely speak. "We?"

"Aye. I can't let you go. I know that now. But I'll tell you this: once we reach the Americas, you'll no longer be a mistress. I plan to wife you proper."

"Wife?" Annie whispered, her belly in icy knots.

"Aye. You'd best start packing, for we leave day after tomorrow, on the dawn tide."

23

ANNIE ducked into her dress. She let it billow down over her shoulders, and then tugged it into place about her waist. Quickly, with shaking fingers, she fastened the button loops down the back and carelessly laced the bodice.

She had no real plan other than reaching Phillip and informing him of Rourke's return, and the man's intent.

Phillip had told her that it would take a week to arrange the theft of the livestock and send a runner to his native friends in the mountains.

But now they couldn't wait a week.

Her color was high as she left the cottage and made her way down the slope to the Officers Barrack and the adjoining stables.

She could feel perspiration running down her back from her shoulder blades to her cinched waist as she nervously waited for her horse to be saddled.

"Ya might watch him a bit, missus," the old convict groom cautioned, leading the gelding toward her. "With all the thunderin' and stormin' he's a bit skittish."

"Aye, I will," she said. "A leg?"

He gave her a leg up, and Annie reined around. Then she rode, mindless of the gelding's footing in the muddy streets, urging him into a high-stepping canter.

Be there, she moaned to herself, dear God, Phillip, be there!

In Rourke's absence, Phillip and two of his convict comrades had volunteered themselves to Duncan for work on River Forks. It was to the farm that Annie now rode, paying no heed to the wind and light mist buffeting her face.

She was sure she was safe for at least a few hours. Rourke and Moran would be busy at Botany Bay the better part of the day, victualing the ship for the coming voyage.

Less than an hour later, she was riding up the wide path leading to the nearly completed house. When she reached the highest part of the plateau, near one corner of the house, she reined the gelding in and slipped from the saddle.

She was scanning the vast fields with darting eyes, trying to spot Phillip's familiar, broad back among the laboring men, when Duncan rode up behind her.

"Good day, missus," the man said, dismounting and moving to her side.

"Good day, Mr. Duncan."

"And a good day it is!"

"Oh?"

"Aye, the Cap'n was here early this mornin' to tell me the news. I imagine ye're a happy lass, about to leave this place!"

"Aye," Annie lied, averting her face lest the overseer notice her anxiety. "Aye, of course."

Intently she kept scanning the knots of men grouped in the fields. And then she saw him. He stood alone, the wind riffling his dark curls. He had been herding several sheep across a shallow part of the river.

Now he stood, gazing toward the house. Annie could almost see the puzzled look in his dark eyes.

"I suppose ye've come out fer a last look see," Duncan said.

"Aye," Annie replied, turning what she hoped was a wistful look in the overseer's direction. "A last look."

Duncan winked at her craftily. "The Cap'n's a smart

one, he is. He'll do well in the Americas. Ye'll be a rich man's wife one day."

Annie shuddered at the thought of being Rourke's wife. She was sure Phillip had seen her. She would have to move quickly now.

"I'll follow the river out to the Hawkesbury now, Mr. Duncan. I'll be saying good-bye to my family."

"Aye," he nodded. "Would ya like a couple of me best to ride a ways with ye? There's been some natives spotted a ways up river."

"No, thank you. That won't be necessary."

Duncan handed her up and mounted himself. "Looks like a storm comin' in," he said, and followed his words with a cackling laugh. "I hope it don't interfere with the Cap'n's sailin'."

"No, let's hope it doesn't," Annie replied, and kicked the horse into motion down the inward side of the slope.

At the river she turned right and rode until she was sure she was lost in the trees. Another hundred yards brought her to a shallow spot, and she crossed.

They had only used this meeting place once before, so it took her several minutes of riding up and down stream to find the narrow break in the underbrush.

When she did, she urged the gelding into the break. Moments later she emerged from the trees into a large, hillside clearing.

Phillip was already there, standing by several felled trees, a scowl on his dark features.

"He's back!" she gasped.

"I know," Conroy replied, reaching for her hips. "He was here early this morning."

Annie slid from the saddle into his grasp. Just the touch of his hands and the feel of his powerful arms sliding around her gave her strength.

He kissed her deeply, one hand coming up, the fingers combing through her wet, windblown hair.

Annie melted against him, needing a moment or two

to collect her thoughts and to draw strength from his love.

He lifted his lips from hers at last, leaving her slightly breathless from the kiss. He still held her, one hand in the small of her back, the fingers of the other entwined in her hair.

" 'Tis in the very wind. Rumors run rampant among the men. What is Rourke about?"

Breathlessly, Annie told him of Rourke's warning from the captain of the *Caroline*. As briefly as possible she related his intent to sail with the morning tide, and his plans once he reached the Americas.

"And . . . and he would take me with him, by force if necessary. He even says he will wife me!"

Phillip released her and stepped back, rubbing the dark stubble on his chiseled chin.

"You can't go back. We shall have to hide you until he sails."

"He won't sail without me," Annie cried, "I know he won't! He . . . he. . . ."

"What, Annie?"

"He even said he loves me."

Something in her voice made him turn. His dark eyes bored into her.

"What happened?"

Annie couldn't hold his gaze. Suddenly she felt unclean, totally defiled. Before Phillip had come, she had accepted Rourke's love-making. She had treated it as payment for the survival of herself and her family.

Now, she felt she was returning to Phillip used and tainted.

"Last night . . . I tried to stop him . . . I fought. He—"

Suddenly his arms were around her again and her sobs were muffled against his chest.

"All the more reason you won't go back. My friend, Gerald Colbert, has a small cottage upriver. 'Tis out of the way. Ye'll hide there."

"But I'm telling you, he won't sail without me. I'm sure of it! He'll turn Port Jackson and the whole countryside upside down to find me!"

Phillip laughed. It was the low, rumbling laugh she had come to know so well. And, when she looked up, she saw it was accompanied by a reckless smile.

"By dawn, you won't be here to find. I'll ride to Port Jackson and alert the others. We'll leave just after dusk. By dawn we'll be well above the Hawkesbury, and in the mountains!"

On the roof of the house, partially shielded by a brick chimney, Steven Rourke lowered the seaman's glass from his eye and passed it to Jack Moran.

The hulking convict adjusted it to his own eye and swept the land beyond the river until he saw the embracing couple.

"Who is he?" Rourked hissed, his tone flat.

"An Irishman, Cap'n, name of Conroy . . . Phillip Conroy."

"So she was out of your sight but the one time, eh, Jack?"

"I swear, Cap'n!"

"Swear nothing to me, you bloody fool!"

Moran recoiled as if the man's words had been blows.

"What ya want me to do, Cap'n?"

Rourke took the glass from the giant's hands and brought it back to his own eye. Though the distance was too far to see the expressions on their faces, he could tell a great deal from the attitude of their bodies.

A cold sweat broke out on his brow and in the palms of his hands as he watched Annie's face turned upward to accept the other's lips.

"Do you remember the Arab seaman . . . from the *Venture?*"

"Aye."

"I want this Conroy to meet the same fate."

Moran turned a thin-lipped smile in Rourke's direction.

"He's as good as dead, Cap'n."

Conroy rode Annie's gelding north to the river at a breakneck pace.

"Hey, Phillip!" Markham cried, his ruddy features breaking into a wide smile as Conroy reined the horse and slid to the ground in one motion.

The smile faded quickly, to be replaced with a sour look of gloom when Phillip relayed the recent events from main camp.

"Damme, man, there's no way we can finish it by dawn tomorrow."

"Are you sure?" Conroy asked.

Markham turned and surveyed the various pieces of the rough-timbered bridge under construction. He had ten men and five women working. The night crew was composed of about the same number.

"Well?"

"Aye, Phillip, it just might be done. But we'll need more hands."

"Bring in the night crew."

"Aye," Markham nodded, "I've thought of that, but it still wouldn't be enough. Can ye get me fifteen or twenty fresh hands from main camp?"

"Nay, 'tis too risky. I'm thinking too many people know what we do as it is."

Markham shrugged.

Conroy wrung his hands together as he paced. Then he came to a sudden halt and whirled, a smile lighting his broad features.

"Have ye a horse ye can spare?"

"Aye," Markham replied. "We've three big Barbaries we use to haul the logs. One is always resting while the other two work."

"And a good rider?"

"Aye, the Spanish woman's wee sister. Rides like the wind, she does."

"Good. Get 'em!"

On a crumpled scrap of paper with a bent quill pen, Phillip scrawled a note to Tom Hollister. He had met Tom only recently, but they had liked each other at once. Also, Tom knew the circumstances between Phillip and his sister, and had candidly told Conroy how thankful he was that Phillip had offered a new life to Annie.

Tom had twenty good men at his farm, and they were intensely loyal. If Tom told them to help with building a bridge to hell, they would.

The older sister translated Conroy's precise directions to the Hollister farm. Ten minutes later the young girl was astride the Barbary and galloping off.

It was near dusk by the time Phillip ground-tethered Annie's gelding on the outskirts of Port Jackson. Quickly he pulled great handfuls of grass and piled them near the horse. He covered the rest of the distance to tent city at a dead run.

It took him less than an hour to locate Colbert.

"I don't know, Phillip, all I can do is try. Rourke took some of our men to Botany Bay for work there."

"How many of our pledged hands are in main camp?"

"Three . . . maybe four."

"Get them together, and their women, if they have any. 'Tis not many, but they'll have to do. We leave just after dark for River Forks."

"I don't know, Phillip. Duncan had thirty men out there—"

"We'll just have to hope there's enough rum flowin', and that only a handful of 'em feel any loyalty to Duncan. Get moving now, lad. I've got to see to the horses."

In long, loping strides, Conroy hurried across main

camp to the communal stables. The youngest of the three grooms, a lad named Bart, had been primed and bribed for weeks.

"But, Mr. Conroy, ya said ya'd gimme three days' notice. . . ."

"How many mounts can ye steal me, lad?"

"Three at best."

"Try to make it four, and there's a chestnut gelding ground-tethered in a clump of mallee just over the inland slope. Bring him in and add him to the string."

Conroy left the lad shaking his head, and moved quickly across the street toward the general store. Once there he avoided the main entrance and moved around behind the store to the makeshift loading dock in the rear.

All was normal. The two wagons were in their usual place. The two wrought iron gates leading to the store's large storage room gaped open, guarded by two lounging corpsmen. That night there would be a third guard on duty, and the gates would be closed and bolted.

Phillip had spent many nights secreted not far from the store, watching the guards' routine. He knew that in the late evening hours they took shifts. Two would sneak off to their beds, leaving one man to guard stores, gates, and wagons.

Overpowering one guard would be no trouble.

He walked back across main camp and over the crudely constructed bridge that connected it to the foul smells and human debris of tent city.

A few hours, he thought, and I'll live no more in this pesthole!

He lifted the flap of his own tent and stepped inside. Odd, he thought, he didn't remember leaving a candle lit.

And then he saw her. She lay sensually posed and completely nude on the cot. Her dark hair lay in a tangle on the pillow and cascaded down across her shoulders. The candlelight danced over her olive skin and seemed to make her small, pert breasts ripple.

He stood at the foot of the cot, gazing down at her for several seconds. before he recognized her.

"You're Moran's woman. Cora Lee, isn't it?"

"Aye, 'tis Cora Lee," she said, casting a smoldering look at him from beneath her dark lashes. "But I'm anybody's woman who's got the price."

"Not interested, Cora Lee."

He reached for her, meaning to lift her from the cot and heave her through the flap. But before he realized it, she was wrapped around his body like a leech. Her olive arms became a tiny vise dragging his lips to hers. Her tongue forced itself between his teeth, and when she spoke the words were accompanied by a mocking laugh.

"Yer a 'andsome one, ye are. Fer you, darlin', 'tis free!"

Phillip gripped her by the waist and pushed her away, holding her body in mid-air. Still clasping his head, she writhed and wriggled like a snake until he found his face pressed between the softness of her breasts.

Then, suddenly, the world exploded in red and there was a dull, throbbing ache between his shoulder blades. The girl flew from his grasp, bounced on the cot, and like a cat was on her feet.

Phillip tried to turn, when a crushing fist landed on the side of his head. He spun like a top across the tent and crashed through the flap into the mud outside.

Shaking his head to clear it, he came to his elbows. Jack Moran stood like a looming ogre in the tent flap. The girl, Cora Lee, cringed, still naked, at his feet. She was babbling, but Conroy couldn't understand the words.

"Have me woman, would ye!" Moran roared.

The giant's eyes gleamed with a devilish glint. Conroy suddenly realized that he had been set up, and was now being baited for the kill.

Out of the corner of his eye he could see yellow-clad convicts converging for the show. They would serve as Moran's witnesses.

It all meant but one thing: Rourke knew.

"Ye're dead, Irishman."

Moran was snaking his belt from the loops around his waist. With a roar he lunged forward, the belt, stretched between his hands, coming directly at Conroy's throat.

Phillip rolled to the side, burying both his booted feet in the man's belly as he came down. Moran landed in the mud and rolled immediately to his knees. There was nothing in his ugly face to tell Conroy that he had even been struck.

The huge man was much quicker than Conroy expected. He had just gained his feet when the belt in Moran's hand came around like a whip. It caught Phillip in the back of the knees, sending him sprawling. He managed to kick out again as he went down. One heel struck Moran's hand solidly, making him lose his purchase on the belt.

Phillip tried to roll free again, but before he could move he was covered by three hundred pounds of roaring, clawing, biting, animal fury.

Every blow from the giant's hamlike fists was like the kick of a horse on his face and body.

Conroy was disadvantaged by a hundred pounds and nearly a foot of height, but pain and anger did strange things to a man.

He curled his right hand into a half-fist and sent it crashing into the other's throat. Moran gagged, and a second blow made him gasp for air. Conroy bucked upward with his knees and torso, throwing the huge bulk from his chest.

But there was no stopping him. Moran could take more punishment than ten men.

He came up from the mud like a spring, his voice roaring with fury, his eyes glazed. Phillip kicked him square in the center of the face. Moran's head went backward and his body followed.

He sat in the mud, merely shaking his head.

Phillip could hardly believe it. Then and there the fight should have been over. But Moran only crawled to his knee and glared at Phillip, flashing him a bloody grim from his ruined mouth. Conroy felt suddenly ill. At that moment Moran was the most grotesque thing he had ever seen.

And, in the same moment, Conroy knew he would have to kill him.

Again the massive, bull-necked head shook and then, from a crouch, he made a powerful lunge. Conroy tried to duck the charge but the giant was quicker. With a gasp of pain caused by the butting head into his groin, Phillip again mired in the mud with Moran's weight over him.

The huge hands closed over his throat. Moran's severed lips dripped a steady stream of blood into Phillip's face as his meaty claws threatened to end Phillip's life.

"Die, ye bloody Irishman! Die!"

Conroy reached up and hammered his fists into the blood and mud-grimed face. Moran only laughed and squeezed harder. Phillip switched his blows to the ribs, pounding, pummeling. He felt several of the big man's ribs break, but there was no let-up on his throat.

There was now no air left in his lungs. Moran's face was swimming before his eyes. As the blackness began to engulf him, he began thrashing wildly with his arms and legs.

And then one of his hands found the wide leather belt.

He grasped it, clawing his way along the leather until he found the buckle.

With all the strength he had left, Phillip arced his arm.

Moran's hands left Conroy's throat and went to the

deep gash in his own. The man's scream was high-pitched and bone-chilling as the huge body rolled away.

Phillip struggled to his feet, took a few seconds to fill his lungs with air, and then turned, only to gasp in disbelief.

Moran was dying on his feet. His face, his neck, and his whole upper body was caked with mud and drying blood.

But again he was stalking.

Now Phillip himself became an animal. All the pent up frustrations of years burst from his throat in an animal roar.

His fist smashed what was left of the giant's face.

Moran toppled, only to be yanked back to his knees. Then, methodically, his arms timing themselves with the thud of his fists on flesh, Conroy pummeled Moran's writhing body.

He lost track of time and place. He no longer knew what he was doing. He felt hands clutch him. He shook them off and returned to his task until his arms would no longer move.

Then he stood, panting.

Shouting, screaming voices were on either side of him. Through the red haze that covered his eyes, he saw the naked body of Cora Lee, her face contorted in a scream.

On his other side he saw Gerald Colbert.

Suddenly the girl's screams became words. "He's dead! Ye've killed him, damn ye!"

Phillip looked once more at the body in the mud, and knew she was right.

Then he pitched forward into Colbert's arms.

Her name was Tobi. She was a small, raven-haired girl with a womanly figure, a wide, engaging smile, and misty dark eyes that seemed to caress everything they saw.

In the few brief hours since Phillip had brought her to the modest hut, Annie had grown to like the girl and know her as if they had been friends for years.

Annie was elated when she found out that Tobi and her husband-to-be, Phillip's young friend Gerald Colbert, would be going over the mountains with them. They planned to marry, even if it was without the church and in the wilds.

"Jest as soon as we're free," Tobi said.

"Free? None of us will ever be free, even over the mountains. 'Tis all one prison, here or there," Annie sighed.

"Nay," Tobi replied, all the optimism in the world in her huge dark eyes. "Anywhere where the land is yers and there's no chains. That's free."

The girl was so convincing that Annie started to believe it.

"Now, everythin's ready. We'll have a bit of sweet tea while we wait." She took a pail and moved to the door. " 'Tis near dusk. They'll be comin' fer us soon. I'll just draw us some water."

The girl had barely touched the latch when the door flew open with a crack.

"Ye'll not go over any mountains, lass. Ye'll to Botany Bay with me!"

Annie screamed as Steven Rourke's powerful fingers curled in her hair and propelled her from the hut.

Phillip Conroy's head felt like the inside of a drum being beaten by the entire Scots Guard marching band. His bruised body felt little better.

The faces of Gerald Colbert and the dark-haired lass, Tobi, swam eerily above his head.

He had heard Tobi's jumbled words, but he couldn't make complete sense from them in his throbbing brain.

"Wha . . . what . . . again . . . tell me again."

Slowly this time, and with more deliberateness, she

again told Conroy of Rourke's arrival at the hut and Annie's kidnap.

"And where are they now?" Phillip demanded.

"I don't know."

Suddenly the tent flap behind them flew open and a blonde, raggedly dressed girl lurched forward.

"I know where they be!" she hissed intently.

The Corpsman on duty at the General Store gates was sleepy. He'd had too much rum before coming on duty.

But he was not too drowsy to appreciate the swelling curves of this raven-haired little lass's breasts. She stood boldly before him, her lips pursed in a provocative pout, her blouse unlaced until he could see her tantalizing olive skin clear to the waistline of her skirt.

"Nay, wench, on duty I am," he said reluctantly.

"What duty can be more important than this, eh?" she smiled.

Her fingers deftly drew the laces free, and she was bare to the waist.

"Damme!"

"A cup o' rum. Isn't this worth a cup o' rum?"

The Corpsman licked his lips and quickly looked around. "Over here," he whispered, "in the shadows."

The girl followed. With catlike agility she jumped up and sat on the edge of the rough plank loading dock. Coyly she began raising her skirt. By the time the hem had reached her hips, the man had his breeches unbuttoned.

"Damme, 'tis worth a whole keg, it is!"

The cosh landed behind his right ear just as he made to move between the girl's knees.

"Damme, lass," Gerald Colbert laughed, shoving the weapon back into his belt, "I'd swear ye were an old hand at this."

"Them that watches learns," Tobi giggled, relacing her bodice. "The others?"

"Out, bound, and gagged. They'll not be discovered 'til dawn. God willin', we'll be in the mountains by then."

"Aye," Tobi replied, the features of her elfin face curling into a frown. "And the good Lord willin', Conroy an' Annie'll be with us."

24

"YOU'LL kill us both!" Annie screamed as the cart wheels skidded sideways in the mud, dangerously close to the cliff's wet, slick rocks.

"Then we'll die gloriously together, wench," Rourke said, throwing his wet hair from his eyes and laughing raucously.

Again the cart swerved, and Annie was sure the wild sound of the surf breaking on the jagged rocks below was coming up to meet them.

She actually didn't care.

Phillip was dead, killed by Moran in the streets of tent city. Cora Lee had met them at the cottage. Annie could still hear her breathless words.

"Killed each other, they did. Ya got ta take me with ya now, Rourke, like ya promised! Me man is dead, ye got to take me with ya!"

Unwillingly Rourke had agreed, and now the girl sat huddled in the rear of the cart, her face white with fear.

"Whoa . . . whoa!" Rourke shouted, sawing the reins until the foam-flecked, frightened animal came to a halt at last.

"Why are we stopping?" Annie asked, more from reflex than any real interest.

"The path down is too narrow for the cart. We'll have to walk. Come along!"

In single file they climbed over the rocks. Rourke

led, with Annie in the middle, and Cora Lee bringing up the rear.

It was as if he knew she would not try to escape now. The news of Conroy's death had taken all the fight from her.

Indeed, as they inched along the rain-soaked rocks, with thunder rumbling above them and the sea roaring angrily below, Annie was tempted to throw herself out into space. There was nothing to live for now. Her family was provided for; even though he had tried to retract his promise at the last minute, Rourke had finally signed over the farm to Tom. So now there was only herself and Rourke. The thought made her shudder.

Anything, even death was preferable to the years she could see ahead of her with Steven Rourke.

"There they lay," Rourke said, stepping into a wide area of the path and pointing downward. "The *Venture* and the *Caroline*."

Annie looked down through the sheets of driving rain. Far below, illuminated in the blinding flashes of lightning, she could see the two ships bobbing at anchor.

It's over, she thought, I'm bound to be a pirate's whore for the rest of my days. She closed her eyes, and felt the darkness overtake her. Oh, how easy it would be, just to take one more step . . . such a simple end to the misery. . . .

"Move aside, Annie, and be quick about it!"

Her head jerked up. From behind a boulder at the rear of the clearing stepped Phillip Conroy.

"Phillip!" she cried.

"Move, Annie!"

Charged by the command in his voice, Annie leapt to the side, barely escaping Rourke's grasping hand.

A brace of pistols filled Phillip's hands. When Rourke missed his clutching at Annie's arm, he drew two pistols from his own belt. He leveled one at her and one at Conroy.

"Damn ye, Cora Lee. Ye said he was dead!"

"He was . . . I could'a swore he was!"

"Phillip! Oh, dear God, Phillip, you're alive!"

"Don't move, Annie," Rourke hissed, and turned back to face Conroy. "How did ye know to get ahead of us?"

"I tol' him, Steven."

From behind a boulder nearer Rourke, to his left, stepped the bedraggled figure of Josie Hunnicutt.

"Dear God," Rourke cried, and then threw his blond head back in a roaring, mirthless laugh. "Will I never be rid of ye, whore!"

Josie advanced a few steps, wringing her hands before her breasts.

"Leave her to him, Steven," she whined. "Let me go with ya. I'll love ya and pleasure ya like she'll never do. Take me with ya, Steven. I wants—"

"Quiet!" Rourke shouted. "Back away, Conroy. We're going on down."

"You have two shots, I have two shots," Phillip replied calmly. "I believe 'tis a stalemate."

"Nay, not so," Rourke growled. "For, as your first ball strikes me, I'll kill her." For emphasis he moved the barrel of the pistol in his right hand upward until it was pointed directly at Annie's breast.

"No, Steven, please," Josie whined, advancing toward Rourke. "Can't ya see, she don't want ya. I want ya, I do!"

"Stay back, you slut."

"I been followin' ya every minute ya been back, cravin' ya with me eyes and me body. That's how I knew about this path. Steven."

"Damn ye for a useless, stupid jade!" Rourke bellowed. "You're no better than her, Moran's slut, and you would presume to have me?"

Josie's eyes seemed to roll up in her head until only

the whites could be seen. Her tiny hands came up to shield Rourke's words from her ears. She stumbled and fell a few steps closer to Rourke.

"Stop there," he hissed, seeing that she was coming between him and Conroy.

"But . . . but. . . ." Suddenly her voice became a high-pitched, wailing scream as she battered the sides of her head with her own fists. "I looooove youuuu!"

Rourke fired.

The ball hit Josie in the middle of her belly. Her hands flew to cover the wound as her eyes grew wide and her mouth dropped open in shock. In seconds a patch of red appeared behind her hands and blood began spilling from between her fingers.

She looked back up at Rourke, her head shaking from side to side in disbelief.

"Cross between us, Annie," Rourke hissed. "If you fire, Conroy, I'll fire at the same time."

"Damme," Phillip growled, lowering his pistols. "Ye're the bloodiest bastard I've ever seen."

"Nay," Rourke laughed, "I'm a man who knows what he wants and takes it. Down the path, Annie!"

She moved slowly between them, her eyes wide with shock at Josie's teetering form. She wanted to cry out in horror, but no sound would come.

Rourke moved to the side.

"Ye shot me, Steven," Josie croaked.

"Damme, will you move!"

He reached out to shove Josie, but her bloody hands came up to grip his wrist.

"Ye shot me!"

"Get back, you fool!"

The words had barely left Rourke's mouth when Josie lurched forward. Her eyes seemed already closed in death, but the grip on Rourke's wrist never slackened. They poised, the two of them on the very edge of the slick cliff, and then they were floating off into space and the blinding sheets of rain.

There was no cry, no scream, indeed no sound at all, as they tumbled into the darkness and disappeared.

Annie's eyes blinked and opened, only to snap shut again to keep out the blinding glare of the midday sun. Slowly she oriented herself and realized that she was sweltering beneath the quilt in the bed of the wagon.

She wriggled from beneath it, and then shielded her eyes before opening them again.

"You're awake!"

She turned her head and looked up into Phillip's smiling face. He sat in the seat of the rocking wagon, munching a dry crust of bread.

" 'Tis noon?"

"Aye, and a sight you've never seen under a midday sun. Climb up here!"

Annie found her bonnet, adjusted it, and then climbed up on the seat beside him.

The splendor before her struck her like a fist in the belly. Vast grassy plains and forests stretched before her as far as the eye could see. Rolling mountains engulfed her, and some, in the far distance, were white-capped with snow.

"Oh, God, it is beautiful."

"Aye, it is, lass, and as much of it as we want is ours."

Her gaze dropped closer, to the cattle and sheep being herded along by the black natives. She found the lithe, chocolate brown body of No-Moonee, and beside her the taller, muscular shape of her husband. The native girl met Annie's stare and waved.

They had met the previous night, when the natives had come out of the trees like spectors to lead them across the mountains.

"He friend," No-Moonee had said to Annie. "You friend, too."

Fifty yards to their right she saw Gerald Colbert and

his Tobi driving the other wagon, their arms about each other.

Then her gaze traveled to the rear of the wagon, and a laugh bubbled from her lips.

"What is it?" Phillip asked.

"Cora Lee," Annie replied. "Look!"

Phillip looked, and he too chuckled.

Cora Lee sat, her legs dangling over the end of the wagon. Her skirt was high on her hips and her bodice was open, baring nearly all of her breasts. Walking behind the wagon were the four young convicts who had helped in the escape. All were paying her enthusiastic court.

Beside Cora Lee sat two other women, one a fragile wisp of a thing with soft, doe-like eyes. She looked very young, a mere girl, actually. The other was a stunning beauty, of obvious Castilian descent, with warm, olive-hued skin and a mass of ebony hair piled high on her regal head. She had her arm protectively around the younger girl, and every now and then Cora Lee would lean over and whisper something to them, and all three would shake with laughter.

Annie sighed. "Cora Lee will be a whore no matter where she goes."

"Aye," Phillip chuckled. "But she'll end up with one of those lads, and, one day, her daughters will not be whores."

They rode in silence for several moments, and then Phillip's arm sneaked around her waist, drawing her close.

"We'll make more than a prison out of this land, Annie. We'll make a home."

She snuggled her breast to his side and moved her arms about his neck. "Aye, that we will. I love you, Phillip Conroy."

"And I love you, Annie Conroy."

"What?"

AMERICAN DYNASTY
Volume Two

THE
CARRICKS

---

by Brooke Miller

Patricia Carrick, beautiful and brilliant, came out of a mill town to create a financial empire, risk it for a reckless love, and continue an American dynasty.

An August 1982 title from DELL/EMERALD 01413-1

His teeth gleamed in a smile as he brushed his lips across the tip of her nose.

"Out here we'll have to do for ourselves," he said. "Since we have no man of the cloth to marry us, I did it myself, at dawn this morning, while you were still asleep."

"And did I say 'I do' in my sleep?"

"Many times over," he replied, leaning his head against hers. "Many times over."